"Department of Homeland Security. Come out with your hands up!"

The shout was cut off by an explosion that made Kate snatch her earpiece off her head, gasping in shock. As she watched the satellite image, the sedan erupted in a glowing, gold ball of flame, forcing everyone to retreat. Kate inserted the earpiece again. "Tracy? Tracy, are you there?"

"Yeah, I'm here. Jesus, he just blew himself up. Must have been a grenade or a bomb or something, I don't know. But he's gone and he took any evidence we might have found with him.

"You need to get out of there. I'm downloading an address and directions from your location right now. Try to coordinate the Border Patrol and any other DHS agents in the area if you can, but go in quietly—we can't tip them off or they might launch early. Brief everyone there on keeping the press out of this for now—we don't want to cause a panic," Kate said.

Before Kate disconnected she heard Nate say, "Hey, that isn't too far from here, maybe about fifteen minutes southwest."

I hope that's quick enough, Kate thought.

Other title[s] in this series:

THE POWERS THAT BE
OUT OF TIME
AIM AND FIRE

ROOM 59

aim AND fire

cliff RYDER

A GOLD EAGLE BOOK FROM

W★RLDWIDE®

TORONTO • NEW YORK • LONDON
AMSTERDAM • PARIS • SYDNEY • HAMBURG
STOCKHOLM • ATHENS • TOKYO • MILAN
MADRID • WARSAW • BUDAPEST • AUCKLAND

First edition July 2008

ISBN-13: 978-0-373-63267-1
ISBN-10:   0-373-63267-3

AIM AND FIRE

Special thanks and acknowledgment to
Jonathan Morgan for his contribution to this work.

aim AND fire

PROLOGUE

As she crossed the border from Mexico to the United States in the dead quiet of a suffocating July night, Consuelo Maria Jimenez didn't thrill to the possibility of beginning a new life, but instead felt the intense dread of entering a strange land. She shifted to a less painful position in the back of the stifling panel truck, filled to bursting with other illegal immigrants and lit only by the shaky glow of a few scattered flashlights. Her gaze alighted on her two children, and as she stared at their wary faces, she wondered again if this hazardous journey into an unknown future was the right choice.

The decision to leave her homeland had been the easiest part. Years of slow, insidious death by corruption from the Mexican government had choked the life out of hundreds of small villages across the country, including her home of San Pedro Canon, forty miles west of Oaxaca de Juárez. The only choices for jobs were either menial work for barely living wages in the city's factories, or joining one of the regional drug cartels, with all of the risk, violence and death that entailed.

Consuelo's sister, who had settled in the U.S. several years ago, had been persuading her to head north and make a new life in America. She had written of the possibilities in Wisconsin, where she and her family had settled, and her persistence—along with the money she had wired each month—had just about convinced Consuelo. The last straw had been when her husband had left without a word, leaving no trace or contact information for her to follow. With two children to support, one look in their eyes was enough to make up her mind.

The trip so far had been long and difficult. She had heard horror stories from the relatives of those who had gone over, being left to die in a trailer or back of a truck, getting lost and suffering an agonizing death by thirst in the desert, being raped or sold into sexual slavery. Consuelo had asked her sister to find a reasonably reliable coyote—one of the men who made their living transporting people across the border. When the same name came up three times by other immigrants, Consuelo knew she had found the right person.

With help from her sister, she paid the fee of two thousand dollars apiece for herself and her two children, more money than she had ever seen in her life. They had left San Pedro Canon late one afternoon, the tears in Consuelo's eyes at leaving her home rapidly drying in the desert heat. From there they had traveled steadily north for two weeks through a dizzying array of cities and towns— Toluca, León, Mazatlán, Torreán, Chihuahua—staying in dingy rooms in small, crumbling motels, crammed with a dozen other people into shacks in festering slums and once even spending the night in the backseat of a car, sleepless, hungry and thirsty the entire time.

But at long last, their journey would soon come to an

end. While crossing the Rio Grande the night before, they had dodged the Border Patrol, which had made a large bust at their planned crossing site, the bright lights and the dark green vehicles forming an ominous cordon on the American side of the border. Instead of canceling the attempt, their guides had simply shifted the crossing point a few miles farther east. Now, about thirty miles outside of the notorious border city of Ciudad Juárez, their long trip out of Mexico was ending, and the journey through America to her sister's family was about to begin.

Still, Consuelo worried about their chances of making it at every moment, what with the increased border patrols and unmanned observation aircraft she had heard the coyotes discussing. The thought of someone watching her, unseen from thousands of feet in the air, made her shudder. The men guiding them had insisted there would be no trouble at all, that "it had all been taken care of." But their furtive glances and whispered conversations to each other did little to reassure her.

"Are we almost there?" her oldest, Esteban, asked, his dark brown eyes shadowed with worry.

"Yes, sweetheart. Drink some more water." As Consuelo looked at her son, she felt a flush of pride. As if they had sensed the importance of what was happening, both of her children had been very good during the prolonged trip, hardly complaining at all and listening to her with unusual patience. Even when they had first boarded the truck, Esteban had staked out a seat on the metal wheel well for his mother. Consuelo had promised herself that one of the first things she would do once they reached their new home of Milwaukee—such a strange name for a city—she would take them to the largest store she could find and let them each pick out one toy apiece as a reward for their good behavior.

Gently shifting her daughter, Silvia, asleep on her lap, to a more comfortable position, Consuelo wiped sweat from her forehead and glanced around at the rest of the people crossing the border. The truck held a mixture of men and women from across Central America—from fellow Mexicans to those from El Salvador, Honduras, Nicaragua and other places, all looking for a new life.

But sitting at the front of the truck were three men who looked markedly different from the others, and whose intense gazes made her flesh crawl. Whereas no one else carried anything with them save the clothes on their backs and perhaps a bit of food and water, the three bearded men had brought a large crate, roughly two and a half yards long. They always stayed close to it, hauling it across the border and through the desert without a word of complaint.

Although the box had attracted curious looks from several people in the back of the truck, no one had asked the trio about it, since they didn't speak to anyone save one another, and then in a melodic language that Consuelo couldn't understand. The only potential trouble had come when everyone had entered the truck for the last leg of the trip. One of the Mexican men had tried to sit on the box, but had been ushered away by one of the three men with a determined shake of his head and violent hand gestures.

Whoever they were, Consuelo was certain they weren't from anywhere in Central America. She wondered why they were traveling this way, but the idle thought passed quickly, replaced by more pressing matters—like the wail of a siren that suddenly pierced the walls of the truck. Her heart sinking, Consuelo knew what that sound meant— they had been caught by the Border Patrol. The truck lurched forward, everyone in the back swaying with the sudden motion, but a cooler head must have prevailed in the cab, for they started to slow down.

Conversation throughout the truck stopped, and all eyes turned toward the large metal door at the back. Several men uttered quiet oaths, but most of the people around her looked resigned to their fate. As Consuelo shook her daughter awake, her eyes strayed to the three men at the front of the truck. They were clustered together, two of them with their backs to the rest of the group. She heard a strange metallic clicking sound, then two of them turned and stood in front of the crate, while the third pushed his way to the rear of the vehicle, his hand resting against the colorful tail of his loose-fitting shirt.

The truck stopped, and the engine died. A loud voice outside called out in Spanish. "Attention, everyone inside the truck. This is the United States Customs and Border Protection. When the door is opened, you will file out one at a time, keeping your hands in plain sight, and kneel at the side of the road in a single line."

Consuelo's son exchanged a troubled glance with her. "What should we do, Mama?"

"Listen to the men, and do as they say. If we are sent back, we will try to find another way across," she replied. She had no idea how they would manage another crossing. It would be months before her sister could send the money to try again, and who knew what might happen to them in the meantime?

A metal rattle echoed through the cargo bay, and the segmented door was pushed up, revealing the bright head-lights of a white SUV illuminating the men and women packed into the truck. An agent stood a few feet away from the back of the truck, one hand hovering above his hol-stered pistol. "Step out of the truck one at a time and take your place over here. Kneel on the ground, cross your legs at the ankles and keep your hands in plain sight," the agent commanded.

Blinking in the sudden bright light, the men and women jumped down to the dirt road and lined up as directed. As the first bearded man stepped off the truck bed, the Border Patrol agent's eyes narrowed. "Hold it—" The bearded man pulled a compact pistol out from underneath his shirt and fired, spraying several rounds at the agent, hitting him more than once and shattering one of the SUV's headlights.

As Consuelo watched in horror, the agent fell to the ground and slowly tried to draw his pistol. The man stepped over him and fired once at the agent's head, stilling him.

The group of immigrants burst into panicked motion, those still inside the truck jumping out while others on the road scattered into the darkness. The gunman continued firing, mowing down several fleeing people. Grabbing Esteban's hand, Consuelo lurched toward the open back as she heard another strange metallic clatter behind her, then the deafening sound of some kind of terrible weapon.

"Run, Esteban!" she shouted. Pulling her son along, she scrambled toward the open door. Around her, men and women died in their tracks, bullets from the chattering, deadly weapons punching through their bodies. Shouts and screams were heard both inside and out, and Consuelo realized one of the voices was her own, shrieking in dazed terror. One arm was wrapped tightly around her daughter, and her other hand clutched Esteban's fingers in a death grip.

And suddenly, they were at the door, miraculously un-scathed. Consuelo didn't stop, but leaped out of the truck, dragging Esteban behind her. She fell hard, landing on her knees, right beside the body of the Border Patrol agent who had collapsed against the side of the truck. The woman's oozing blood stained her uniform black in the bright lights and heat. Around her, the three foreign men methodically killed everyone in sight. The first one now stood on the patrol vehicle's hood, shooting anyone who moved. Bodies were strewed everywhere, cut down as they tried to escape.

Sucking in a breath of hot night air, Consuelo staggered to her feet, helped by Esteban, who was now tugging on her. "Hurry, Mama, hurry!" She let him pull her into the darkness, stumbling past yucca plants and Amargosa bushes. She saw a thick cluster of *guajillo* a few yards away, and knew if they reached the thicket, they might be safe.

A shot cracked out from behind her, and Consuelo felt something punch her hard in the lower back. All of the strength drained out of her legs, and she collapsed in a heap, still holding Silvia, who was clinging to her neck.

"Mama, get up, we have to get out of here!" Esteban pulled on her hand, pleading, tears streaming down his face.

"Esteban, take your sister and go." Consuelo shook her head, trying to think. "Follow the—the road." Scattered shots came from behind them, the cries and pleas of the others falling silent. Suddenly she was tired...so tired.

"No, I won't let you. Don't hurt Mama!" She felt Esteban drape himself over her back, and all Consuelo could think to do was to huddle over her daughter, who had suddenly turned limp and heavy in her arms. Consuelo tilted her daughter back and saw Silvia's head loll on her shoulders. Looking down, she saw dark blood from where the bullet had passed through her and into her daughter's body.

"Oh, no...no, not Silvia..." She felt Esteban, still yelling and struggling, suddenly lifted off her, and then a single, sharp crack, punishing her ears. Strange, but she couldn't hear her son's voice anymore. The shot has deafened me, she thought.

Consuelo drew her daughter close again, wrapping her arms around the small body as footsteps crunched in the sandy soil next to her. She looked up to see one of the men, his eyes expressionless, a pistol held at his side.

"Please…my daughter…she is hurt…."

He spoke to her in mangled Spanish. "Your son had heart of warrior. I give him quick death. Good death."

"Please…help my baby…let her go…."

He raised the pistol again. "They will be at peace, if Allah wills it."

Just before she saw the blinding muzzle-flash, she heard him say one last thing in that strange language, and in the flash of a second before Consuelo's death, she somehow understood the words, although they did not ease her passing one bit.

"*Allahu Akbar.*"

1

Nathaniel Spencer tilted his cowboy hat lower over his pale blue eyes and leaned back in the seat of the battered, primer-gray Ford Bronco. He appeared to be just another gringo taking a siesta in the ovenlike afternoon heat on the road in front of a line of small businesses along Oregon Street. But Spencer stared through the loose weave of his straw hat at the auto parts shop and attached warehouse across the street. He also kept one hand on the small, discreet earbud to monitor the reports from his men. He and several Customs and Border Protection agents had been stationed around a drop point for one of the dozens of local drug-smuggling rings that infested El Paso and its poorer half to the south, Ciudad Juárez, for the past four hours, and Nate would stay there until their quarry showed up.

"I still don't see why I have to sit back here and suffer. I think I've lost five pounds just from sweat alone." Nathaniel's new partner, George Ryan, was a big, green recruit not even six months out of training. He was huddled in the backseat, out of sight, but not out of smell. Nate wrinkled his nose at the sweet-sour stink coming off the other man.

"Because two men in the front would arouse suspicion. Now shut your trap and drink more water. At least you're still sweating, so consider yourself lucky. I don't need my backup keeling over from heatstroke." Nathaniel eased the straw of a plastic sport bottle underneath his hat and took a long, warm gulp. After dozens of stakeouts just like this one, he knew all too well the stealthy danger of the life-draining heat. He keyed his radio. "Anybody got anything yet?"

A chorus of negatives answered him, from two agents posing as loitering day laborers in front of the hardware store next to Hernando, the unlucky guy who had drawn the short straw and had to dress as a homeless person. He had spent the past few hours alternating between rooting through a small grocery store's garbage and wandering up and down the alley.

Nate would have preferred to have an extra half-dozen agents on this raid, but they were stretched thin as it was, and he'd been lucky to get the three additional agents in the first place.

"Jesus, these guys are seriously late." George sucked down tepid water, draining the bottle. "Bet they ain't coming at all."

"Slow down, Tex—drink too fast and you'll give yourself cramps." Nathaniel heard the growl of a truck coming up the street, and his eyes flicked to the rearview mirror, spotting a rumbling cargo truck turning the corner, heading toward the back of the building. Emblazoned on its side was the name of the auto parts store they were watching.

"Everyone look sharp. I think they just arrived. Hernando, get your head out of that Dumpster and see if you can verify that license plate."

"With pleasure—you had to pick the day they threw out their old meat, didn't you? My wife's gonna make me sleep in the den again. Okay, Lima Juliet Kilo five-one-niner. That matches the truck we're expecting."

Nate sat up and pushed his hat back. "All right, everyone. Get ready—the cargo has arrived. We'll give 'em a few minutes, then move in after the truck has docked and they've started unloading. Carter, Juan, you guys take the front. Hernando, move to the back corner and keep an eye on the truck. Ryan and I will circle around the block and take them from behind." He clicked off his radio. "All right, George, get up here." He leaned toward the door as the stocky man clambered into the front seat.

"Damn two-door," he muttered.

"Hey, do not insult the vehicle. This little son of a bitch has gotten me through hell and back." Firing the engine, Nate pulled a U-turn and headed past the grocery store, then turned right down the side street.

Hernando's voice came over the radio. "Nate, I'm in position. The truck just parked in the loading dock, and it looks like our boys are in quite a hurry for some reason."

"We'll be there in thirty. Front team, you ready?"

"Give the word, and we'll be inside in ten seconds."

"Copy that. No one moves until my signal." Nate turned right again, aiming the Bronco down the alley toward the auto parts store and pulling forward until he could just see the white snout of the truck's hood. Drawing his .40-caliber HK P-2000 pistol, he chambered a round, waiting until George did the same. "We'll pull in front of the truck as Carter and Juan sweep from the front, round everyone up and be done with it. You remembered your vest, right?"

George thumped his chest. "You mean the thing I'm swimmin' in here? Hell, yeah."

"Good man. Get ready." Nate hit his radio. "Hernando, are they unloading yet?"

"Looks like it."

"Okay, follow us as soon as we're in front of the truck, and the three of us will go in together. Carter, Juan, on my signal."

The three other agents confirmed the orders, and Nate slipped his SUV into gear, creeping down the alleyway until he judged he was close enough, then flooring the accelerator. The Bronco rocketed down the alley, and Nate squealed to a stop in front of the truck, trapping it between his vehicle and the building.

"Go, go, go!" he shouted. He yanked the key out of the ignition and slipped out the door, running around the hood, his cowboy boots slapping the pavement. George was already covering the driver, and Nate headed around the passenger side of the truck, seeing Hernando running down the other side of the vehicle.

The truck had backed up to a concrete loading dock that let people walk from the truck into the building without climbing up. Approaching it at a full run, Nate leaped up between the truck and the side of the building, squeezing through the narrow gap, pistol first. "U.S. Customs agents. Nobody move!"

The interior of the warehouse was large, easily several thousand square feet, and was filled with rows and rows of metal racks, stacked full of cardboard boxes and wooden crates of every size. Five shocked men, all standing in a line ready to relay the cargo into the warehouse, stared back at him. The second-to-last man had just tossed a box to the next guy, who had looked over in surprise, only to have the heavy container smack into his chest, sending him to the ground with a surprised grunt.

Nate heard the footsteps and shouts of his agents as they came through the front door, but knew it would be at least a minute before they secured the area and got to his location. He knew that was plenty of time for something bad to happen. He peered into the gloom, waiting for his eyes to adjust and not liking what he saw. There was too much cover where more men could be lurking, too many shadows to hide people.

Nate's gaze flicked over to the other side of the loading bed, expecting his partner or Hernando to come barreling through at any second. He turned back to the five men, three of whom had put their hands up. *Any day now, guys,* he thought. "Everyone down on your knees and raise your hands—you know the drill." He repeated the command in Spanish, trying to keep all of the men covered. The man farthest inside the warehouse edged a step away, then another.

"Buddy, you take another step you'll be missing your knees something fierce," he growled. *Where the hell is he?* "Agent Ryan, report!"

A shadow fell over the other side of the loading dock, and George Ryan forced his way inside. His face was red and he was panting with exertion. "Sorry, bastard driver… didn't wanna…come outta the…truck. Hernando's takin' care of him."

"All right, read 'em their rights," Nate ordered. Keeping his pistol trained on them, he walked to the other agent and removed two pairs of handcuffs from his belt. "I'll start trussin' them."

His pistol in one hand, George took the laminated Miranda rights card out of his pocket and held it up. "You have the right—"

The loud, unmistakable sound of a shotgun slide being pumped echoed throughout the warehouse. Ducking, Nate barely had time to yell "Get down!" before the dark interior lit up with a booming flash as the scattergun let loose. He twisted around to see George stumble and go down, a cloud of buckshot tearing at his body. The five men scattered in different directions as Nate squeezed off several shots in the direction of the ambush.

"Shots fired, shots fired! Hernando, get in here, Ryan's down! Carter, Juan, watch for suspects coming out the front!" Nate crawled over to George and dragged him behind the nearest metal rack, his chest hitching as he struggled for breath. He checked George's vitals, seeing blood stain his fingers. It looked as if the vest had stopped most of the pellets, but at least two had penetrated. "You're gonna be all right, buddy," he said.

The shotgun boomed again, and a shadow fell over Nate as Hernando hit the floor beside him. "I called for backup and the medics. Jesus, boss, what did you get us into this time?"

"Just the usual—hip-deep in shit." Nate heard a flurry of shots from the front of the store, and knew the other two agents had bottled up anyone trying to leave—at least he hoped that's what was happening. Another boom from the front made him wince. "Goddammit, these bastards are fuckin' with the wrong guys. Take the right, I'll take left, let's see if we can pin 'em in a cross fire," he said.

Hernando nodded and rolled over to a rack of crates, rising and ducking into the shadows of the warehouse. Nate checked George again, finding his breathing had steadied. "How you doin'?" he asked.

"All right—just prop me against the jamb, and I'll cover the back."

Nate nodded admiringly. *He's tougher than I thought.* "You got it. Let's give 'em something to think about first." Sticking his pistol around the corner, he shot three times toward where the shotgun blasts had erupted. He propped George against the back wall. "Medics will be here soon enough. Keep your powder dry."

George coughed, but held his pistol steady. "Go get 'em."

Nate fired two more rounds, reloaded, then ran to the other side, hunching against the expected fire. Just as he ducked behind the parts rack, the shotgun roared again, and the corner of a wooden crate exploded into jagged splinters. But the shot had given him valuable information—he now knew the shooter's location.

Nate looked up at the sturdy shelves around him and decided to take the high ground. Holstering his gun, he had just gotten a firm handhold when a shape barreled out of the shadows toward him. Caught in the act of lifting himself up, Nate had just turned his head when the man tackled him at the waist, shoving him off the rack and to the concrete floor. The breath rushed out of Nate's lungs, and pain stabbed through his elbow and knee. Pinned by his attacker, he couldn't snake an arm around to his pistol, and was forced to throw up his hurt arm to keep the man's clutching hand away his throat. Squirming, he ended up flat on his back, with the attacker sitting on top of him and throwing wild punches at his face. Dodging a swing that grazed his cheek, Nate lashed out with his fist, clouting the man's head so hard he rocked back. The agent hooked his arm underneath the smuggler's leg and heaved him over. Rolling, Nate threw a knee into the man's chest, doubling him up, then scrambled to his feet and slammed his opponent in the head twice with his boot heel. The man struggled to his hands and knees, but Nate put him right back down with another hard shot to the back of the neck. He checked his pistol, then keyed his mike.

"Hernando, come in. Hernando, do you read?"

Nate didn't even hear the hiss of static, but instead

caught a rattle of something broken inside the radio. He dropped the useless device and hoisted himself up the shelves while ignoring his throbbing elbow and knee. Scrambling up and over the final row of boxes, Nate began creeping in the direction he had last heard the shotgunner fire from. It had now gone ominously silent.

Geez, I could really use that radio now, he thought, since he had no idea who was dead or alive, who was shot or not. He couldn't even hear any sirens in the distance, and wasn't sure when any backup would arrive. For all he knew, he was on his own.

He heard the noise as the shotgun slide racked again and another boom thundered through the cavernous warehouse. Nate homed in on the sound, climbing over the uneven terrain of boxes and crates, his pistol always pointing toward the direction of the shotgun fire. At one point he had to leap from one rack to another. He barely made it, dangling from one arm for a few tense moments. When he was safely positioned again, he took a second not only to listen, but also to try to calm his jackhammering heart.

Should be close now, Nate thought, peering over the edge to see if he could spot the gunner in the gloom of the warehouse. In the sudden quiet, the faint scream of sirens reached his ears, and he knew if they didn't take this guy soon, he would bolt. He reached the end of a row and looked over again. Spotting a crouched form, he raised his pistol and aimed, but pointed it toward the ceiling when he saw Hernando moving cautiously through the racks. Nate instinctively reached for his radio again, silently cursing when he remembered it was on the floor. He considered trying to get the other agent's attention, but didn't want to risk giving away his position.

Standing slowly, he looked in all directions, wondering where in the hell their common enemy was. The slam of a door at the front of the warehouse drew his attention, along with Hernando's, and another loud blast echoed as the jumpy shotgunner loosed more buckshot in that direction. This time it sounded as if the guy was directly below him, and Nate stepped to the far side of the rack in time to see the man taking cover behind a pile of boxes, his scattergun aimed at the end of the row. Nate glanced over to see Hernando appearing from around the end, squinting to see the smuggler in the gloom.

Nate extended his gun and yelled, "Drop it!" The shotgunner blinked in surprise and raised the scattergun. Nate squeezed the HK's trigger twice and two 165-grain hollowpoints smashed into the man's chest, dropping him where he crouched.

Hernando ran up and kicked the shotgun away as the sirens finally echoed off the buildings as cars pulled up. "I got mine on the other side. You?" he asked.

"Number three's sleeping off a kiss from my boot up front. The other two probably lit out for the front." Nate clambered down the rack, sliding the last several feet. "Cuff him, and I'll clear the store." Running from rack to rack, he reached the set of double doors, which now sported several bullet holes and a spiderwebbed Plexiglas window. "Carter? Juan?" he called out.

"In here!" Carter replied.

Still keeping his pistol ready, Nate eased the door open, not wanting to walk into another ambush. The storefront looked like a war zone, with damaged cardboard display racks lying on their sides amid fluttering car-parts brochures. A black puddle of oil slowly grew from rows of blasted, leaking containers. As Nate walked forward, he heard Carter's voice counting steadily.

"One-and-two-and-three-and-four-and-five." Pause. "One-and-two-and-three-and-four-and-five—come on, dammit, breathe! Where's the damn medics?"

Nate ran through the racks to the far side of the store, where the damage was even worse. The counter had taken so many bullets and shotgun blasts that it had broken in two, the pieces leaning against each other. An overhead fan lazily stirred the smoky air. Nate spotted two bodies right away, one behind the counter, the other near the door, brought down while trying to make a break for it.

Seeing his two remaining men on the floor in the center of the room, however, chilled Nate's heart. Agent Juan Menendez lay unmoving, his side a soaked mass of blood. Next to him, his partner leaned over and performed chest compressions, stopping after every fifth pump to breathe into his partner's mouth.

"We need those medics in here now!" Nate shouted over his shoulder as he ran to them. "Stay on mouth-to-mouth—I've got this." Locking his arms, he began chest compressions, leaning in to drive the wounded man's breastbone down and manually keep his heart pumping blood. "Come on, Juan, you still haven't given me that damn barbeque recipe yet, and I ain't lettin' you go until I get it!"

The two agents continued CPR until the medics arrived a few minutes later, but Nate knew it was a lost cause. Juan had shown no response to their ministrations, and even electric shocks directly to the heart had done nothing. In the end, the agent was taken out in an ambulance with the lights flashing on its way to the hospital, but Nate was pretty sure they would call it on the way. He put his hand on Carter's shoulder. "Sorry, man."

"There's still a chance—they might save him at the hospital…."

"Yeah, he might pull through—Juan's a tough old bastard." What else could he say? he wondered. "Come on, we better get back and clean up the rest of this mess."

He helped the shaken Carter through the ruined shop and into the back room, where apparent chaos was unfolding. Uniformed El Paso police officers were everywhere, cordoning off the area, taking pictures and trying to keep some semblance of order. "Aw, Jesus Christ." Nate shook his head as he surveyed the scene.

"Nate, over here!" George, who was being pulled out on a guerney, was holding on to the side of the garage door while the medic tried to dislodge his hands. "I didn't want to leave until you'd secured the scene," the big man said.

"Okay, I'm here now, so settle down, George, and let them take you to get checked out." He made sure his partner was on the way to the hospital, then turned to the rest of the men and women on the scene, holding up his badge. "Everyone listen up! I'm Customs and Border Protection Agent Nathaniel Spencer, and this is my crime scene, so would all of you please clear out so our guys can process it, thank you very much!"

The police officers filed out, grumbling at missing out on the bust. Nate and Hernando made sure all of them were gone, then turned to the half-loaded truck.

"Well, let's see what we got," Nate said. Pulling on a pair of latex gloves, he grabbed a crowbar and pried open a large crate. The stenciled lettering on the side claimed it contained a pair of automatic transmissions. Clearing out the packing material, he saw two shiny metal casings, as promised. He pushed one to see how heavy it was. The round metal housing shifted easily under his hand. "Looks like they're importing something more than metal here." He scrounged up a wrench from the warehouse and unscrewed bolts until the housing came apart. Instead of the gears, clutches and bands that would have been inside a normal transmission, this one was filled with dozens of bags of white powder. "Hey, Carter, Hernando, take a look at this." The other two agents walked over. "Must be five kilos in here easy, and more in the rest, I'll bet. We got 'em dead to rights."

Hernando smiled and nodded, while Carter just looked numb. They all glanced up as more footsteps approached, and several other agents came in, including the crime-lab group.

One of the agents, a tall, bony redhead, took off his mirrored sunglasses and surveyed the scene. "Heard something about a war breaking out over here, and look who we find—Shootin' Spencer."

"Aw, Billy, don't be so sad—after all, you did arrive just in time to help clean up," Nate said. He held up a plastic bag full of white powder. "And you certainly can't argue with these results."

Billy Travis—the department's hotshot until Nate had arrived eighteen months earlier—snorted. "Maybe, but I could have done the same job without sending two agents to the hospital."

Carter started at his words, but it was Nate who carefully set the bag down and strode toward Travis. He was intercepted by Hernando, who put a hand on his shoulder. "Hey, big guy, it's not worth it."

Nate shrugged him off and walked up to the other agent, pinning him with his gaze. "You best take that cork out of your ass and shove it in your mouth, 'cause if you ever accuse me of being sloppy on a bust again, we're gonna have more than just words about it."

Travis looked around for support, but Hernando and Carter studiously ignored him, and the rest of the team busied themselves with processing the scene. "You're a goddamn hot dog, and everyone knows it, Spencer. It's only a matter of time before you really fuck up, and I hope to hell I'm there to see it," he snarled.

"Well, son, you do what you gotta do, and in the meantime, I'll be busy doing my job. By the way, if you want to see what twenty kilos of coke looks like—you know, to refresh your memory—they're in the truck there." Turning away from the other agent, Nate headed outside to cool off. He pulled a battered cheroot from his pocket and lit up, jetting the pungent smoke out of his nostrils.

Standing by the front of the truck, he climbed on the external gas tank and peered into the cab. He shoved aside a layer of fast-food bags and empty soda bottles, looking for anything interesting. He found a clipboard with the bills of lading on them, no doubt forged, and which should match the numbers on the boxes in the back. He bagged it and was about to jump down and give the board to a tech when a soft beeping sound caught his attention.

Leaning back in, he cocked his ear, trying to pinpoint where the noise was coming from. Running a hand between the seat cushions, he was rewarded with the feel of smooth plastic and withdrew a small handheld device.

"Looks like our smuggler got himself an e-mail," he muttered. Nate bagged that, as well, and walked back inside the warehouse, finding one of the techs he trusted, a short, stocky brunette named Claire.

"Do me a favor. Give me all the e-mails on this when

you have a chance—and don't let the walking asshole over there get wind of it, okay?" he said with a wink.

Claire nodded, and Nate turned to help with the rest of the crime scene, throwing Travis a cheery false smile as he did so. He had a feeling that the e-mails would take him further up the smuggling chain—and while he loved to bust the bad guys, it would be even sweeter to throw that in Travis's face, as well.

2

Kate Cochran, the director of Room 59, stared straight into the muzzle of a sleek SIG Sauer P-229 9 mm pistol.

"Just stay cool and do as they say. He's bluffing, trying to rattle you." She sucked in a breath and waited, unable to do anything else. "Keep it together and stick to the plan."

The man she was speaking to—who couldn't hear her at all—was in a small building in the town of Panamik, on the Nubra River in Kashmir. He kept his hands raised as he said in perfect Pakistani, "I am unarmed—I am just a college professor. I was hoping this kind of treatment wouldn't be necessary."

The man holding the pistol nodded to two other men, who grabbed the speaker's arms and spun him around, smacking his hands against the wall of the abandoned building where they all stood. One of the men patted him down for weapons. The other reached for the briefcase at his feet. He then shoved the professor away, whirling him to face the pistol-wielding man, who shoved his weapon right into the Pakistani's face.

"That is not for you! Not until you show me what I have come for!" the professor said.

Half a world away in New York City, Kate held her breath, hoping that her floater hadn't just bluffed himself into a bullet in his brain. Although she could see and hear everything, she couldn't lift a finger to help him. There were two other men who were supposed to be working with him, but they also had pistols pointed at their heads and couldn't come to his aid without getting shot. The entire deal now hinged on a stare-down with a ruthless Russian arms merchant who had already proved he would kill if he suspected even the slightest hint of a double cross.

For a long moment, no one moved. The Russian shifted his grip on the pistol, his eyes emotionless. "I should kill you where you stand for such an insult. But you also show courage to stand up to an armed man with nothing but your conviction to protect you. I can respect that." He lowered his pistol, and both the Pakistani and Kate breathed a sigh of relief.

Room 59 had spent six months subverting elements of the Pakistani terrorist group Lashkar-e-Omar, which had coalesced out of at least three smaller terrorist groups in 2002. Since then, the organization had been linked to several bombings, including a hotel and the U.S. Embassy in Kashmir. The terrorists also had ties to the men involved in the abduction and murder of the journalist Daniel Pearl. Now they were planning to up the stakes of their game considerably.

The group, which was battling for control of the disputed region of Kashmir with several other factions, had been negotiating to acquire a nuclear weapon on the black market for several months. Room 59 had placed an operative close to a nuclear scientist, Professor Osman Shirazi, a zealous patriot who wanted Kashmir brought into Pakistan's fold by any means necessary. Through a carefully arranged series of meetings, the Room 59 operative had finally learned the master plan to acquire a nuclear weapon and set it off while planting evidence that the Indian government was responsible for the attack. The goal was to begin serious talks with pro-Pakistani elements in the Kashmiri government to unite against India.

Professor Shirazi thought he was purchasing the weapon on behalf of Lashkar-e-Omar, but in reality he was being played by the operative in hopes he would lead him to senior members of the group. The terrorist group's ultimate plan was to absorb Kashmir into Pakistan, but if Kate and her people had their way, the weapon they planned on using to set that in motion was about to disappear.

The ultrasecret nongovernmental agency Room 59, charged with keeping peace throughout the world through just about whatever means possible, always had an interest in removing nuclear bombs from the world stage. The easiest way to do this was to simply purchase them from whoever was selling, and dispose of the weapons at a top-secret facility designed for just such a purpose. If they could strike blows against both the terrorist groups looking to buy or sell these weapons, as well as the arms dealers who trafficked in them, then it was three birds down with one well-placed stone. However, that assumed that the floater didn't get himself killed, as Shirazi almost had a few seconds ago. But as on several previous occasions in the past months, the uptight professor's strange knack for wriggling out of mortal danger had saved him again.

"It is good that you see reason. Tell your associates that there is no need to hold my friends hostage. I am here for a simple business transaction, that is all," the professor said.

"This man still might talk himself into a shallow grave before this is over," Kate said. Her gold-green eyes glanced at another window, where a lean, fox-faced Chinese man was also observing. Pai Kun, Room 59's director of Asian operations, had been instrumental in helping insert their operative, who was waiting to take delivery of the nuclear device as soon as the transaction was completed. It was the epitome of a Room 59 operation—using local resources who didn't even know they were being used to complete the mission, which had been going smoothly, except for the momentary unpleasantness just then.

"Shirazi's psych profile indicated he would react to a threat by not backing down, but he also wouldn't turn completely belligerent, either. If he had caved, they would walk all over him. Hard as it is to believe, he's doing exactly what we need right now," she said to Kun. Although when this is over, someone should talk to him about his negotiating tactics, Kate thought, sweeping a lock of platinum-blond hair out of her eyes. She watched the situation through Shirazi's glasses, which had been replaced by their operative and contained a miniature camera that recorded everyone the professor looked at. The signal was transmitted back to Room 59 analysts so they could match the faces with known terrorists and arms dealers.

Kate was particularly interested in this seller. Alexei Kryukov, a former Spetsnaz commander, had found the black market much more lucrative than working for his government. He'd made tens of millions buying and selling weapons. He had already fought his way out of one bust set up by Room 59, leaving an operative in the hospital, and had relocated to Southeast Asia, playing the local sides against each other and profiting every time.

The heavy-set Russian's eyes narrowed, but he nodded

at his men, who lowered their pistols and stepped away from Shirazi's companions. Everyone in the room visibly relaxed, and the professor picked up the briefcase and walked over to the Russian.

"So, where is it?"

Kryukov shook his head. "You will need to open that case and show me the diamonds first. Your purchase is nearby—that I guarantee."

"All right, Shirazi, give them a taste," Kate said. Her breath caught as she steeled herself for another outburst from the Pakistani, but he nodded and gave the case to one of his associates to hold while he spun the combinations and opened the catches, revealing a half-dozen velvet bags, all nestled in cutouts in a block of foam padding. Selecting the one on the lower right, he opened it and poured out a dozen glittering, clear gems in his palm, holding it out to the arms dealer.

"Examine any one you wish," he said.

Kryukov had already taken a jeweler's loupe from his pocket and placed it over his right eye. He plucked a small stone out of the other man's hand and held it up to the broken window, letting the sun's weak rays shine through the diamond. He turned it one way, then another, examining every facet. He did this with two more, then lowered his hand and nodded. "They are acceptable. Come with me into the next room so you can verify your merchandise."

Kate and Pai Kun watched as Shirazi trailed the Russian into a smaller, windowless room containing a wooden table and a metal-framed, aluminum-sided case about fifteen inches long, a foot wide and six inches high. There was no indication that it held something that could destroy a medium-size city or lay waste to twenty blocks of a major metropolitan area.

"The case is lead lined, so we are perfectly safe. I have left it unlocked so that you may examine it to be sure it is what we had agreed upon," Kryukov said.

The nuclear scientist flipped open the catches, his eyes never leaving Kryukov's face as he opened the top. "Part of the arsenal created in the 1980s, yes?" he asked. After the other man's nod, he continued, "The power source is still viable?" He took a small Geiger counter from his inside jacket pocket and ran it over the top of the case, apparently satisfied with the reading.

Kate stared at the open case in detached fascination. The interior was framed in about two inches of metal all around, and contained a tube about two inches in diameter that rested diagonally in the case. She knew exactly how it operated— the discus-shaped plutonium core was surrounded by a cylinder of high explosive, that, when detonated, would create an implosion that compressed the plutonium on all sides, making it a perfect sphere, and causing it to reach supercritical mass, with a mushroom cloud to follow.

"The battery system has been maintained on an annual basis, the explosives have been verified, as well, and the transmitter that would normally alert my former employers of low or failing power has been disabled—no sense in having them track this down before you are ready to use it, *da?*"

"And the yield?" Shirazi asked.

"Ten kilotons, suitable for any purpose from urban terrorism to the destruction of infrastructure or other targets of opportunity. But of course, that is none of my business," the Russian replied.

"True. It is perfect, and is certainly acceptable." Shirazi closed the case and snapped shut the latches, then held out the briefcase full of diamonds. "I will have my men take this out immediately. Thank you very much."

"It has been my pleasure." Kryukov hefted the case, which, along with the four million dollars in diamonds, also contained a transmitter that would enable Room 59 to track his location at all times. Kate expected him to get rid of the case as soon as was practical, but she hoped he would take it to one of his hideouts in the area, enabling them to set up surveillance there.

Although they had considered using their operative to make the buy, the ex-Spetsnaz's legendary ability to smell a setup, coupled with his earlier escape in Russia, had convinced Kate to use a committed floater who had no idea of the true nature of his mission. The buyer had to believe his own story down to the last detail, and Shirazi's fanaticism had shone through every second.

"All right, now get out of there before the Russians—or you—decide to pull something stupid," she muttered. Kate leaned forward as if she could force the professor out of the building by sheer willpower alone.

Pai Kun sipped from a china cup before replying. "That is hardly likely. It wouldn't help Kryukov's reputation if his clients ended up dead."

"No, but if he was already gone when his backup team terminated Shirazi and his boys, he'd get his nuke back to resell and could blame the deaths on the Indians. That's the problem with this business, Pai—you just can't trust anyone." Kate knew what she spoke of all too well. She'd seen many good operatives lost in the line of duty. Although they all accepted the risks of the job, it was always a blow to Kate. No matter what, they couldn't afford to lose Shirazi until after he had delivered the nuke to her operative.

She watched as Shirazi brought his two men in to carry the case to a waiting car and told them to stow the weapon in the trunk. "Notify Alpha they're on their way. ETA ten minutes," she said. Once he had the weapon and was away, they could either burn the professor, leaving him to be killed by the Lashkar-e-Omar members once he failed to deliver the device, or attempt to openly recruit him by providing protection or even exfiltrating him out of the country if necessary in exchange for information on other terrorist members and future plans.

The Room 59 comm operative signaled for Kate's attention. "Alpha has received and confirmed delivery time of package. Primary, you may want to hear this—the men in the car are talking."

Kate enhanced the audio as she watched one of the men in the backseat draw a pistol and pull back the slide. "You're sure he is a traitor?" Shirazi asked.

"I spoke to our contact in al-Rashid, who assured me that this Muhammad Alavi is not a member of the Islamabad cell as he had claimed. We are to capture him and find out whom he is really working for, then dispose of him."

Kate and Pai Kun exchanged glances. "Our cover package was supposed to be airtight," Kate said.

"Unfortunately, it seems that wasn't the case," Kun replied, sounding alarmed.

Kate raised her communications suite. "Notify Alpha that his package handlers are hostile—repeat, the handlers are hostile. He is to terminate all of them upon delivery and proceed with secondary departure plan. Pai, your men are in place?"

"Of course. All Alpha will have to do is head north to the Chinese border. My men will handle the rest. We'll be able to get him and the package safely off the continent."

"Good. Has the message been transmitted?" Kate asked.

The young woman in Australia who was serving as

Room 59's communications suite operator replied, "I have transmitted the message, but have not received the acknowledgment yet."

"Why not? Is he off air?" Kate asked.

"It appears that the satellite we were routing through has malfunctioned somehow. Am moving to backup communications system."

"I do not want to see our operative killed or this loose nuke slip through our fingers. Keep trying until you raise him. Pai, can you establish contact on your end?" Kate could only watch as Shirazi led the two other men in prayer, asking for strength as they prepared to capture the infidel plotting against them. Her stomach twisted as she watched the three men pervert the essentially peaceful message of Islam to suit their own twisted ends.

"My people are working on it now. Although the area is remote, we shouldn't be having this much trouble."

The seconds stretched out into longer silence as Kate and her counterpart in China waited for word that their operative had been warned, all the while keeping their eyes glued to the rough mountain road the professor's car traveled along on its way to capture their man.

"Primary, this is comm. I've established contact with Alpha and have received confirmation that he has received the message. Repeat, he has received the message."

"Comm, acknowledged. Let him know that the two men in the rear seats are armed, and the one on the left should be considered the primary threat." Kate sat back in her chair and opened a split screen on her touch-interactive monitor. It allowed her to keep tabs on the professor, her operative, Kryukov's location and the route her man would follow out of Kashmir, via satellite feeds all on one screen in real time.

The car turned onto a small dirt road that led into the surrounding mountains. White-capped peaks were visible in the distance. They continued up the road for another few minutes, then pulled into what barely qualified as a clearing in the road, more of a wide spot where the steep walls receded slightly.

Standing near the wall was Room 59's operative, a man whose real name was Robert Lashti. He huddled in a hooded parka, hands in his pockets, shifting from one foot to the other to keep warm. His car, a four-wheel-drive Range Rover, was parked on the other side of the space. The sun was setting as the three men got out of their car, and Professor Shirazi hailed him with the traditional greeting.

He reached out to shake Lashti's hand, most likely to distract him from the other two men, who would then subdue him, Kate thought. She watched as Lashti extended his right hand to clasp Shirazi's, and as he gripped it, Kate saw a puff of down feathers erupt from the left-hand pocket of his coat as he shot the Pakistani professor in the abdomen. Shirazi stumbled away and collapsed as his two henchmen, their eyes wide with shock, struggled to draw their own weapons. Firing from the hip, the Room 59 operative dispatched the man on the left with two shots to his chest, leaving the third man to sprint to the still-running car. Diving into the driver's seat, he gunned it and aimed straight for Robert, who had taken his pistol from his pocket and sighted down the barrel at the driver.

"Somebody tell me that man isn't playing chicken with a live suitcase nuke in the trunk of his car." Kate gritted her teeth in anticipation of her operative getting mowed down by the wildly plunging vehicle, but the real-time satellite feed showed a different story.

Lashti fired one shot as the car hurtled toward him. The bullet punched through the windshield and into the driver's skull, causing him to slump over the steering wheel. Immediately the car began slowing, and Lashti stepped aside to let it pass. Gravity and lack of acceleration completed his job as the car crunched into the wall of the pass at about fifteen meters per hour, then stalled.

Exhaling a white plume of breath into the night air, Lashti checked the two men on the ground, ensuring that both were dead and snatching the glasses off Shirazi's nose as he did. He walked to the car, opened the trunk and lifted out the metal case, carrying it to his Range Rover. Opening the back, he set the case down inside, then slid open a hidden compartment in the side wall of the SUV's cargo area. He withdrew a device resembling a large, smooth steel can set on its side. It had a handle on top, with two smaller cylinders sticking out of its back, and rested on four short legs. Flipping a power switch, he waited for it to warm up and flipped open the catches on the case. After checking a small display screen, he picked up the device and played the large end over the entire case. Frowning, he did so again, then a third time.

"This does not look good." Pai Kun's normally calm features shared a furrow of unease with their operative, who had flipped open his encrypted sat phone.

"This is Primary. Go, Alpha," Kate said.

"Primary, this is Alpha at Mountainview. The handlers are dead. However, the package is a fake. I repeat, the package is a fake. This is U-235—my guess is from spent fuel rods. I'll bet the detonation material is also fake, as well. We've been scammed."

"Alpha, say again—are you sure?"

"I've scanned this three times, and I get the same exact

reading. That suitcase nuke is still out there somewhere. Either Kryukov was running a double cross or he thought he had the real thing and didn't, but if that was the case, it was good enough to fool him, as well."

Pai Kun stroked his chin. "If the case and workings are the real thing, and it gave off radiation, why would he have any reason to believe that this was not an operational weapon?"

"True—assuming he wasn't pulling the double cross in the first place. Alpha?" Kate said.

"I'm here. What are your instructions?" the operative replied.

"Sanitize the area, then head back to Panamik. We'll put you on Kryukov's trail as soon as possible. Good work."

"Thanks, but not good enough. Will await further instructions in Panamik. Alpha out."

Kate killed the connection, her mind racing with possibilities. Did Kryukov double-cross the terrorists? Why, other than the obvious reasons? If he did or didn't was almost irrelevant. *Who has it now?*

She sent a quick message to all of the Room 59 analysts scattered around the globe. "Keep alert for any mention of loose nukes originating either from Russia or Pakistan, no matter how tenuous or far-fetched. Alert me priority with any information you come across."

3

The three bearded men drove through the desert landscape, dotted with the hardy scrub vegetation and stunted trees that looked relatively familiar to all of them. No one commented on the similarities to home, however; they were all completely focused on the job at hand.

After the slaughter on the deserted road where they had been pulled over, one of the men had loaded the bodies of the two Border Patrol agents into the SUV, driven it into the middle of the desert, wiped it down and set fire to the vehicle. Meanwhile, the other two men had hauled the bodies of the luckless illegals and their coyotes several dozen yards off the side of the road and had cleaned up the truck as best as they could before leaving the scene. The third man had met up with the other two a few miles down the road, and they proceeded together to their destination.

The farmstead they pulled up to had once been a thriving ranch in the middle of the south Texas plain. It had been abandoned decades earlier, and was now a waypoint on the illegal-immigration highway. Every so often the

Border Patrol would stake out the place, and the three men had stopped a few miles away and watched the buildings for two hours until the sun came up. During their surveillance, they took turns performing the predawn prayer.

When they were satisfied no one was there, they drove the truck up the long driveway, past the leaning, window-less, two-story house, its drab wooden siding stripped clean of every speck of paint by decades of dust storms. At the sagging wooden barn, two of the men got out and walked to the door, machine pistols in hand, and checked the interior. Finding it empty, they waved the truck forward, closing the doors behind them.

The temperature inside was already stifling, but the men didn't notice as they pulled on latex gloves and got to work. In one corner was a green tarp, underneath which were cans of spray paint and other supplies. After moving the long box out of the back of the truck, one of the men washed out the back with a strong bleach solution, then soaped it down, as well, finally rinsing it clean. Mean-while, two of the men wiped off the thick layer of dust, then covered the truck's lights, windows, bumpers and trim with paper and tape. After the cargo bay was clean, the third man prepped the cans and laid out large decals to complete the truck's transformation.

When everything was ready, they spray painted the truck, starting at the front and moving back, taking breaks every few minutes to let the fumes dissipate. Gradually the panel truck turned from white to a flat gray, which dried quickly in the heat. Two of the men methodically covered every inch of metal with the paint, while the third scrubbed blood spatter from the cab's interior and covered the bullet-torn bench seat with a blanket.

At noon, they stopped to pray again and eat a lunch of

flatbread, hummus and cold falafels. Afterward, they checked the paint job, and stripped off the paper. The third man measured carefully and applied the decals, making the truck appear to be just another vehicle that belonged to one of the hundreds of private companies in El Paso. Lastly, he switched the license plates with ones that had been supplied along with the paint and other materials. He sent the other two to dispose of everything left over, warning them to travel at least a mile away from the building before digging, and to bury everything at least four feet deep.

Once they were finished, the three men walked around the truck, examining their handiwork. The driver nodded with satisfaction, and motioned for the other two to open the double doors. He drove to the end of the driveway, then went back and helped the other two sweep away the tracks leading from the barn to the road. Taking one last look around, the driver was satisfied that everything looked exactly as it had when they had arrived. He got into the cab, joining the other two men, and drove away, heading down the highway toward El Paso.

4

Nate Spencer pushed through the doors of the Customs and Border Protection Office of Field Operations that evening after staying at the parts-shop scene for several hours, making sure every scrap of evidence had been bagged, labeled and processed correctly. He was greeted by enthusiastic applause from most of the day shift, with a few holdouts, notably Billy Travis, glaring at him instead.

Shaking his head, Nate held up his arms to quiet the clapping. "Hey, it wasn't just me out there, but Hernando, Carter, Ryan and, most of all, Juan Menendez. All of them helped bust these guys and recover more than one hundred kilos of uncut cocaine—the biggest haul this year, I might add."

"Yes, but unfortunately, it cost the life of one of our own." Chief Patrol Agent Roy Robertson had been leaning against the door frame of his office, but now he walked into the center of the assembled men and women. "I'm sorry to tell you that Agent Menendez passed away an hour ago after participating in the successful raid on the smuggling ring. The funeral will be held on Saturday, and all off-duty personnel are expected to attend. Agent Spencer, I'll want your report on my desk by noon tomorrow."

The celebration suddenly over, Nate caught Travis's eye, who shook his head with a frown. Reaching up to scratch his cheek, he flipped the other man off, then turned and went to his desk.

A stack of printed e-mails was there, along with a note.

Here you go—the encryption was a bitch! E-files are on your computer. You owe me—Claire.

Nate made a mental note to buy her dinner sometime, then leafed through the messages. It soon became obvious that the device had passed through several hands. Only a few dozen of the messages were from Jesus, the driver they had arrested from the smuggling group. The majority of the e-mails were from a man named Arsalan Hejazi to an address simply titled "freedomfighter" at a common Web address. Several were copied to Jesus at an El Paso e-mail address. Nate read the most recent message.

Dear Yousef,
Our plans are progressing well. Soon we will have everything we need to strike at our enemies. Our men are coming to you soon across the southern border. Be strong, and keep working toward our common goal. *Allahu Akbar.*

Attached to the message was a list of machine parts and pieces, none of which were immediately recognizable to Nate except for one—the chemical symbol for plutonium. Is this a list of parts for a bomb? he wondered. Nate reread the message, something about it niggling at the back of his mind. The name of the sender—he couldn't quite grasp it.

He searched through the detritus in his desk drawers, looking for a notebook from one of his older case files. Scrabbling among the copies, he came up with his logbook from the previous year. Flipping through it, he looked through his notes until he came across the entry he was looking for.

Almost a year earlier…another warehouse. Nate had been involved in a large bust that had brought in the FBI and ATF, as well. A fringe group of Muslims had been suspected of stockpiling weapons on the Mexican border in preparation for an incursion into the U.S. An informant had given them the address, and the three U.S. law-enforcement departments had swooped down on the place. But the terrorists had been forewarned, and had detonated explosives inside the building, demolishing it and also blowing themselves up. The ringleader had been a man named Sepehr al-Kharzi, a longtime member of al Qaeda, and a most-wanted member of the organization. Nate had seen him go into the building—had actually looked into the son of a bitch's expressionless brown eyes, he recalled—before it had vanished in a huge fireball. While they had uncovered evidence of an underground escape tunnel, there was no evidence that anyone had used it, and it was presumed that al-Kharzi had been vaporized along with the other terrorists. However, as Nate stared at a copy of the terrorist's wanted poster, he saw a familiar name among the known aliases al-Kharzi used—Arsalan Hejazi.

Nate checked the date of the sent e-mail. Three months ago. He leaned back in his chair, absorbing the information. Flipping through the rest of the e-mails didn't reveal an answer from the mysterious Yousef, nor any more communication from al-Kharzi, Hejazi or whatever he might be calling himself nowadays.

Nate got up and headed to Robertson's office. His superior was on the phone, and held up a finger while he finished. "Yes, sir…no, everything was done by the book. There won't be anything of the sort. Yes, sir, I will, sir. Thank you, sir. Goodbye." He hung up the phone and frowned at Nate. "If that's your report, it's the fastest typing I've ever seen from you."

"Yeah, you'll have that soon enough. Look, I found something in the evidence from the bust, and wanted you to have a look." He placed the printed e-mail on Robertson's desk.

His boss picked it up and scanned the brief message. "And?"

"Arsalan is an alias for Sepehr al-Kharzi, the terrorist."

"Yeah—isn't he the one that died in the warehouse explosion last year. So?"

"This e-mail is only three months old," Nate pointed out.

"So one of his cronies has picked up his handle, trying to make people believe he's still alive. You know this happens all the time, Nate," Robertson said.

Nate put his hands on the desk and leaned forward. "This doesn't feel like a fake, Roy. My gut tells me this is the real thing. They're talking about some mission, and one of the addresses was here in El Paso. And look at this parts list—including plutonium. I think he's still out there, and still planning something."

Robertson rubbed his hands over his face. "Shut the door, Nate, and take a seat."

He complied and returned to the battered chair in front of the chief's desk. "Look, we've just lost three agents in the last twenty-four hours—"

"What, who were the other two? What happened?" Nate asked.

"Early this morning, Agents Morton and Delaney were killed in the line of duty by unknown persons, who also seem to have massacred at least twenty illegals."

"Jesus, why ain't I workin' that case right now?" Nate said.

"Dammit, Nate, you know you're on administrative leave until your case is cleared. The person I was talking with on the phone was the deputy commissioner, straight outta D.C. Now, I've kept as tight a lid as possible on that illegal incident, but the shit's about to hit the fan, and we're all standing downwind. What I need from you right now is cooperation, and your word that the auto-parts bust went down legally and by the book."

"Hell, yeah, it went by the book—the book that says agents will defend themselves when they are fired upon. Menendez got killed, and Ryan is in the hospital right now as a result of our 'by-the-book' bust."

"Right, and the drugs you recovered is the kind of press we need right now to counter this slaughter in the desert. If too much of a big deal is made out of that, everyone's going to think we're doing a worse job than some people already do. Our stats are up where it counts in all areas, but it just takes one of these incidents to blow out of proportion, and no one remembers the twenty good things we do every day—they just see the one operation that went wrong."

"Yeah, I get that 'the press is our best friend and worst enemy at the same time' BS. Look, Roy, you know how wide-open the border is, even with the additional men and the National Guard people we have. A lot of guys think that it's only a matter of time before someone sneaks something more lethal than immigrants through, and this could be it. Do you want that to go down on your watch?"

"Jesus, Nate, you know that's not fair—I'm doin' everything I can, but the government wants us to do more with less every day, and I can't have my men chasing down cold leads just because your gut says something's going on." He held up his hand to forestall Nate's protest. "Look, there's nowhere I'd rather have you be than out in the field, but that just ain't gonna happen right now. If you say the bust went down clean, then I'm sure the clearance team will come to the same conclusion. But you know the drill—shots were fired and one of our guys died. Since those incidents with that pair of illegals a couple years ago—where he got shot in the ass, then turned around and sued us—"

"Putting two of our agents in jail for no goddamn reason, too," Nate gripped.

"Yeah, that too. Anyway, the brass has been breathing down our necks about executing clean operations, and we need to do that as best as we can. So do me a favor—finish your report and get out of here. The minute you can come back, I'll let you know."

Nate ran a hand through his crew-cut, salt-and-pepper hair and sighed. "You're the boss." He rose and walked back into the office, only to find Travis leaning against his desk.

"Looks like ol' Shootin' Spencer was the one who got tagged this time." Travis smirked as Nate walked around him and sat down.

"If I'd wanted any more shit from you, Travis, I'd squeeze that big greasy pustule you call a head and see what came squirtin' out. Now get the hell out of here. I got work to do."

Travis stuck his face right next to Nate's. "Yeah, you get back to your real important report, buddy. Me, I'm headin' out to work that slaughter case in the desert. I just wanted to tell you personally. Have fun holdin' down the fort."

Nate stared at the retreating back as Travis swaggered out of the office, willing the punk-ass agent to drop dead with his next step, but to no avail. The office was almost deserted, with only a few agents still finishing up their paperwork. Nate blew a breath out and dug in, as well, pecking out his report with two fingers on the ancient computer he had been handed down from God knew where. At least the damn thing had e-mail, although it was balky and slower than hell. He finished his report, then leaned back in his chair and snuck a peek at Robertson, who was still working at his own desk.

Nate considered his options. *What do I have to lose by kicking this up the chain? Well, for starters, Roy won't be too thrilled. But he'd be less thrilled if this turned out to be something, and downright furious if it was something big. What the hell—at least they can't say I didn't try.*

He found the copies of the e-mails on his computer and attached the one from Arsalan, along with his thoughts on it, in a message to the Department of Homeland Security. He hoped they'd give it to an analyst who'd be able to think at least halfway outside of the box. But this is going to Washington—what are the odds? he wondered. He shrugged and hit Enter, shaking his head as the message flashed into cyberspace.

5

"My God, some days working here is just like any other large corporation, except we're supposed to be keeping three hundred million people safe every single day," Tracy Wentworth said as she walked back to her cubicle at the ramshackle headquarters on Nebraska Avenue. She was annoyed after yet another pointless two-hour meeting on analyzing strategic weaknesses in America's private infrastructure. Everything she'd heard was a repetition of things she already knew. They had just tried to package it in yet another new "assessment procedure."

Only 1:00 p.m., and already her day was an exercise in futility. Two of her requested follow-ups on what she had thought had been promising leads had been denied due to "lack of feasibility." This was primarily due to her boss, a politicking butt-kisser who squashed anything he didn't regard as a "slam-dunk," to parrot a certain high-level intelligence chief's unfortunate choice of words a few years back regarding WMDs in Iraq. Since then, Tracy suspected that all of America's intelligence agencies had become paralyzed by fear—the fear of not connecting all of the dots fast enough, or even worse, getting something wrong, and having the press lambaste them for not doing their job properly. That especially went for the one she worked for, the Department of Homeland Security.

When she had come to DHS two years ago, Tracy had been filled with the desire to join a department that would fight the real threats that America faced. She had hoped this new agency wouldn't be hampered by the baggage of the Cold War and the continued focus on potential-threat nations and their standing armies. She wanted to tackle fourth-generation warfare and the emerging terrorist networks spreading from the hotbed Middle East to ensnare other countries in their multitentacled grasp of drugs, money and suicidal ideology.

Unfortunately, that had not proved to be the case. From its once-promising beginning, the DHS had rapidly become stuck in the same operational quagmire that hobbled most other government departments. Small-minded career bureaucrats wielded their power like tyrants, rewarding loyal followers and punishing anyone they didn't agree with almost at whim.

In particular, there was a terrible lack of information flowing from the top officers down, which was, in Tracy's and many other analysts' opinions, crucial to effectively gathering intelligence to identify and stop threats to the nation. Personality clashes and conflicting interpretations of rules, regulations and even the DHS's role in homeland security were everyday occurrences. It all served efforts to get vital programs off the ground.

The department's creation by squashing together twenty-two separate agencies under one roof meant there was often confusion as to what section would handle a particular project, which led to even more delays. Certain departments, such as Immigration and Customs Enforcement, operated under severe budgetary limitations, to the point where the agents could not execute their duties effectively. The problem was later revealed to be infighting among various departments for budget allocation. Tracy had heard the horror stories, and had unfortunately been a part of some of them, as well, as she fought for information, access and resources, along with the other 180,000 people in the sprawling department.

When she got back to her desk, she found an e-mail from her supervisor, Brian Gilliam.

Tracy,
See me soonest regarding your sewage threat analysis.
Brian

"Fantastic, this is exactly what I need right now," she muttered. Tracy had been analyzing unconventional attacks on metropolitan areas, and had come to the conclusion that there could be a risk—small, but definitely a possibility—that terrorists could attempt to contaminate water supplies of major cities using waste products. The companies that handled raw sewage were often even more poorly guarded than chemical plants, and the waste material could be released into aquifers with relative ease. She had worked up a solid list of facts to support her case, including three known plots that had been foiled in the past five years. She included lists of various treatment plants that were most vulnerable, and their proximity to major supplies of freshwater resources. It wasn't a glamorous job, but that's what she was paid to do, and Tracy thought she did it pretty damn well. At least, until her boss came in and crapped all over her carefully researched analysis.

She pulled the leather holder and hair stick from a tight bun, letting her glossy black hair cascade down to the middle of her back. She wasn't a fool. She figured Gilliam let her do the reports primarily because she made him look good in his interdepartmental progress reports. And every so often he actually sent one up the chain, where it usually died a slow, painful death in one of the various committees that had to approve it. The fact that she was both a woman and part Mexican—her father was a blue-blooded Bostonian, hence her last name—didn't hurt, either, given the DHS's dismal record on both minority and gender-equitable hiring. Just what you wanted to be when you got into intelligence analysis—a good-looking figurehead.

She rose and stretched her back, feeling the kinks pop out, then smoothed her skirt. Across from her, Mark Whitney raised a quizzical eyebrow. "You just got back. Now where you off to?"

Tracy nodded at her supervisor's office. "I'm about to go zero-for-three with Gilliam. Bet you a grande latte he's going to flush my sewage-contamination report down the toilet."

"What? I thought that was a great piece of work. You sure? He just sent one of mine on securing the Canadian border up the chain."

"Yes, but you're his fair-haired boy, remember?" Tracy said this without a trace of rancor. She knew Mark was a very good analyst. Tracy strongly suspected her boss was sexist, but he had never given any proof of it, other than the strange priority he gave some reports and not others—coincidentally the reports turned in by the men in the department, in particular. The fact that Mark was gay—and that Brian had never noticed—was a private joke shared between the two of them.

"Here goes. Wish me luck," she said.

"Tracy, you work for the government—if they'd wanted you to have any luck, they'd have sent you a memo assigning you some," Mark said with a grin.

"Ain't that the truth?" Unable to delay any longer, she began the trek to Gilliam's office at the end of the long, cubicle-filled room, each one manned by an analyst busily crunching the never-ending avalanche of data that poured into the DHS every day. She knocked on the door, and a terse voice called, "Come in."

Tracy opened the door and slipped inside. Unlike the rest of the stark, gray-walled cubicles, which were only personalized with whatever an employee brought from home, Gilliam's office was furnished well, if not plushly. Tracy always felt as if she were entering a bank officer's workplace. The caramel-colored carpet was thick enough that she barely felt the concrete floor under her leather pumps, and the walls were actually paneled with a light-colored wood. His desk wasn't a standard-issue metal-and-partical-board affair, either, but also made of wood—cherry, she thought. The surface was spotless, not even a piece of paper on it, only a flat-screen monitor attached by a sleek swivel arm so it could be pushed out of the way when necessary. Gilliam claimed that he had inherited the furnishings from his predecessor, but Tracy knew differently; she had seen the order invoices. Yet another efficient use of the company budget. *Executives never learn that they can't hide anything from a computer geek,* she thought.

"Ah, Tracy, thanks for dropping by."

When she had first met Gilliam, Tracy had searched for the one word that described him best, and had come up with *unctuous,* since it sounded slightly better than *oily.*

Dressed in a pinstriped shirt with coordinated suspenders, and sporting gelled, dark brown hair that was never out of place, with gold, wire-rimmed glasses on his pale, round face, Gilliam was the epitome of middle-management bureaucracy.

"My pleasure, sir. You wanted to discuss my latest report?" Tracy knew from long experience that it was best to keep her boss focused on the task at hand, the better to get it over with as soon as possible. If she didn't, he might make an attempt at small talk, which would be a punishment worse than receiving bad news in the first place.

"Yes, the waste-contamination analysis. First, I'm pleased to say that it was very good work—I really liked what I saw there."

"Sir?" The curveball threw Tracy. Normally Gilliam was bluntly dismissive of anything that he didn't automatically jump all over. The hair on the back of her neck rose; something was up, but she didn't know what.

"Unfortunately, your threat-assessment estimate is too low at this time to forward this through the proper channels. However, I'd like to table it for a revisit in about three months. I'll just hang on to this version, and we'll see about further consideration when the proper time comes up," he said.

Well, a partial victory was better than none at all, Tracy thought as she nodded. "Thank you, sir. I'm glad to hear that. Is there anything else?"

"No, you're free to go." Having summarily dismissed her, his attention had already returned to the computer monitor. Tracy knew that this was as good as it was going to get. She rose to leave, and was halfway to the door when he spoke again.

"Oh, there is one more thing."

She turned and waited for him to speak.

"Your application for one of the next fusion centers that is about to open—I thought you'd like to know it's coming up for review in the next few days."

The fusion centers were a new program, the DHS's version of boots on the ground. In effect, they were localized offices in each of seventeen sectors across the country, where staff would work local law enforcement and private-sector companies in a more closely coordinated joint effort. Tracy had been working toward a position in one of them from the moment she'd heard about the plan. The way Gilliam had brought it up was just like him—wait until she'd thought the meeting was over, and then spring this bit of news as a surprise.

"Yes, sir?" she said, waiting.

"I was wondering if you'd given any thought as to where you'd like to be posted. Although I'd hate to see you leave my team, I could put in a good word if you had a particular assignment venue in mind."

Tracy's instincts screamed at her to proceed with care. *He's never this nice. What's going on?* "Thank you, sir. I understand that an office will be opening in Virginia at some point, and I was hoping that could I transfer there."

Gilliam removed his glasses and polished them, then did something Tracy couldn't remember seeing since she had come to work for him—he smiled. Instead of reassuring her, the expression filled her with a vague sense of unease, especially since he looked like a cat that had just eaten a dozen canaries. She resisted looking down to see if there were any yellow feathers on her lapel.

"Well, I'll see what I can do—pending HR's approval, of course."

"Of course, sir. Thanks again." She walked to the door and let herself out, all the while wondering what trap she may have inadvertently stepped into.

6

Kate Cochran pushed up her viewscreen glasses and rubbed the bridge of her nose. She had just logged out of a quickly convened meeting with the members of the International Intelligence Agency, the governing body that had set up and now oversaw Room 59's operations. The shadowy figures—literally faceless silhouettes in a virtual, heavily secured conference room, which was all Kate or anyone else who worked in Room 59 ever saw of them—met to deliver assignments, or, in this case, to discuss a potential mission that any sector director brought to the table.

Kate had conferenced in Pai Kun for support, and the diminutive Chinese head of Asian operations had performed with his usual spotless efficiency. Kate had also done well, opening a continuing surveillance file on Kryukov to find out what he knew about the suitcase nuke, and to try to track it down. The board, as concerned as the two directors were about missing nuclear weapons, voted both missions green with no opposition.

Kate had gotten what she wanted; now the only problem

was trying to find a nuclear needle among the world's hay-stacks. But that was why she had the world's best analysts on her payroll. *At least, I hope that's the case,* she told herself. She was about to slip the viewscreen glasses back on and dive back into the virtual world to see what her Web scourers had brought up when there was a knock at the door.

"Kate, you really need to take a break." The slip of a girl who peeked into the room was Arminda Todd, Kate's live-in housekeeper and, she often half joked, her link to both the outside world and sanity. Dressed in a red-and-black-plaid pleated skirt and a white boys'-cut button-down shirt, with her normally dark blond hair accented with streaks of black this month, she looked exactly like the moonlighting college student she was.

"Hi, Mindy. Come on in. I assume it's lunchtime?" Kate asked.

"Do you ever look out those fabulous windows of yours? Try about three hours past dinnertime. I made you a plate." She set a tray down with a heaped plate that gave off a spicy, heavenly aroma. "I was cooking with Grand-mama, and of course, anything she makes will feed twenty, with leftovers."

The main course, what looked like zucchini halves stuffed with ground lamb and baked in tomato sauce, didn't look all that appetizing, but the smell was irresistible. It was accompanied by a small green salad and still-warm flatbread. Once Kate dug in, the first bite awakened a ravenous hunger. "Thanks," she mumbled around a mouthful.

"Oh, I should warn you—" Mindy began just as Kate's eyes widened, and she grabbed the glass of ice water, downing half of it in huge gulps "—Grandmama likes things spicy."

"If that's 'spicy,' I'd hate to see what she considers hot." Kate paused, took another drink and eyed the plate dubiously. "It is good, once my tongue recovers from, what was that, a pound of paprika?"

Mindy shook her head, making her long pigtails swing back and forth. "Grandmama's secret recipe. She says she will give it to me only on her deathbed, and that I can never write it down, but can pass it on to my own daughter when the time comes."

"That sounds like her, all right." Kate tried another bite, and was pleased to find that her mouth had grown accustomed to the pungent blend of spices. "Delicious."

A soft chime from her computer brought Kate's head up. "That's what I've been waiting for. Give me a minute to see if I'm right, and I'll quit for the night, I promise."

Mindy scrunched up her face in what passed as a stern expression, but only made her young face and china-blue eyes look even more adorable. "All right, five minutes, but that's all. Otherwise I'm coming in here to drag you out."

"Deal, cross my heart." Kate wolfed another bite while sliding the glasses down over her eyes. With precise movements, she navigated to the new message and opened it.

Hey K,
This slid into a DHS server twenty minutes ago. It isn't much, but it's the best lead so far. With the Rio Grande still leaking illegals like a sieve every day, maybe some homies from a bit farther east—like Mideast, if you know what I mean—are making a run for the border, too, before it really gets closed up?
Let me know if you need follow-up or anything else, okay?
B2S

Kate smiled. She'd figured that Born2Slyde, as the hacker called herself online, would come up with what looked like a solid lead first. The eighteen-year-old girl could whiz in and out of supposedly secure mainframes and security systems with unparalleled ease.

Room 59 had been organized as a decentralized operation, with no main ops center, like other agencies worked from, the better to not find it. Kate's New York City town house, where she lived and worked, was the closest thing to one, and that was primarily because she hardly had time to leave the luxurious suite of rooms. Terror and threats to world security rarely took days off, so she didn't, either.

She opened the triple-encrypted, compressed data file. That brought up two e-mail messages, along with an itemized list, including plutonium, that had been highlighted by the sender. B2S had also included current statistics for incidents of violence or large drug caches coming across the U.S.-Mexican border. The name of the sender caught her eye, and a quick check of a top secret deceased-terrorist list confirmed her first suspicion—that the man using the alias Arsalan Hejazi was supposed to be dead.

A deceased man placing an order from beyond the grave? Someone wanted to make a bomb, but what if they got the chance to pick one up that was assembled and ready to blow? All they'd need to do was get it across the border, which, while difficult, wasn't impossible, according to the most recent border security review, Kate thought.

She used one of the installed back-door programs that enabled her to access any government network without being detected. Bringing up the network for the U.S. Customs and Border Protection department of the DHS, she entered the keywords *Mexico, nuclear, border, kill* and *terrorist,* and directed the system to scan all files accessed within the previous forty-eight hours.

Hundreds of messages back and forth between station offices and Washington filled her screen. Kate sat back and used a trick she had learned during grad school. She let her eyes wander over the long list, relying on her subconscious to home in on the message that would be most useful. Her gaze alighted on one subject line. Two Border Patrol Agents And Multiple Illegals Killed North Of Border Outside El Paso. Opening the message, Kate read a concise summary of an incident involving a pair of Border Patrol agents and twenty-three illegal immigrants, all shot at what should have been a routine stop. What was strange was that the coyotes had been killed, as well, and everyone had been shot multiple times, many in the back of the head at close range. The Border Patrol SUV had been found several miles away, a burned wreck, but the truck that had been carrying the human cargo had disappeared. It wasn't just a random murder; it had been a massacre.

Who would go to such lengths to kill everyone at the scene? she wondered. The answer came to her immediately. Someone who had something to hide, and when their cover was compromised, they didn't hesitate to kill everyone to insure that they wouldn't be seen. What could be that important? A suitcase nuke?

Kate leaned forward again and brought up the e-mail from the Border Patrol agent, putting the two side by side. She felt a familiar strange fluttering in her stomach that heralded a leap in her intuitive logic. She knew the two incidents were connected, although she couldn't explain why. It just felt right; that was all. But that was enough to start on, anyway. The proof would have to come later.

She looked at where the agent's e-mail had ended up—the in-box of an analyst named Tracy Wentworth. *My dear, I think you may be doing a lot more than you expected tomorrow,* Kate thought, letting the rest of her dinner grow cold as she made preparations to travel to Washington the next day. *Hope you're up for the challenge.*

7

The man known as Narid al-Gaffari had driven more than twenty-five hundred miles over the past three days, but instead of exhausted, he felt more and more invigorated as he neared his final destination.

Traveling down the highway at a steady seventy miles per hour in his nondescript Honda Accord, Narid took a moment to marvel at the diversity of the land he had spent every waking hour driving through so far. This was a far cry from his first visit to America, more than a decade earlier. Then he had been much more cautious, seeing enemies around every corner, the specter of police surveillance on every block. Now he looked back on those days as the easy times. After 9/11, there were still plenty of opportunities to sow the seeds of fear throughout the bloated American infrastructure—seeds that were still bearing fruit. But the paranoia, even if justified, had increased, and then the U.S. agencies had also started getting things right, so much so that al-Gaffari had resorted to what some might have considered desperate measures to rid himself of the surveillance. Desperate but effective—after all, few people spent time looking for a dead man.

This time, he had landed on the rugged coast of British Columbia in the dead of night, transferring from a freighter to a fishing boat that had dropped him off on shore. From there he had driven east, through the thick forests and the Cascade Mountain range and over the Rockies into the Great Plains, where the elevated beauty of the mountains that reminded him of home was replaced by the endless, flat grasslands that reminded him of the arid plains of Afghanistan that bloomed briefly in spring.

His map had been clearly marked, and when he'd reached the correct point, he turned south and followed a small maze of back roads to find what his contacts had said was an unwatched route into the United States of America. Although he had initially expressed doubt about this plan, he had been delighted to discover that it was exactly as promised—unrestricted access to the U.S. Although the passport and identification papers for his alias would stand up to determined scrutiny, he had decided to enter the country this way, not willing to risk being matched to a watch list and compromising the entire reason he had taken this trip in the first place.

As it turned out, he hadn't had much reason to fear. After the crossing, his trip through the former breadbasket of America had been uneventful, even dull. The next few days had followed the same pattern—driving interspersed with sparse meals—halal food was hard to come by out here—brief breaks for his daily prayers until stopping at small, privately owned motels off the highway that were just glad enough to have a customer prepay in cash that they would overlook the securing of the room with a credit card. The fact that Narid spoke impeccable English, with a genteel British accent, did much to put the proprietors' minds at ease.

For his part, he was a model tourist—quiet, neat, polite and minding his own business. Even when three drunken good ol' boys had tried to play "rag the raghead," as they had jeeringly called it before being stopped by a sheriff's deputy—which gave Narid his only real fear of discovery during the entire trip—he had thanked the khaki-clad officer and declined to press charges. He had, however, gotten out of town immediately, and hadn't stopped driving until he was three hundred miles away. Allah would certainly not have looked favorably upon him had he let the entire operation be jeopardized by a chance encounter with those uncultured thugs.

Winding his way through the Dakotas, Wyoming, Colorado and New Mexico, Narid had passed plenty of empty land, and the peace and quiet he experienced while driving through those areas reaffirmed his determination to carry out the mission. He knew that the dividing line of the Mississippi River bisected this country to the east, and on the other side were tens of millions of people, crammed into their sprawling cities, half-clad in their revealing clothes, eating their artificial food, watching their mindless entertainment, listening to their banal music, smug in their complacency because they lived in what they thought was the most powerful nation on earth. It was a notion Narid would be only too happy to disabuse them of soon. But in a way, he was glad to see that this heartland wouldn't be as affected by what he was about to set into motion. The people out here had been unassuming and friendly, men who worked the land and the women who stood by them. For the most part, they had let him go about his business with hardly a raised eyebrow, even given his obvious heritage.

Crossing the border into Texas had lifted his spirits immensely, and now, only a few dozen miles from his goal, Narid's pulse quickened as the city of El Paso appeared in the distance. He resisted the urge to press the accelerator down, but left the highway and headed east instead, traveling on a series of progressively smaller roads until he turned down a narrow dirt road surrounded by featureless brown plains, broken only by an occasional small rise or hill. He followed it for another five miles, pulling up to a small complex of buildings on ten acres, ringed by a ten-foot-high chain-link fence topped with razor wire. Large signs in English and Spanish warned that the fence was electrified. But what truly made the business unique was the white, three-story rocket that rose like a narrow finger on a launch pad in the middle of the buildings, pointing toward the heavens. A sign on the hill outside the perimeter proclaimed the company's name—Spaceworks, Inc.

As he approached, Narid looked up at the clear azure sky, imagining the path the rocket would soon take over the eastern United States, and of the mass destruction and terror it would sow when it reached its final destination. And although he was not doing this for fame, everyone around the world would soon be speaking of a new mastermind who had wreaked an even more devastating assault on the world's last remaining superpower than the destruction of the Twin Towers.

The front gate of the grounds had a small guardhouse, manned by a pair of guards, both of Middle Eastern descent. Narid pulled up to the post and lowered his window. "*Assalamu Alaikum.* I am Narid al-Gaffari. I have an appointment with Joseph Allen."

"One moment please, sir." The guard closed his window and spoke into a microphone on his shirt. Narid had no doubt that both men were armed, and doubtless had access to more than just pistols. With the flood of illegal immigrants coming over the border, the fence, guards and other methods to dissuade people from trespassing were simply the cost of doing business out here on the plains.

The guard slid open his window again and handed Narid a small static sticker. "Thank you for waiting, Mr. al-Gaffari. Please affix this to your side window so it is plainly visible. Mr. Allen will meet you inside the main building, which is straight ahead. Parking will be on your right. Have a good day." He pressed a button that raised the heavily reinforced metal barrier.

Narid nodded and drove ahead, pleased at how Americanized the young man sounded; blending in with this culture was vital if they were to subvert it. Every man who worked here had been chosen for their dedication to the cause, his education and his unmarked records, having never appearing on any watch list. Many had actually studied in the United States, acquiring the necessary degrees in engineering, physics and sciences to set their plan into motion.

Pulling into a parking space near the building, he stepped out into the blazing heat, so like the summers back home. The dry, hot environment was like a furnace, and Narid welcomed the warmth enveloping his body. He walked to the main door, which buzzed as he approached.

Inside, the temperature was at least twenty-five degrees cooler, and he shivered in the chilly air-conditioned interior. The small foyer was unassuming but comfortable, with a man standing behind a chest-high console at the far end in front of two thick double doors. Narid noticed two cameras in corners of the room, their unblinking black eyes sweeping back and forth, and nodded again. No doubt he had probably been monitored as soon as he had approached within a few miles of the site.

"Mr. al-Gaffari, I have your security badge ready." The receptionist, also a man, handed him a laminated card, which Narid affixed to his pocket. "If you will please follow me." The young man spoke into a cell phone earpiece, then swiped a card and led him through the double doors, which clicked as they automatically unlocked and slid into the walls. The man walked down a hallway with pictures of a smiling, light-skinned man of Middle Eastern descent shaking hands with various people, including the current governor of Texas.

The opposite wall had several large windows set into it, and Narid glanced into the room to see at least a dozen men in what looked like a smaller version of the control room at NASA, with computers and large plasma-screen monitors everywhere. Some displayed the rocket outside on the launch pad, while others showed a map of the United States with trajectory arcs from Texas to various destinations in the eastern United States, including estimated flight times. And on the far wall, high above everything, was a large red digital timer that was currently set to forty-eight hours. The men inside were of different nationalities, from Middle Eastern or Indian to Spanish, Mexican, British and even one white-blond Scandinavian, and each was intent on his task, whether that was programming, running three-dimensional models or conferencing with one another.

The receptionist walked to the end of the hall and swiped his security card through another slot. "Please go inside. Mr. Allen is waiting."

Pushing open the door, Narid walked into the office. The room was comfortably furnished, with thick carpet, wood paneling and no windows. In the center were two upholstered chairs facing a desk with a computer and a man sitting next to it. On the wall to his right were three monitors, one showing the rocket, the other two each divided into four quadrants that flashed on various security cameras around the area, including outside the perimeter. Another door to his left was open, revealing a small but meticulously clean bathroom.

The man on the other side of the teak desk was dressed in a button-down, dark blue oxford shirt with his sleeves rolled up, a silver tie neatly knotted and dark gray slacks with black wingtips. He was in his early forties. His face lit up as he saw his visitor, a broad smile revealing perfect, capped white teeth. He rose and held his arms out wide as he came toward Narid, who embraced him and returned the traditional, formal Islamic greeting wishing peace, Allah's mercy and blessings on the other person.

"It is good to see you. We were worried after not hearing from you for so long." As he spoke, Joseph took a small device from his desktop and walked around the room, studying the needle with every step. Narid watched him pace the perimeter, moving the sensor over the walls, pictures, chairs and desk. He completed his circuit and nodded to Narid, indicating that it was safe to talk. "Something to drink or eat? You must be hungry—believe me, I know how impossible it can be to find decent meals on a trip like that."

"Perhaps a bit later, after *wadu*." All of the travel and motel rooms had left him feeling unclean, and Narid was looking forward to performing the ritual Muslim cleansing. He sank into an overstuffed maroon armchair, luxuriating for a moment in its soft embrace before leaning forward, his expression intent despite his exhaustion. "Do you do that often?"

Joseph Allen tossed the bug detector on his desk and sat

on one corner. "Twice a day. In this business, everyone is looking for an advantage. The private space race makes the one between the U.S. and the U.S.S.R. look like child's play. Sure, everyone smiles for the camera and says they are doing whatever their program's goals are to benefit humankind, but the truth is that everyone's fighting for the same piece of the pie here, whether it's for an X-Prize award—still a drop in the bucket compared to what we spend on R&D in a year—or federal grants and loans, there's still only so much to go around. That's why our security is so high for such a small company, but you already know that."

Narid was fully aware of the reasons, along with many other things about Allen and his leading-edge aerospace company. The man in front of him was a second-generation American citizen who had spent the past fifteen years founding and building the space-exploration company, getting his master's degrees in astrophysics and engineering to build the next generation of lightweight, fuel-efficient rockets to carry payloads into space. He was well-known in the field, had published papers on aspects of rocket telemetry and aerodynamics and had received awards ranging from business accolades for minority hiring to recognition from a national science organization for advances in fuel efficiency that had been adopted throughout the burgeoning industry.

He was also one of the deepest cover terrorists working in America.

Allen had been raised in the strictest *sharia* ways by his father, who had been one of the founding members of the first American al Qaeda cells, established even before the World Trade Center bombings in 1993. His father had understood the struggle and the sacrifices that would have to be made, and had chosen to have his son learn from their enemies, to use their own knowledge against them to carry out an attack that would be unlike anything anyone had ever seen. He had changed his name and worked at a factory in Texas, saving every penny he could while indoctrinating his son.

Allen had founded Spaceworks with two goals—build a legitimate company with absolutely no ties to any publicly known terrorist operation, and develop the next generation of rocket technology—but for a far more glorious purpose than taking humankind to the stars. His success as a businessman was ironic, since the attack on the United States would come from within, and was being financed, constructed and carried out with backing from the unknowing U.S. government and various venture capitalists.

"I understand that it arrived before me. May I see it?" Narid asked.

Allen smiled. "Not even here for five minutes and already you're asking about it. The Barretts arrived safely, as well, glory be to Allah." Allen went to a locked cabinet, opened it and removed the only item inside, a locked aluminum-sided chest. He brought it out and set it on the desk. "There it is."

Narid slowly rose and stood over the case. He flipped the latches and opened the top, revealing the inner workings of the ten-kiloton nuclear weapon that an al Qaeda cell had risked their lives to steal from the Russian arms dealer. It was beautiful.

"We shall fight the pagans all together as they fight us all together, and fight them until there is no more tumult or oppression, and there prevail justice and faith in Allah." Narid bowed his head over the case, and when he raised it again, the tears of true belief shone in his eyes. "My friend, we are about to embark on the greatest mission of the jihad our people have ever known. Prepare the installation immediately. In three days, the world will know of our might—and this nation will be forever changed."

Narid—whose real name was Sepehr al-Kharzi—bowed his head over the case again and intoned his pleasure at seeing his plan coming to fruition, *"Allahu Akbar."*

"God is great."

8

Tracy's morning hadn't started well at all. On her way to work, she had picked up the *Washington Post* to see a below-the-fold headline—DHS Warns Of Potential Water Contamination Plots.

What the hell—I thought Gilliam said this wasn't "actionable" enough, she thought. Skimming the article, she found that it delineated exactly what she had laid out in her report. The article painted a chilling picture of what could happen in the event of a water-supply contamination, including the strain on local hospitals and emergency personnel in an area. There were even ominous quotes from Gilliam himself, warning that the DHS "was on top of the situation," and "already working to strengthen security at waste-treatment plants around the country. This simple plan could incapacitate hundreds, perhaps thousands of people, and we must make sure that won't happen on our soil."

Aren't you the noble mouthpiece, she thought. Of course, there was no mention of the DHS analysis—not that Tracy would have cared. Besides, the tone of the article said it all. He'd sent the report upstream anyway yesterday. But why? *And why lie to me about its importance?* There could have been any number of reasons, she supposed. Perhaps he didn't want a leak to be revealed before the article was published. Was there some kind of turf battle at headquarters? Most likely, the top brass was pressuring him for something they could show to the press, and he had seized on this. But she couldn't understand why he'd told her he was going to delay it, then pass it up the chain right away. *Is he just that much of a glory-hogging dick? Maybe they're pressuring him for something from the department, and he's parading this out as his own idea,* she thought.

After clearing security, Tracy walked to her cubicle to find a triple latte sitting at her desk, and Mark sitting across from her with a copy of the *Post* in his hands. "Congratulations, you really nailed that one." His expression, however, was hangdog.

"Thanks, but at my meeting yesterday, Gilliam told me the actual threat level was too low for review, and he was going to sit on that report for the next few months. I don't understand why he told me that, then rushed it upchannel so fast."

"So you haven't heard? Gilliam's taken the credit for your report internally. He's saying it was his idea from the start, and that you had expanded it only under his explicit direction."

"What? That's totally untrue! I can't believe he'd stoop to…" Tracy trailed off as she replayed the conversation in her mind. "Oh, my God."

Not catching her last words or the incredulous look on her face as she sank into her chair, Mark kept talking. "What I can't believe is why he thinks you won't contest his version of events—I mean, by all rights, he should be trumpeting your work on the project all over the place. This is low, even for him."

"Because he knows I won't say anything, that's why." Tracy shook her head in despair. "At our meeting yesterday, he said that my app for the fusion center was being approved, and asked if I'd thought about where I wanted to be stationed. He claimed he'd put in a good word for me. Like an idiot, I said I was looking at the Virginia center. If I speak up now, he'll be sure to kill any chance I have of getting the assignment. There must be something else going on above us that we don't know about."

"What, you mean like everything? All I can say for sure is that I can smell the stench of backroom wheeling and dealing from here." Mark spun around in his chair and woke up his computer. "I'm just sorry you got caught in the cross fire, or whatever's going down with this."

"Yeah, me, too—maybe I'll get lucky, and can work this into that fusion center assignment anyway. After all, he needs me to remain quiet about this, as well, else I could raise a big stink about it." She raised the steaming cardboard cup of coffee with a malicious grin. "Thanks for the java, by the way."

"I figured you'd need it, especially after you saw that headline."

Tracy killed the screensaver on her computer and scrolled through her e-mails. The first one from Gilliam was as terse as ever, making her brow furrow in annoyance.

Send all related data on sewage-contamination analysis to me ASAP.

He hadn't even bothered to sign it. Now Tracy's blood began to boil. *It's bad enough that he snakes this report from me—now he's treating me like his personal secretary,* she fumed. She compressed the hundreds of pages of technical analysis she had used to generate her report into a single file and sent it off, wondering all the while why he had requested it, since there was zero chance he'd even be able to comprehend it, much less utilize it in a manner that would make any sense. "I hope he chokes on it," she muttered.

Still angry, she scanned through her other messages, sorting items that needed immediate attention from the usual stream of interoffice detritus that flowed around the system. One message in particular caught her eye—a summary report and attachments from the El Paso Customs and Border Protection office. She opened it, scanned it quickly and then began researching.

Like many analysts at DHS, there were certain topics Tracy kept track of on a more-than-professional basis, and one of her hobbies was missing nuclear weapons. As soon as she began delving into the data package from Agent Nathaniel Spencer, she thought he was on to something. Accessing her files on Sepehr al-Kharzi, she reviewed what she had learned about him. He had been attempting to procure nuclear materials for three years prior to his death in a warehouse explosion in Texas. But who could say if it had been his remains recovered from the wreckage—there was no way of testing what was left by fingerprinting or dental records, since nothing was on file for him. This Nathaniel Spencer had been the last one to see the man alive, and his suspicion that the terrorist was actually alive and up to something again was a good start. But if all he had was a gut feeling, that and her own twinge about this wouldn't buy them a cup of coffee. The problem was that there was no hard evidence except for the e-mail message he had sent, which could very well be someone else using the name as a pseudonym.

Playing her hunch, she brought up the last picture of al-Kharzi, a grainy airport shot taken about four years earlier, and tasked her computer to search for any matches to anyone entering the country within the past thirty days who resembled the photo. Even attached to the DHS mainframe, this would take hours to compile, so she tackled other paperwork while waiting for the scan to finish. With literally millions of faces to review and compare using the biometrics face-scanning software, she could be waiting for the rest of the day—if she was lucky.

With noon approaching, and no matches in sight, she stretched her arms above her head and contemplated taking her lunch break when her computer suddenly chimed. She leaned forward to see the notice.

"Biometric match on subject—sixty-six percent."

She compared the data from the new picture—taken with a hidden camera at an unmanned border crossing near North Dakota three days ago. That familiar thrill of discovery fluttered in her stomach. Could this be him? She studied the two photos side by side, magnifying them as much as she could without sending them over to the lab for refinement. *It looks like him, but these damn camera angles make it so hard to see,* she thought. If he was alive, he had certainly kept a low profile, since his name hadn't come up on any recent watch lists. *But how hard would they be looking for a dead man?* Still, a man who resembled a suspected target was crossing the border illegally, and the program, which was twitchy on the best of days, had still managed a sixty-plus percentage of accuracy.

The call was hers to make, and she did, preparing an e-mail to the department heads at intelligence and analysis, the Domestic Nuclear Detection Office, U.S. Customs and Border Protection, the Transportation Security Administration, the Border Patrol office in El Paso and, as an afterthought, her immediate superior. She outlined the possibility that a known terrorist had not been killed in the Texas warehouse explosion, and had instead entered the United States approximately ninety-six hours ago, and may be intending to carry out an attack on infrastructure, possibly involving nuclear material. All DHS personnel should be on the lookout for Sepehr al-Kharzi or any of his known associates.

When she got to that point, however, Tracy brought herself up short. She had just put forth all of the evidence she had, and had based it on what? Two grainy photographs and a Border Patrol agent who'd gotten hold of an e-mail from a supposedly dead man. Was she about to cause an alert across all of the departments over these few scraps? The issue with Gilliam was one matter, but was she willing to risk her career over a cobbled-together analysis based on incomplete data? Of course, the suspect had been in the U.S. for more than ninety-six hours, and if he was planning something, that was more than enough time to get started….

Although relatively young in the analysis field at thirty-one, Tracy had learned the first lesson of intelligence gathering—cover your ass. If she was going to buck the boss on this, she had damn well better have a good excuse for going over his head, and the window of entrance into the U.S. was it. If it was nothing, she could simply claim that his being here for so long undetected was cause for concern.

Her index finger poised over the enter key, Tracy weighed the consequences of sending the message, then stabbed down. "Screw it," she muttered.

She stood up and nodded at Mark's back. "I'm going

to grab some lunch. If you hear a scream from Gilliam's office, that's probably my fault."

"Tracy, what did you do?" Mark asked, but she was already on her way to the drafty cafeteria.

WHEN SHE RETURNED FROM lunch, Mark looked even more worried than usual. "Gilliam wants to see you *now*."

"Of course he does." Tracy checked her makeup and made sure there were no crumbs on her suit jacket. She was sure he knew she was back at her desk. If she was going to be chewed out, she might as well make him as upset as possible. Who knew—maybe he'd do something that would be grounds for a lawsuit. "Mark, I may not be long for the department. If I'm escorted out, it's been great working with you," she said.

"Aw, Trace, you didn't go and get yourself fired, did you?" Mark shook his head. "If you land a cushy private-sector job, remember your friends, 'kay?"

"If my fiancé had anything to say about it, I'd already be gone." Her phone rang, and Tracy knew who was on the other end. She straightened up, ignoring the flashing light and insistent tone. "Here goes everything."

She walked to her superior's office and knocked.

"Come in."

Feeling like a condemned prisoner about to face her own judge, jury and executioner, Tracy opened the door and strode in, planting herself squarely in front of Gilliam's desk. "I received a message that you wished to see me, sir."

Other bosses she had worked for got redder as they got angrier, but the more furious Gilliam was, the paler he turned. Judging by the pallor of his chubby face, Tracy figured he must have been about to explode. But when he spoke, his voice was calm, with only a hint of underlying tremor. "Do you like working at the Department of Homeland Security, Ms. Wentworth?"

In for a pound, in for a ton, she thought. "Sometimes," she said slowly.

"Explain your answer."

"I do not appreciate being deceived, sir," she said.

His brow furrowed. "What are you referring to?"

Tracy kept her voice level with an effort. "Yesterday you claimed that my analysis wasn't at a threat level sufficient enough to move forward with, yet this morning's *Post* splashed it all over the front page. In this line of work, there's no such thing as coincidence, *sir.*"

"What, that? I got a request from the Health Affairs Department yesterday afternoon requesting information, then the public-affairs office sent some follow-up questions from the reporter on an article they were already doing. You know how fast things move around here sometimes."

His words sounded plausible, and yet Tracy knew enough about the man to know that he wasn't telling the whole truth. "Why didn't you have them contact me directly? I could have provided more depth to the analysis."

"After reading your summary, there was no need. Really, Tracy, I cannot believe that you would let that cloud your judgment so much that you would send this—" he tossed a sheaf of papers that she recognized as her analysis of al-Kharzi's movements "—around me to the major departments."

"It wasn't that at all, sir." Tracy prided herself on how rational she sounded. "After I got the hit, and realizing that this terrorist had already been in the United States for more than ninety-six hours—"

Gilliam's hand slammed down on his desk, making her jump. In her two years there, he had never shown that much emotion. "Ms. Wentworth, no matter what you think may be the proper course of action, I remind you that the only channel you are to follow in your analysis and reports is directly to me. *I* will determine what is to be followed up on and what isn't. There is much more going on here—much more at stake—than you could possibly know."

What, like your next raise? Maybe even your job? she thought. "Regardless, sir, I thought it appropriate to warn the pertinent departments as soon as possible, before more time elapsed and the subject would be able to launch whatever operation he has planned." *Now just try to sit there and tell me it wasn't justified.*

"Ms. Wentworth, that would have been fine, except that Sepehr al-Kharzi has been dead for the past nine months."

"With all due respect, sir, the biometrics scan on the suspect entering illegally from Canada—"

"Is notoriously unreliable, and only came up with a sixty-six percent chance of a match—hardly what I could call a definite hit. Also, your corroborating evidence is a simple e-mail message from three months ago, from one of this deceased terrorist's aliases?" Gilliam said.

"Along with a list of materials for constructing a nuclear weapon or dirty bomb, including plutonium—"

Gilliam held up his finger and Tracy fell silent. "And on that basis, and your—what would I call it? intuition, I suppose—you felt justified to alert our other departments, diverting them from other, more critical operations? Ms. Wentworth, I've just spent the past hour recalling your so-called report from those departments. I told them it was a preliminary study only, and not meant to be disseminated at this time. I also told the other departments that in your exuberance, you had mistakenly sent the report before it was in final form. This is not the competency level I have come to expect from you, which is why it led me to believe this had to do with a more personal disagreement. Now that you've made the reason for this insubordination plain, I have a hard time believing that we're even having this conversation in the first place."

"If I overstepped my bounds, then I apologize." Tracy bit off each word, staring at the wall behind him, not wanting to give this detestable man the satisfaction of seeing her anger. "Will there be anything else, sir?"

"You'd better believe there is. I've shunted the kook file to your desktop alone. I want you to evaluate and forward every single threat that we've received before you go home tonight. Is that clear?"

"As crystal, sir." Tracy turned on her heel and left the office, only exhaling once she was outside with the door closed behind her. She shook her head and trudged back to her desk where, as promised, her in-box was overflowing with what agents referred to internally as "the kook file." Every immediately nonverifiable threat made against the U.S., the President, the government or any other landmark or public place was kept in the kook file until it could be assessed. Every threat was investigated, and either appended and filed or forwarded to the appropriate department for follow-up. Once the chuckles stopped from reading the fiftieth misspelled diatribe against the government, it turned into the monotonous, grueling work that it really was.

With a sigh, Tracy opened the first one and got to work, knowing she would have to call Paul and let him know she would be late—again.

9

Nate opened his eyes to the blaring alarm clock, its insistent buzz reverberating through his hungover brain. Reaching out a long arm, he smacked around the nightstand until he hit the snooze button, knocking over an empty Jack Daniel's bottle in the process. The sudden silence, broken only by the rattle and hum of his window air conditioner, was almost as loud.

Raising himself up on his elbows, Nate rubbed the sleep out of his face, then looked twice as he noticed the sleeping woman lying next to him. He tried to remember where he had met her or, for that matter, what her name was, but came up blank on both accounts. His recollection of the previous night was a blur of whiskey and beer, beer and whiskey. And apparently he had brought home more than just a raging blackout yesterday evening. *Holy shit, just how much did I have?*

Slipping out of bed with an ease born of years of practice, Nate was unsurprised to find himself naked. Besides his pounding head, his teeth felt furry. He padded to the bathroom, closed the door and leaned over the sink until the dizziness passed. Splashing cold water on his face, he squeezed the last of the toothpaste out of a rolled-up tube into his mouth, but couldn't find his toothbrush, and settled for running a wet finger across his teeth. Spitting, he rinsed with mouthwash next, the sting opening his eyes wide.

A knock at the front door made his tired eyes open even wider. Who the hell can that be? he wondered. He crept out of the bathroom, crossed the bedroom and walked through the living room into the kitchen. Snagging his jeans from the floor and his shirt from where it had ended up on the table, he cracked open the apartment door.

"Jesus, Nate, you look like warmed-up shit."

"Good morning to you, too, Beth."

"At least you know what time it is," she said sarcastically. His ex-wife stood with her arms crossed, her foot tapping and her black eyes flashing. Her dark Cherokee features glowered at him, but to Nate she looked just as beautiful as the day they had met. "I kept getting your voice mail, so I thought I'd stop by. Are you going to let me in?"

Nate glanced over his shoulder at the disheveled apartment. "You see how bad I look? Well, the apartment looks worse."

"Why am I not surprised? You drink yourself out of a job yet? That's supposed to come from my side of the family, you know."

"They're still keepin' me on for now. Speaking of, I should be gettin' on back there, so what can I do for you?"

She held up a printed form. "The alimony is screwed up again. I need another hundred."

"Sure, sure, just a minute." Closing the door, he rooted around on the table until he found his checkbook.

"Baby? Who's there?"

His head snapped up, and the checkbook flew from his suddenly fumbling fingers. He trotted back to the bedroom, where the sleepy-eyed blonde's head was poking out of the sheets. "Someone at the door?"

"Yeah, just a deliveryman. He'll be gone in a moment. Stay here for a bit, okay? You can grab a shower if you want."

"Hmm." She disappeared under the sheets, just as Beth banged on the door again.

"How do I get myself into this shit?" Nate muttered as he ran back to the table, his bare feet skidding on the dusty linoleum. He scribbled out a check for $150, leaving him twenty-seven until his next payday. *Jesus, I hope I didn't drink the rest away last night.* Going to the door, he opened it again.

"Is someone in there with you?" Beth asked.

"Just me and the TV." He handed her the check.

Beth's eyes narrowed, and for a second Nate thought he was busted, as she had a pretty good bullshit detector. She took the slip of paper, and her face softened. "You eaten anything solid in the past few days?"

"Yeah, I do all right. I'm still seeing Bobby this weekend, right?"

"If you're not called in, yes." Beth's eyes clouded even more. "He sure misses you."

"Yeah, I miss him, too. Tell him we're going fishing Saturday, so make sure he has his gear."

"All right." She stepped in close and kissed his stubbled cheek. "Try not to get yourself killed between now and then, all right?" she asked.

The corner of his mouth crooked up at their private joke, which had started when they were newlyweds, and had grown progressively less humorous over the years. "You doin' all right?"

"I get by. Take care of yourself now." She strode down the apartment hallway, her hips swaying as she went. Nate shook his head as he watched the best thing that had ever happened to him walk away again.

As he closed the door, he heard the shower going, and trotted back to the bedroom, looking for clues. He picked up the woman's purse and expertly rifled through it until he found her identification, replacing it as the water shut off. Nate started to clean up the bedroom, but realized he didn't know where he'd begin, and settled for lighting a cheroot and waiting for her to come back in. A few minutes later, she came out, dressed and drying her hair with a towel.

"You, uh, want to get something to eat?" Nate shifted on the bed, never comfortable with this part of the dance. His one-night stand looked older in the afternoon light, he mused—with crow's feet and laugh lines that had been artfully disguised the previous evening. Maybe five years younger than his own forty-four years, she was thicker in the hips and legs than he'd remembered, too. But she wasn't embarrassed, just gave him a weary smile.

"Shoot, honey, I got just enough time to get back home and cleaned up before I go back to work."

Jesus, did I pick up a waitress? Nate wasn't sure to whether to laugh or blush. "Well, it was quite an evening, Sharon."

"Oh, you remember? I'm flattered, Nate. Make that impressed, after everything you put away last night."

"Um, yeah, well, yesterday wasn't the best of days for me, at least till I met you."

"That's what got me here, you silver-tongued devil. I

gotta run." She walked over and patted him on the cheek. "If you ever get shot, have them bring you to Providence Memorial—I work the night shift there."

Ah, a nurse, he realized. "I'll keep that in mind, but why do you think I'll be shot?"

"You're Border Patrol—at least, that was what you said last night—so it'll probably only be a matter of time. I'll let myself out. See you around, Nate."

When she was gone, he locked up and took a shower, then got dressed again and grabbed some water bottles and a bag of beef jerky and headed out to his Bronco. Getting in, he headed south out of town, keeping an ear on his scanner for border chatter.

He stopped about two miles from his destination. Pulling a pair of binoculars from the backseat, he walked out into the scrub and found a good vantage point on a small rise. Making sure the setting sun wasn't reflecting off his field glasses, he raised them and scanned the area to the south, looking over the cordoned-off crime scene where the Mexicans and the border agents had been killed. He watched Billy Travis strutting around as if he owned the place, barking out orders.

After watching the scene for a few minutes, he panned right and left, searching the horizon for anything out of the ordinary, but he was too far away. *I can either cool my heels in the desert, or I can go piss Travis off some more,* he thought. That was no choice at all. He walked back to his Bronco and drove over to the crime site, pulling up near the crime-lab van. Grabbing a cold bottle of water from his cooler, he walked up behind the van, keeping out of sight of Travis for the moment. "You look thirsty, Kottke," he said.

The balding, bespectacled tech mixing up a batch of plaster of paris glanced up to see the sweating bottle hovering above him. "Hey, Nate, thanks." He drained half the water in long swallows. "Aren't you on leave pending that drug-bust investigation?"

"What can I say, I happened to be in the neighborhood."

Kottke handed the bottle back and kept stirring the plaster. "Better check your zip code, then. You're aimin' to bust Travis's balls again, aren't you?"

"Won't be a need to as long as he don't come around and try stickin' them in my face. What you got so far?"

"Right now, just the three Bs—bullets, blood and bodies. Looks like one of the agents spooked someone they shouldn't have, and got perforated for his trouble. Second one came around to assist, got the same thing, then the perpetrators—anywhere from two to four—went to town on the illegals. Looks like machine pistols of some kind, all 9 mm. Different kinds of weapons, Ingram M-11s, maybe a couple of Uzi pistols. No survivors—these guys were thorough."

"What about the truck?"

"Wheelbase and axle width indicate it was a 1.5-ton panel truck, probably a Chevy G30, maybe a small IH model. We'll know more once we run the tread pattern. The two agents were dumped in the SUV, which was driven out five miles to the middle of nowhere and torched. Second team's working that now—at least they were dead before they burned."

"Amen to that." Nate repressed a shudder at the thought of how the Colombian and Mexican cartels killed undercover agents or screwups. One of the most common methods was to hang a tire soaked in gasoline around the victim's neck and light it, guaranteeing a hideous, drawn-out death.

"That's about all we've got right now, until we can get everything back to the lab—"

"Kottke, where the hell are you, that tread was supposed to be cast—"

Travis barreled around the corner of the van pulling up short when he saw Nate. "Goddammit, get that plaster over there and take those tire casts now."

"Yes, sir." Kottke shot Nate an apologetic glance, then scurried away.

"Now, what in the hell is an agent who's supposed to be on leave doing sniffin' around a crime scene he's got no business being at?"

"Aw, Billy, don't get your tighty-whities in a bunch. I just thought I'd drop by to see if you guys could use an extra hand, us being so short staffed and all."

Travis got right in Nate's face, his words spraying out only inches away. "Jesus Christ, Spencer, what part of *on leave from active duty* do you not understand? I am not going to have this investigation fucked up because of an off-duty agent who doesn't know when to quit! Now go home and crawl into your bottle, or whatever the hell it is that you do when you're not making everyone's job harder."

"By God, Travis, you best step back before you find yourself flat on your ass. And if anyone asks, you can say you tripped and fell against the van door," Nate growled.

The other border agent glared at him for a moment longer, then stepped back. "Get out of here right now, Spencer, or my next call is to Roy, to tell him to put a leash on his dawg."

"Piss on you, Travis." Nate spun on his heel and stalked back to his Bronco, hoping the other agent would push it and give him a chance to knock him on his can. But the expected hand on his shoulder never came, and Nate opened the door of his little truck and stopped to look through the window at the busy agents and technicians working the scene.

Goddammit, that should be me in there, not that sanctimonious prick, he knew. He got into the Bronco, slammed the door and drove away in a cloud of dust.

10

The sun had long disappeared by the time Tracy walked out of DHS headquarters. The old Navy complex had been given to the new department when the deal for their new quarters in Chantilly, Virginia, had fallen through just before they were to go live in 2003. At first there had been talk of moving to newer quarters later, but as time passed, those intimations had slowed, then stopped altogether. Now the behemoth department was stuck in the decrepit collection of buildings that were supposed to be refurbished when time and budget allowed, which, in government parlance, meant never.

After clearing security, which had been rigorously improved since someone had walked out with four pistols from the secure vault the previous year, she walked out to her six-year-old Nissan Altima, keeping an eye on her surroundings all the while. Just because she worked at DHS didn't mean something bad couldn't happen there. Driving off the lot, she headed north on the always busy highway toward Chevy Chase and her fiancé's condominium.

During the week, she stayed with him, since his place was closer than her apartment on the south side. Although Tracy always tried to let the stress of the day drain away on her drive, her shoulders were still tense as she pulled into the driveway, got out of her car and headed up the walk.

As she reached for the door, it opened and there stood Paul, who greeted her with a kiss. "Hey, there. Another long day, huh?"

"Yeah." She slipped off her pumps and hugged him for several seconds, then slipped free and walked into the living room. "Late enough for a beer, I think."

"Come on, you need something to eat, too. I kept a plate warm for you."

"Is that the scrumptious aroma in here? Smells heavenly," Tracy said.

"Just shrimp scampi with linguini and steamed vegetables. Nothing fancy."

Tracy raised a skeptical eyebrow. Paul was an avowed foodie, and a "simple" dish for him often involved handmade noodles, seafood caught less than twelve hours ago and fresh herbs from his own garden. As usual, she marveled at how he found the time to do all that and work his day job, as well.

Sitting, she allowed him to serve her with a flourish, capping the simple yet elegant meal with a cold Heineken. "This is wonderful," she said between mouthfuls. "I almost feel like I don't deserve it."

"Why would you say that?" Paul turned a chair around, sat and clinked his beer bottle against hers.

"Oh, I baited Gilliam again." She summarized the day's events to him as she polished off the pasta. "But he deserved it, dammit, no matter what he claimed he was going to do."

Paul shook his head. "Sweetheart, you're never going to get anywhere looking for trouble and butting heads like that." Seeing her head come up, he held up his hands. "Not that I'm saying it wasn't justified, but really, don't you think you should pick your battles more carefully?"

Tracy rose to take her plate to the dishwasher. "Yeah, but I'm just so tired of the whole thing. I know we analysts are supposed to be behind the scenes, but still, when the behind-the-scenes people don't get the credit for a job well done, what else is there? Even though a lot of people would consider that a little thing, it was the thousandth little thing, and I've just had enough."

Paul got up, as well, moving behind her to rub her shoulders. "Well, if it's that bad, like I've said before, you could always come to work for Globeview. With your experience, we could have you briefing units in the field in about two weeks, and actually making a difference where it counts, instead of battling the inexorable DHS bureaucracy."

Tracy leaned back into him, trying to remain focused on the conversation but becoming more relaxed under his ministrations. Paul was a lawyer for Globeview Security Systems, one of the new wave of private security companies that had sprung up in the wake of the expanded global war on terror that was stressing America's armed forces to their limits. Ever since they had met at a military defense convention in Las Vegas two years earlier, he had been working on bringing her over to the company, and although she couldn't help but feel a distinct dislike for what was essentially a mercenary outfit, there were times—like now—where it sounded better than heading back to the office in the morning. That thought also brought a stab of guilt with it.

With an effort, she pulled away from him. "Paul, we've been over this before, and you know how I feel. There are just some things I think our government should handle, instead of outsourcing them."

"It's the wave of the future, Tracy. You of all people should know that there will never be a standing army large enough to cover all the potential conflict areas, and there are plenty of other areas where the U.S.—or other countries—will want to have influence without being directly involved."

"You mean carrying out whoever's orders, no matter what the consequences are to the indigenous people and country. That's how coups are carried out, Paul, as we both well know."

"So you would rather have hundreds of thousands of people suffering every day, while some insane dictator subjects millions to countrywide hell?"

"Of course not! But what I don't want to see is corporate boards of directors profiting from going in and toppling those governments, either, and then double-dipping by providing security to the personnel of the private companies awarded the 'no-bid' contracts to rebuild these places. After all, look at the Middle East, where contracts were just handed out to anyone who knew the right people."

It was an old argument between them, and Tracy knew her comment hit Paul where it hurt—his company had landed several lucrative reconstruction projects, all fairly bid for—through their connections on Capitol Hill. However, the no-bid scandal had tarred all of the PSCs with the same suspicious brush, and Globeview was feeling the pressure, as well. "Paul, it's too late to get into this right now, and besides, we both know where the discussion is going to wind up anyway."

Paul sighed. "I just wish you'd be a little more flexible in your thinking. We're doing a lot of good in Iraq—helping where the military can't, and taking on considerable risk while doing so."

Crossing her arms, Tracy leaned against the table. "I'm not saying they're all bad, but it's an unregulated industry, and there are more than enough examples of PSCs overstepping their bounds and even participating in criminal behavior—I know, I know, not Globeview."

"Damn right not Globeview." Paul was fiercely proud of their spotless record—while his company had been investigated for several instances of wrongdoing, no charges had ever been filed, and none of their employees had ever been tried by an international court of law. Several had either been killed or imprisoned in some of the Third World countries they had been working in, however, and Paul had been involved in assisting with their defense in those cases, facing kangaroo courts and bribed judges. "Tracy, the future belongs to—"

"Well, it's not a future I want to face tonight!" she snapped.

"Tracy? Is that you?" A small voice came from down the hallway leading toward the bedrooms.

Exchanging an accusatory glare with Paul, she peeked around the kitchen door into the night-lighted hallway. "Jennifer, sweetheart, what are you doing up at this hour?"

The little girl tottered into the room on sleepy legs, her eyes fighting a losing battle to stay awake. She clutched a ragged blanket as she headed to Tracy. "I heard you talking with Daddy, and you sounded mad."

Tracy bent down and hugged her tightly. "Oh, no sweetie, your daddy and I were just discussing work. Now come on, it's time for you to get back to bed. You've got a big day tomorrow." She picked up the seven-year-old, managing not to grunt with the effort, and carried her back down the hall to her bedroom. Tucking the girl back into bed, she pulled the horse-emblazoned comforter up to her chin and kissed her on the forehead.

Jennifer's eyelids were already drooping. "You're gonna come to the recital, right?"

"I wouldn't miss it for the world, sweetie."

"You know I'm playing the fairy queen, right?"

"Yes, and I'm sure you'll be magnificent. I'll see you onstage with your wings tomorrow."

"Okay. Night." Her eyes closed, and her breathing deepened into the regularity of sleep. Tracy gently swept a lock of blond hair off her forehead and watched her for a minute. While she cared deeply for Paul, and knew she loved him, her feelings for his daughter went far beyond a simple stepparent-and-child relationship. Jennifer had been terribly hurt by her parents' divorce, and Tracy had taken care to let their relationship grow slowly, trying not to pressure the girl or to grow too attached herself. But the strategy had backfired on her, and now she loved the impish child's every move. Indeed, she had bonded with Jennifer more quickly than she had ever thought possible—which frightened her sometimes. Although Paul and she were engaged to be married the following spring, and she was certainly committed to it and him, enough doubts niggled at the back of her mind so that she wasn't absolutely sure it was the right decision. But where Jennifer was concerned, there was no hesitation at all.

A shadow in the doorway made her look up to see Paul standing there, a smile on his face. Rising, she left the room and closed the door, leaving just a sliver of light from the hallway to fall across the bed.

Paul shook his head. "Sometimes I think she loves you more than Marilyn."

Tracy slipped her arm around his waist. "I doubt that."

"I don't—I see the way she looks at you—pure, unadulterated love. By the way, we *are* on for tomorrow afternoon, right?"

"Yes, I cleared that time three months ago, and have rechecked it every week for the past month. I'll be there. Now come on, let's go to bed." Sneaking one last glance at the bedroom, and the sleeping angel within, Tracy led Paul across the hallway to the other bedroom.

Traveling to Washington D.C. always left Kate with mixed feelings. While she loved the city where she had gone to school and gotten her start in intelligence analysis, there were also enough bad memories there that set her teeth on edge whenever she visited. Like the time she had just spent—*wasted* was more like it—with her soon-to-be ex-husband, Conrad Tilghman.

She leaned back in the passenger seat of the Lincoln Navigator SUV and drummed her fingers on the armrest. "One thing I never missed here was the traffic."

In the driver's seat next to her, handling the steering wheel with expert flicks of his hand, her bodyguard, Jacob Marrs, regarded her from behind mirrored aviator sunglasses. "You in that much of a hurry to pop some brass? Tillie must have been more annoying than usual." His opinion of her husband was just a shade higher than the respect he had for pond scum.

Kate grimaced and stared out the window at the Washington monuments. "It's bad enough I had to sit across from him and his phalanx of lawyers for the past two hours. The last thing I want to do is rehash it. Let's just get to the range—I'm sure I'll feel better after emptying a few magazines."

"You're the boss, so exercise your administrative powers and move this snarl out of our way." Assigned to protect Kate ever since she had come to work for Room 59, Jake had taken it upon himself to train her in the fighting arts of all kinds, from unarmed combat to firearms. Since she was already going to Washington on business, he had suggested that they kill two birds with one stone at the range. Knowing how irritated she would be after the divorce proceedings, Kate had readily agreed. "At least it will be good to see Herbert again."

"You got that right."

The rest of the trip passed in silence until they reached the Maryland Small Arms Range, one of the few public firing ranges near the notoriously firearm-averse city. Jake pulled the SUV into the parking lot and waited for Kate to retrieve her gun case from the back. Room 59 operatives weren't required to carry a weapon 24/7, but many did, with the appropriate concealed-carry paperwork, as well.

While she enjoyed shooting, Kate rarely felt the need to carry in public, especially with Jake always on her heels. It was an attitude they had disagreed on more than once, and the former army Ranger hadn't won her over yet, although he kept trying. Today, however, he didn't say a word, but just followed her inside.

Like many shooting ranges around the country, this one was utilitarian, stressing function over form. Kate walked through the door, her heels clicking on the concrete floor. Pale cinderblock walls surrounded them, and they could hear the rapid bark of several pistols firing.

Confirming their appointment at the front desk, Kate led

Jake to the lounge, where an older man dressed in casual but expensive khakis, a long-sleeved shirt and a shooter's vest was seated at one of the battered Formica tables. His eyes, slightly magnified by the gold-rimmed bifocals he wore, widened with pleasure when he caught sight of her.

"Kate, so good to see you." He rose and came over to embrace her. "Jake." The man exchanged nods with the bodyguard. "Still keeping her in one piece, I see."

"Hell, just keeping up with her is a full-time job, but I do all right." Jake's respect for the man in front of them was as deep as his disdain for Kate's husband, as evidenced by letting the gentle jibe pass without a riposte.

Herbert Foley had been the director of the Central Intelligence Agency when Kate had first gone to work there, and had taken her under his wing during the turbulent 1990s, when the agency had attempted to redefine its mission in response to the rise of global terrorism. He had been instrumental in helping her move to Room 59, and had also served as a sounding board and mentor for her since his retirement a few years ago. Resembling a kindly grandfather with his thinning gray hair and soft-spoken manner, his appearance disguised one of the sharpest minds in the city, undiminished by age, and still relied on by many in the intelligence community, all of which made him an excellent contact for Kate.

"It's good to see you, too, Herbert," Kate said with a bright smile.

"Well, we didn't come all the way out here to stand around. Let's get to the range. I'm looking forward to seeing what Jake's been teaching you," Foley said.

They put on their ear and eye protection and entered the range, where several other men and women were already shooting, filling the air with thunder and clouds of burned

powder. Kate stepped up to a booth and opened her case, revealing a 9 mm HK USP, along with a Bianchi 3S pocket
holster. She attached a paper target to the track and moved
it out to twenty-five yards. After checking to make sure she
was cleared to fire, she slid a loaded thirteen-round magazine
into the pistol's butt, chambered a round and holstered the
gun at her side, adjusting the rig for the easiest draw.

Taking a deep breath, she drew the pistol in one smooth
move, cupping her right hand around her left to brace the
weapon securely, lined up the three-dot tritium sights on
the target's center mass and squeezed the trigger repeatedly,
riding the recoil up and back down to empty the magazine
as quickly as possible. When the slide locked back on the
empty chamber, she set the pistol down and hit the button
to bring the target forward, examining her handiwork.

Beside her, Herbert nodded approvingly. "Nice grouping."
And it was, with most of the bullet holes in the bull's-eye and
9-ring. "You did well enough at the academy, but nothing like
this."

Kate smiled, remembering her disdain for the pistol
range all those years ago, although she had tackled learning
to shoot with the same intensity she did everything else.
"I find it a lot more enjoyable shooting now than with a
CIA instructor barking at me. Jake also taught me a few
techniques to sharpen my shooting posture and aim."

Herbert had brought his own weapon, as well, a SIG
Sauer P-229 9 mm, and they spent the next hour doing a
variety of target shooting.

After they were finished, many of the other shooters had
left, and Kate was able to bring up the real reason for her
visit. "Have you heard anything about warnings of loose
nuclear devices in the United States?"

With a wariness born of decades in spycraft, the older

man put his weapon away while checking all around them for anyone who might have been eavesdropping. "That's a rather sensitive subject for a public place, don't you think?"

Kate grinned as she stowed her pistol. "On the contrary, I can't think of a better place than this. Besides, we're just talking hypothetically."

"Hmm. What type, specifically, are you referring to?"

"Not dirty or waste. Suitcase."

Herbert regarded her over the rims of his glasses. "Kate, you know as well as I do that the Russians have never officially acknowledged that any of their small-yield devices are missing."

"Yes, but we also know that in the nineties the army officers were selling anything that wasn't bolted down just to survive. Some of them, like General Kryukov, apparently liked it so much that they decided to go into business for themselves."

Her mentor's eyebrows rose. "He's still around, eh?"

"Yes, and doing what he does best. Recently he's been busy in Pakistan and India. However, on one of his recent deals, someone managed to outfox him and switched a ten-kiloton device with waste. So it's loose, and I think it's either headed here or already inside our borders."

"My dear, surely with your resources, you'd have far more access to this sort of information than I." Tucking his case under his left arm, he offered his right to Kate, who linked hers through it as they walked to the lounge, Jake trailing them like a very solid shadow.

"Herbert, what's the first thing you taught me?"

"Analysis and secondary data never equals information gained firsthand."

"There you are. Don't worry, I've got folks sifting

through everything they can get their hands on, but there are those sources that simply cannot be accessed with computers. Now, since I'll be getting this from you, it's not the firsthand info that you always preferred—" Kate smiled again "—but I'm willing to take that chance."

"You are, are you?" Herbert sat down at a table and set down his gun case. "When I headed the CIA, we estimated there were anywhere from fifty to one hundred portable tactical nuclear devices that had been moved out of Russia, both before and after the Curtain came down. The majority of those are either nonfunctional due to degradation of the various power or detonation systems, or have been lost around the world."

"But?"

"*But,* in a no-limit, table-stakes Omaha poker game I was in with an ex-KGB general last month, he may have alluded to the fact that there are still a dozen viable devices floating around out there, and if any of the fundamentalist Muslim groups get their hands on one, they'd either try nuclear blackmail, or take it a step further and carry the jihad to our very shores."

"The simulations we've seen never look good. A detonation near a city puts casualties in the tens of thousands. Considering that once it's in the country, there's very little to prevent a cell from transporting it to a major metropolitan area and setting it off, the best bet is to stop it at the border. But again, that's a problem in and of itself, given the still-porous state of both the north and the south.

"Did you hear about the incident near El Paso?" Kate slid her BlackBerry over to him, but he waved it off.

"The twenty-plus illegals killed? Yeah, it trickled into the news even up here, then got pushed aside just as quickly. You think there's a connection?"

"I can't think of much else anyone would kill so many over, unless they were hiding something. Even drug smugglers usually aren't that ruthless—why kill their mules? It sounds like it's linked to something bigger. It's my next appointment in town. I'm sending someone down to look into it."

"You're sending a Washington person down to the Tex-Mex border to look into the slaughter of illegal immigrants? That's what I would call counteranalysis indeed."

"I'm not worried. This young woman is very capable. Besides, she'll be assigned to an experienced Border Patrol agent who will keep an eye on her. I'm sure she'll be fine."

Herbert folded his hands over his trim stomach. "Any asset in a storm, right? From what I hear, it's still the Wild West down there. I'm sure you know what you're doing, but be careful."

Kate leaned over and took his hand. "Don't worry. The second lesson you taught me was to do everything in your power to make sure an agent or asset comes back alive."

Herbert fixed her with his blue eyes, and for a second, he looked like the steel-hard director she had known fifteen years ago. "Yes, but sometimes everything you do still isn't enough."

Kate just nodded. There wasn't anything to say to that truth. After a moment lost in thought, she said, "I'm afraid we have to get moving if we're going to get there on time. It's been a pleasure, Herbert, as always."

"When you get that all taken care of, you should come down to our Hilton Head cottage for a few days, take it easy. You look tired, Kate."

Rising, she shrugged. "No worse than you when you were in the thick of it—pots of coffee and thirty-six-hour days. It's the life we chose."

He rose with her. "That we did. Good luck with this—and for all of our sakes, I hope you're sending that analyst on a wild-snipe chase."

"So do I, Herbert, so do I."

12

Tracy had finished her actionable tasks, and was closing the last files on her desktop. Just a few more minutes, and she'd be home free. The soft trill of her phone froze her in the midst of her efficient maneuvering. Oh, no, not now. Any other time but now. "Yes?"

It was Gilliam. "Tracy, a situation has come up that needs your immediate attention. Someone is waiting to brief you in Conference Room B. You are to extend them every courtesy, understand?"

"I…" She trailed off, knowing the futility of any protest. "Yes, sir, I'll be there in just a moment. I'm just finishing up at my desk."

She dialed Paul's cell phone, knowing what his reaction was going to be even before he answered.

"Hi, Tracy, you on your way?"

"Paul, I—something's come up at work. I hope it won't take long, and I'll be there as soon as I can." She hated the pleading tone in her voice. "It's beyond my control."

"Tracy." Paul's voice was a mix of resignation and controlled anger. "You know how important this is to Jennifer."

"Of course I do. You think I want to be here instead of there? You know as well as I do that these things happen—remember our one-year anniversary? I'll try to make it as soon as I can."

"Well, wish Jennifer luck, will you? Hold on."

She heard muffled voices, and silently cursed again. *I didn't think she'd be next to him.*

"Tracy?"

"Hi, sweetie."

"Daddy said you might not make it."

"Sweetheart, they need me at work just a little while longer, but I'll be there as soon as I can, okay?"

There was a long silence, every second breaking Tracy's heart. Then Jennifer's small voice replied, "Okay. I have to go backstage now."

"I'll be in the audience by the time you make your entrance, okay?" Although her tone was light, part of Tracy's mind was aghast at what she had just promised. The school was a half hour away in light traffic, and afternoons usually doubled the travel time. "Bye, sweetie."

"Bye, Tracy." There was a click as the connection was broken, and Tracy took a moment to get herself under control again. Deep down, she had known it was too good to be true, that something would come along to sabotage the outing. For a moment, she wondered if Gilliam had orchestrated it, but dismissed the idea. He thought he was Machiavellian, but this didn't sound like him, especially since he wouldn't be there to see her squirm.

She got up and headed for the small conference rooms used for breakout meetings and group briefings. All of them were dark except for the second one down. Resigning herself to an afternoon of monotonous briefing, she took a deep breath and knocked.

"Please come in."

Opening the door, Tracy walked in and closed it behind her. The room was its usual barren self, with an oval table surrounded by ten wheeled swivel chairs. Sitting in one of them at the head of the table was her appointment, who looked nothing at all like Tracy had expected.

Instead of a harried, rumpled, middle-aged Washington bureaucrat, she faced a trim, well-dressed woman she estimated was in her late thirties. Her platinum-blond hair was cut stylishly short, closely framing her face and making her appear even younger. As she looked up, her eyes seemed to shift from gold to green, unsettling Tracy even more. Dressed in a navy blue suit that accentuated her short frame, the woman rose and extended her hand. Her FBI badge, with its matching blue letters against a white background and the woman's picture in the lower half underneath her signature, was clipped to her lapel.

"Ms. Wentworth? Nice to meet you. I'm Stephanie Cassell, with the Federal Bureau of Investigation, National Security Branch, Weapons of Mass Destruction Directorate. Yes, it's quite a mouthful. I'm sorry to have to interrupt your workday like this."

Tracy disguised her momentary surprise at the other woman's politeness and humor, and shook her head. "Not at all. I'm happy to assist the FBI in whatever way I can."

"And we appreciate that." Stephanie checked her watch. "Have you been briefed as to the subject of this meeting?"

Oh, great. Tracy hated these kinds of questions. If she said she hadn't been briefed, and it got back to her boss, she'd be in even more trouble than she was now. If she said she was briefed, and couldn't tell any pertinent details, then she'd look like a fool in front of the analyst. Just another intelligence catch-22.

"I haven't been informed as to any recent details, ma'am," she bluffed.

"That's fine. Your superior seems like the type that doesn't give up any more information than necessary."

Tracy made a noncommittal noise in her throat, neither confirming nor denying the statement.

Agent Cassell fixed her with those peculiar eyes. "I mean, he seems to be the type that if you shoved a lump of coal up you-know-where, you'd have a diamond in a month," she said with a laugh.

Tracy was startled, but recovered quickly. "I'd never quite thought of it in those terms, ma'am."

"Please, call me Stephanie." The FBI agent checked her watch. "This is going to seem a bit strange, but my schedule has gotten a bit jammed, and I'm supposed to be heading to the station to catch my train. Would you mind coming with me? I can drop you wherever you like, within reason."

Tracy stared at the women in disbelief. Had she stumbled upon the Holy Grail—a government agent who didn't have a stick up her ass? Would she actually take her to the school? She could catch a ride back with Paul—

Blinking, she wrenched herself back to reality. The federal government didn't run a taxi service—at least, not for GS-10 personnel. "Ma'am—Stephanie—as I'm sure you know, classified, top-secret or eyes-only materials cannot be discussed off the premises in nonsecure locations," she said, relieved she hadn't fallen into the trap.

"Don't worry, Tracy, my ride is probably more secure than this building. Come on, let's go." With that she rose and picked up her soft-sided leather attaché case, which,

Tracy realized, she had never opened. She was planning to leave the entire time, she thought. *Who is this person?*

They headed out of the office, with both Mark and Gilliam giving them puzzled looks. Tracy responded with one of her own and a shrug. With Stephanie leading the way, the two women passed through security and out the main doors, where a black Navigator with tinted windows awaited them, its engine purring softly.

"Let's talk in the back, shall we?" Stephanie walked around to the far side, leaving Tracy to climb into the rear passenger seat. As soon as she was settled, she fastened her seat belt and looked up at the driver, a tall man with military-issue hair and a stone-serious demeanor. He screamed ex–elite forces and was obviously a bodyguard, which jangled Tracy's senses even more. Although his eyes were hidden by mirrored sunglasses, she had the feeling he had glanced at her and assessed her threat capability in an instant. Even through the silvered lenses, she had felt the dispassionate coldness of his gaze before he turned to check the street all around them. *Compared to him, I'm probably no threat at all,* she thought.

"Let's go. Shields up." Stephanie smiled as the SUV pulled away from the curb. "I love saying that." She waited a few moments until the driver nodded at her. "Okay, you may now talk freely in here. Also, he is cleared for all security ratings, just like I am, so pay him no attention. One more thing before we begin—where did you want to be dropped off?"

"I can catch a ride back from the station." A part of Tracy's mind screamed at her to take up the other woman's offer and head to the school before it was too late, but she didn't.

"Very well. The reason I'm here today is that we believe there is a high probability of a nuclear device having been smuggled across the Mexican border into the United States, and that it will be used against our country in the next few days."

Tracy frowned. "How did you—did you get a copy of my report?"

"Among other things. You do good work, by the way." Stephanie pulled out a thick envelope and rested it on her lap. "We'd like you to go down to El Paso and investigate this incident."

"Me? Excuse me for asking, but wouldn't this be better suited for the domestic nuclear detection office?"

Stephanie's expression turned, if not sour, then definitely not approving, either. "We're coordinating the investigation with them, as well. However, they're not equipped to handle a field investigation at this time, and are handling things on the research and theoretical-response side of things."

A bit of hostility there, Tracy thought. Apparently the interdepartmental cooperation only went so far.

"Since a Border Patrol agent initiated the message that started all of this rolling, we feel that pairing that agent on scene with an outside analyst is the best course of action at this time. And after reading your report on the subject and the potential threat, we believe you are the best-qualified person to carry out the assignment, rather than starting someone cold. That is, if you accept. It is, of course, strictly voluntary." Stephanie held out the large envelope. "Everything you'd need right now is in here, in hard copy and also on a flash drive."

Tracy automatically reached out and took it while trying to parse what had just happened. Of all the various possibilities that could have come up, this one was not among those she'd anticipated. "So you're treating this as real—that al-Kharzi isn't dead?"

"If we weren't, I wouldn't be sitting here. Al-Kharzi was supposedly killed attempting to use a WMD against the U.S., and we have every reason to believe that, if he is back, he'll try again."

Tracy drummed her fingers against the envelope. "If I accept, when would I leave?"

"We'd need you on a plane tomorrow morning. That's one of the issues, the time frame we're up against. If the agent down there is correct, and a device is in play in the U.S., then it may be a matter of weeks or even a few days, depending on how they intend to use it."

Tracy nodded as she weighed the package in her hand. "This is all so sudden—I mean, I'm an analyst, not a field agent."

"Some of the best work for our country has been done by analysts working in the field. Often, people like yourself bring a new perspective to an operation, looking at things from a new angle or finding what others have missed." Stephanie leaned forward. "I understand if you need to think about this. However, we need an answer from you as soon as possible."

"Of course." Again, Tracy was torn. She wanted to accept the assignment immediately. On the surface, there was no reason to turn it down, since it could only help her career. However, the logical part of her mind urged her to think it over more. "If you wouldn't mind, can I let you know before the end of this evening? If my answer is yes, I could be ready to go early tomorrow morning."

"I understand. Here, take this." Stephanie held out a small cell phone. "You can contact me on this anytime, day or night. It's secure, so you don't have to worry about security protocol."

Tracy took the device, slipping it into her inside suit jacket pocket, where it rested against her chest. "You sound pretty sure that I'm going to say yes. Otherwise, why give me this?"

"I never assume anything—it's simply an easier way to get in touch with me, and, should you decide to accept, then I don't have to drop it off. If you decide not to take the job, DHS will send it back to us."

"I wouldn't count on getting it back in a timely fashion." Tracy grimaced as she thought about the long delays in getting even the simplest tasks finished.

"We'd be able to keep track of it regardless. I think we're here," the FBI agent said.

Tracy looked up to see not the train station she had expected, but a single-story redbrick elementary school that looked very familiar. "This is—"

"North Chevy Chase Elementary, if the directions were right. I think the program has just begun, so you shouldn't have missed much," Stephanie said.

Tracy looked from the school to the blond woman and back again. "But—how did you know?"

"You know that old cliché that says the U.S. government is supposed to know everything? Well, in certain very small areas, that happens to be true." She leaned back in the leather seat. "Your boss said you had to miss a school recital to meet with me. He seemed very pleased by the idea, so I thought the least we could do was get you here on time, or as close as possible. Finding your fiancé's name was easy, and the rest came from the school's Web site." A faraway look crossed her face for a moment, then disappeared as quickly as it had come. "I know all about making sacrifices for the job, Tracy, and even with the importance of what we've just discussed here, you shouldn't have to make this one." She smiled and patted the seat beside her. "Leave the folder here—we'll messenger it back to your department. Go on, and please don't let this influence your final decision in any way."

"Thank you very much." Tracy got out of the SUV and reached back in to shake Stephanie's hand. "I'll be in touch as soon as I've made my decision."

"I look forward to hearing from you."

Tracy hurried into the building, eager to surprise Paul and Jennifer, but also dazed to be pondering the momentous decision before her, and wondering how she would explain it to both of them.

13

Sepehr al-Kharzi sat on a wooden stool in the spotless bathroom at Spaceworks and inhaled a deep breath of the white-tiled room's fresh scent. He was barefoot, with the sleeves of his shirt rolled up past his elbows. One of the twin sinks was filled with warm water, the other was empty.

"Bismillah," he said softly, bowing his head briefly before beginning *wudu,* the ritual Muslim ablution, which started by washing his hands in the water three times. Cupping a handful of water, he filled his mouth, rinsed it thoroughly, then spat it into the other sink and repeated the process twice more. Next he gently sniffed water up each nostril to clean them, repeating that process three times, as well. He washed his face from ear to ear and from his hairline to his throat, cleansed his arms up to the elbows, then ran his wet hands over his hair from his forehead to the back of his head. Placing his index fingers into his ears, he washed the inside and outside of them three times, as well. Finally, he completed his task by washing his feet to the ankles.

Driving across the country, al-Kharzi had barely had time to perform the washing ritual. But now, for the first time in several days, he felt clean.

Joseph Allen was waiting for him in the office. "Better, I trust?"

He nodded. "How is it going?"

"We're running tests on the device now. The most worrisome issue was the condition of the case—we found a small crack along a bottom seam, which may have released a minuscule amount of radioactive material. We've sealed it, and so far there seems to be no further trouble with it."

He raised a hand to interrupt. "Is there any danger that the leaked material will be discovered?"

Joseph considered that, then shook his head. "The estimated amount was so small that it would be almost impossible to filter out from background radiation that is encountered every day. The Americans would need the latest technology to isolate it. The other matter was a power drain on one of the battery connections, which is being examined now, and will be replaced if necessary. Everything else is in order—including the plutonium. The last steps will be to install the altitude detonator, place Allah's Fist into the rocket, and then it will be ready to go."

"Allah's Fist—I like that. Good, very good. Were there any problems getting it into the country?" al-Kharzi asked.

Joseph looked slightly pained at the question. "The team did have to go to their contingency plan when the vehicle was stopped shortly after crossing the border. Despite reassurances from our transporters, the Border Patrol found them. They eliminated all witnesses, then took the vehicle and completed the transfer. I'm surprised you didn't hear anything about it on the news—there has been coverage on the major networks for the past twenty-four hours."

Al-Kharzi shook his head. "I haven't had much access to television lately. Is there a concern about discovery?"

"No, current reports indicate that they believe it was a fight among drug smugglers, and even if they did figure out what might have happened, it will be too late."

Smiling, al-Kharzi clapped his fellow terrorist on the shoulder. "Good, good. All the same, I would feel better if you strengthened the guard rotation. I trust the cameras are all in place and working?"

"They are tested every week, and I will order the perimeter patrols increased to around the clock until our launch."

"Thank you, my friend. I do have one other request at the moment—the rocket that you're using to deliver our device—may I have a closer look at it?"

"I thought you would never ask. Come." Joseph led him through the main building to the entrance, nodding at the man behind the desk. They walked outside and across the grounds to where the sleek, gray, three-story rocket rose into the air like a steel finger pointing toward the heavens. Four slender fins protruded from the lower half, and al-Kharzi bent down to see a complicated-looking flared nozzle underneath. It was mounted on a joint that allowed the controllers on the ground to direct the thrust, steering the rocket, in effect. He shook his head in admiration—while he was a master of armed insurgency, terrorism and fourth-generation warfare, he would be the first to confess that he did not have the slightest idea how this vehicle worked beyond a very basic explanation. However, he could certainly tell anyone what it could be used for—sowing terror across half a continent.

Joseph had put on a pair of sunglasses, and stood with his arms folded across his chest, like a father watching a favored child. "Built with the most generous assistance of the United States government. We were scheduled to try for the X-Prize last year with a manned model, but unfortunately, our rocket developed an oxidizer-flow problem, which necessitated our dropping out of the contest." The grin on his face belied the truth of his words.

"How does it work?"

"We use nitrous oxide as the oxidizer, which is forced into the combustion chamber, where it is ignited to burn the fuel—in this case synthetic rubber—that lines the chamber. Once that reaction happens, the hot gases produced are channeled out of that nozzle at the bottom to provide thrust. However, it is our guidance system that is the company's pride and joy—we even hold two patents on the refinement of the system. With a range of twenty-five hundred miles, just about any target east of the Mississippi is within reach."

"And you know that I want as many of them blanketed as possible." Al-Kharzi frowned. "Aren't you concerned about being discovered?"

"My friend, you are too used to working under the fear of constant scrutiny. Here, we labor in plain sight every single day, and until twenty-four hours ago, there was absolutely nothing to hide anywhere on this property. I pay the taxes for our land and assets every year, and my employees do the same. They contribute to the company's 401K plan, and we even give to local charities. My people are using the degrees they received from universities here to create the next generation of technology. We are the model of every American company chasing after its piece of the so-called dream." His genial smile turned grim, like a predator's. "The only difference is that we have a much different interpretation of how that dream will play out. Once the payload is inserted, and our holy vessel takes to the skies over this nation, our own dream, one that you and I have been working toward for the past fifteen years, will be realized, and this nation will know our might and tremble like it never has before."

The main door of the complex opened, and an engineer dressed in a white lab coat walked out to them. "Dr. Allen, all modifications to the payload are complete, and it is operating within normal parameters. We are ready to begin the loading with your permission."

"Go ahead." Allen turned back. "Would you care to begin the countdown to put our operation truly into motion?"

Taking one last look at his instrument of destruction—hidden in plain sight in the very nation he was about to attack—al-Kharzi smiled. "I would like that very much."

14

The school play was an amazing production of *The Fairie Queene* by Edmund Spenser. The gifted and talented class had been delightful, and Paul had been extremely pleased when Tracy had slipped into the seat next to him as the curtain rose. Regardless, Tracy had been distracted by her conversation with Agent Cassell and the decision that lay before her. Her desire to accept the job was overwhelming—a success could only help her career—but every time she looked at Jennifer's face as she pirouetted and ruled over the rest of the cast as Gloriana, the title character, her heart almost broke at the thought of leaving her, even if only for a few days.

She clapped at the right places, and gave Jennifer a big hug when she came down off the stage after taking her bows before the enthusiastic audience, but let Paul take the lead in the after-play celebration. She did not hesitate to lavish praise on Jennifer's performance, which had been very good, but all the while a part of her wished the day would come to an end so she could discuss the offer with her fiancé.

With an exhausted Jennifer tucked into bed, she and Paul could finally relax in front of the plasma television. Her head rested on his shoulder as they listened to the light rain on the living-room windows. Now that the moment had arrived, she was unsure as to how to bring it up. Better just to come right out with it, she thought.

"Paul?"

"Hmm?"

"The reason I was late was because I had a visitor today. From the FBI."

"Oh, what did the feebs want?"

"You're incorrigible." She took the remote and hit the mute button. "They offered me a coordinated assignment out of town."

He looked directly at her. "Where?"

"I can't go into specific details, but it would be on the U.S.-Mexico border."

"What? Why did they ask you—never mind, you probably can't tell me."

"Afraid so. I would be gone for at least a week, maybe two."

He sat up. "And you said?"

"That I would think about it and let them know tonight."

"That isn't a lot of time."

"It's important that I give them an answer right away. I would be leaving as early as tomorrow morning."

"I take it you're seriously considering going?"

"I wouldn't be talking about it with you if I wasn't. This could give my career a boost, and, let's face it, I need it right now."

Paul turned off the television, darkening the room a bit. "Or it could get you shot or killed, as well. I mean, have you been keeping up on events down there? There's been reports of the Mexican army providing escort for drug smugglers, special-forces soldiers going over to work for the bad guys. It's dangerous down there, I mean really dangerous. You can't tell me exactly where?"

"Sorry. But this isn't any different than when you're packed up and sent off to Bahrain or Somalia or somewhere equally dangerous. And don't even think of trying to play the gender card on me," she said.

"I wouldn't dream of it, but keep in mind that when I go to these places, I have bodyguards accompanying me for safety. I hope to God that they're providing you with a contact down there."

"The briefing agent said I'd be working with the Border Patrol agent who first brought this to our attention."

"One guy? That's reassuring. Will you be carrying? When's the last time you qualified on the range?"

"Possibly, and I requalified last month. I shoot monthly, as you well know."

He rose from the leather couch and paced the room, running a hand through his already-tousled blond hair. "I don't know, Tracy. We were going to take that trip to the coast next weekend. Now we'll have to postpone it."

"Paul, tell me you're not using Jennifer as a reason I should turn this down."

"No, but our schedules are crazy enough that it was hell just getting that time off together. And as for Jennifer, I'm not using her. I'm telling you that she is a reason. Look, Marilyn was a workaholic—twelve-hour days, extended business trips—she only took two weeks off to have Jennifer, then she was running around the world again. When I found out my newborn daughter was being nursed by a nanny, I dropped everything, came home and took care of her for the next three years. Fortunately, the firm I was with was very understanding."

Paul ran a hand across his face. "Once I realized that Marilyn had agreed to have a child primarily because she thought it was what I wanted, and that she really had no maternal attachment to Jennifer, that's when we started talking seriously about splitting up. And, well, you know the rest. I swore that I would never put my daughter through that again. I know government work comes with a price—I've worked plenty of late nights, too, but I always made time for my daughter, as well, even though it almost killed me sometimes. Now I—we—have finally got Jennifer to where she's accepting you not just as my girlfriend, but as a mother—" He paused at Tracy's surprised look, then continued. "Yes, she's called you that more than once. Anyway, out of nowhere comes this trip—one that could get you killed. I mean—and this is not meant to be an insult—you're an analyst, not a field agent."

"I know that. They said they wanted a fresh viewpoint, which is what I bring to the situation, I guess. But keep in mind this is just one trip, Paul."

"Sure, for now. But what happens when they ask you next time? I appreciate that you try to make time for Jennifer and me, but we've had to reschedule or cancel things so many times in the past year alone. And what happens if the DHS assigns you to a fusion center across the country? I love you, but I'm not sure I could uproot Jennifer at this point in her life and start over again."

"You know I've been angling for a spot at the Virginia center once it's online. That's why this is important—I have to look to the future, as well. I'm not just doing it for me, but, I hope, for all three of us."

Paul stopped to stand in front of her. "What if I said I didn't want you going?"

She stared up at him, her brow furrowing. She knew Paul cared deeply about her, but sometimes that came out in what she saw as ridiculously protective actions or thoughts. "I'd say this isn't your decision to make."

"I figured you'd say that. You know, I was first attracted to you partly because you're so damn hot, but also because of your huge independent streak. However, at times like this it can certainly be a pain in the ass."

She smiled sweetly. "Just like your overprotective nature can be, too."

"Well, I don't think I'm wrong to be concerned. I know you can take care of yourself, but this is a completely unfamiliar area you'd be heading into."

"No, it's not, Paul. It's intelligence gathering and analysis, which is what I've been trained to do in my job. Only the geography changes—that's all."

"And the people you have to work with, and the job itself once you get there and any number of other things, any of which can bite you in the ass. I've been to places where there was no support staff on the government side or among our own people, mainly because they were cooling their heels in jail. And I certainly don't like what I'm hearing about the Border Patrol lately—seems a lot of them don't like the head guy very much, and there's rumblings of an internal revolt coming."

"None of that impacts how I do my job or how this agent I'd be paired with should do his," Tracy said.

"It shouldn't, but it does."

"So you'd rather have me stay here and keep my head down until a *safe* position comes along?"

"I thought we had discussed both of our career tracks

trying to mesh as closely as possible so we could both stay in the D.C. area."

"This would help me do that."

Paul stalked across the room. "Dammit, it would put you at risk! This isn't crunching numbers on a computer screen about something that happened a thousand miles away. If they want you there, then it's something local, and if it involves the border, then it's most likely something dangerous that they don't want leaking to the press." He took a deep breath, obviously trying to rein himself in. "When you said where the job was, the first thing I thought of was you lying dead in the desert somewhere, and I don't want that to happen."

"Oh, for God's sake, Paul, now you're being melodramatic." Her words trailed off as a thought came to her. "Jesus, you don't think I can do this, do you?"

"That's not it at all—"

"No, that *is* it. You think I should stay in my safe little cubicle and crunch data and not stick my head out at all, don't you?"

"Being concerned about you and thinking you can't do something are two very different things, Tracy."

"If you're trying to seriously talk me out of this, you're doing a piss-poor job," she shouted.

"It's hard to do that when you've practically made up your mind already. Jesus, why discuss it with me in the first place if you're just going to go off and do it anyway!" He crossed to the window and stared out at the drops gathering on the glass. A bolt of lightning flashed across the sky, the silver-white light revealing the emotions on his face—anger, concern and fear all warring with one another. At that moment, Tracy felt closer to him than ever before.

She got up and walked behind him, slipping her arms

around his waist. "Paul, nothing's going to happen to me. Most likely they'll set me up in an office to crunch data on a computer, but I doubt I'll ever be in any physical danger." Even as she spoke, she realized the ludicrousness of what she was telling him—after all, if that was the case, she could have conferenced in from D.C.

He stiffened at her words, but turned and enfolded her in his arms. "Come on, Tracy, I'm your fiancé, not an idiot."

"Then I'd appreciate you treating me as such, and not like a child. I'm telling you not to worry, I can take care of myself."

Paul sighed. "Just like talking to a brick wall. You're going to do whatever you damn well choose, aren't you?"

"If by that you mean I'm going to make the decision I feel is best, then yes."

"Of course, it's not like I'd be able to change your mind, but I do wish you wouldn't take this."

"Duly noted, and I haven't decided one way or the other yet. I'm surprised you've thrown in the towel so early."

He leaned back and looked at her. "You've got that scrunched little line at the bridge of your nose, which means you've already dug in your heels. I recognized that by our second argument."

"I'll have to work on that. I don't want to give you any more tells. Look, would you mind if I borrowed your car? I'm going to head home tonight—get some time to think on the way."

"You know you can stay here. I could run you back in the morning."

"No, staying here will just give me more reasons not to go."

"So much for my cunning plan," Paul said.

"Yeah, and don't think I hadn't noticed. Look, if I decide to go, I'll stop by and say goodbye, and if I stay, then our own trip is still on, so don't let Jennifer know about this just yet, okay?"

He held up his keys. "All right, all right. You'd better go before I try something really silly, like keeping you here against your will until the feebs find someone else."

Tracy snatched them out of his hand. "In that case, I'm gone." She stood on her tiptoes and kissed him, holding on to the moment for as long as she could. "I'll call you regardless."

He hugged her again, holding her to him before letting go. "You'd better get a move on if you plan on getting any rest tonight."

"It's a foregone conclusion I'm not going to get much anyway." She walked to the door, opening it and letting the crisp night air in, redolent with the fresh smell of the rain. "I'd certainly miss this down south."

"Hopefully that's not all you'd miss. Tracy, just—give me a call later, will you?"

"I will." Tracy walked to the car and got in, adjusting the seat to fit her smaller frame, and pulled out of the driveway. She navigated the maze of suburban streets around his condo, breathing in Paul's unmistakable scent in the car. Only when she reached the highway did she allow herself to think about their conversation.

She hadn't been lying to Paul. The decision still wasn't clear in her mind. The practical choice would be to take the assignment, but practical didn't count for much when staring into the eyes of a little girl and telling her you were going away for a while. Indeed, a part of her couldn't believe that she was this wrapped up in making the call, and all because of a little girl. All her life Tracy had prided herself on being able to make rational decisions, unclouded by emotion, unlike so many other women. Yet from the first time she had looked into Jennifer's big blue eyes, she had been lost. And even stranger—she actually enjoyed the feeling of being depended on, of having someone in her life who needed her. Not like Paul—their relationship was different. Jennifer was a force unto herself, one that could divert Tracy from the goals she had set for herself, and the direction her career was heading.

And ultimately, that is what it is all about, she thought as she reached into her jacket pocket for the sleek black cell phone the FBI agent had given her. Flipping it open, she listened as the phone automatically dialed a contact number. Oddly, the small screen remained black, the phone not showing the number it was calling.

The phone rang once before it was picked up. "Special Agent Cassell."

"Stephanie, this is Tracy Wentworth."

"Yes, hello, Tracy, how are you?"

"Fine, thank you. I've thought over your offer and decided to accept. When do I leave?"

"Very good. We have tickets held for you on a morning flight."

"That will be fine. Thanks very much for the opportunity—I'm looking forward to working with you."

"Same here. You'll be taking a company laptop down with you, correct?"

"Yes."

"Good. I'll send your itinerary, as well as that file over to your address at DHS—a little light reading on the way down. The phone will connect you directly to me anytime you need to make contact. I suggest daily reports unless something breaks earlier. Good luck, Tracy."

"Thank you." She closed the cell phone and tossed it on the seat next to her, then stared straight ahead, putting off the conversation with Paul until she got home. Might as well let him hope for a little while longer.

15 ‖ ‖65 ‖‖ ▪ ‖ 59‖ ‖‖ ▪‖ ‖‖ ▪

Kate switched over from Stephanie Cassell's cell line to the next incoming call, from her agent in Pakistan. "Alpha, this is Primary, go."

Robert Lashti's voice sounded winded, as if he had been running. "I've been made, Primary. After initiating contact using the disposable asset, she lured the subject back to the room. However, she was caught administering the drug, and gave me up under duress. Subject terminated asset after getting my description, then swept the room and located our surveillance equipment. I've left the hotel, but the town isn't that big, and they're looking for me."

"All right, Alpha, time to pull out. Can you make it to your vehicle?" As she spoke, Kate pulled up a window on the touch-sensitive screen that allowed her to juggle multiple projects, conferences and data streams at once. She contacted the Room 59 hacker on duty and requested a satellite map of the town of Panamik, as well as the quickest route north to China.

"Negative, subject's men are watching it. They're good, too—I almost walked right into them," Lashti said. "Probably ex-military, more Spetsnaz if we're really unlucky."

Swearing under her breath, Kate opened a new window to Pai Kun in Beijing to apprise him of the situation. She never liked bringing in more Room 59 operatives to assist with an extraction, but since their Asian director was only half a continent instead of half a world away, he needed to know what was happening to carry the ball when she handed it off.

"I'm attempting to procure another vehicle. However, everything around me seems to be limited to tractors and oxen—hardly suitable for the trip."

"How did subject and his men arrive?" Kate asked.

"I had thought by SUV, but I am currently unable to locate it."

"Okay, just keep your head down for a moment." Kate brought up the overhead view of Panamik, finding it to be indeed a one-ox town, although the largest in the area. There was a main road that bisected the sparse business section, and off to the northwest was a military base, which was of no help to her operative at all. He needed reliable wheels, and fast.

Kate opened a voice channel to her hacker. "Can you run a thermal scan on the buildings around that hotel? I'm looking for a still-warm engine," she said.

"I'm on it," came the reply.

"Damn, where'd they come from!" she heard a muffled shout in her headset, followed by the thuds of several running feet.

"Alpha, what's happening?"

"They spotted me…kids ratted me out…gonna try to… lose them—"

"Hold on, I'm going to visual." Kate popped open a third window, this one showing her the view through Lashti's glasses camera, the rough walls of the buildings on either side of him bouncing up and down as he pounded down the dirt road, trying to outdistance his pursuers.

A soft chime announced that Pai Kun was online, as well. As usual, he wasted no time on inconsequential matters. "Alpha will have to get himself out of town at the very least before we can extract him. I can do a lot, but I don't have anyone that close at the moment, and the region is volatile enough without anyone thinking the Chinese may be involved in covert activity there."

"That would be the last thing we need," Kate replied, then switched to the hacker. "Got anything yet?"

The words "It's coming up now" appeared on her screen. The regular street map disappeared, and an eerie blue-and-black thermal view of the dark town appeared instead. Kate saw a tiny red-orange figure running down a narrow alley. He was chased by two others across a street and into another alley. She quickly scanned the buildings around the hotel, looking for the telltale heat bloom of an idling car. *There!*

"Alpha, turn left at the next intersection, and head back toward the hotel. Their SUV is in a building approximately twenty-five yards south of it. I'll guide you to it."

Kate drew on the monitor, tracing the route her operative would have to take. As she plotted the route, the computer used the satellite imagery to give her the precise distances of each leg, as well as visual points to lead him through it. "Move forward ten yards, then turn left again. Circle around the hut you're near…cross the road ahead of you…they're about thirty yards back. Checking cross alleys, looks like you've lost them for now."

Lashti had stopped in the deep shadow of an overhanging hut roof. "Dawn's going to be breaking soon, and there won't be any place to hide. Primary, if I don't make it out of here, you need to know that all of the data I've collected indicated that our subject thought he was selling a live device. He had no idea it was a fake."

Kate didn't let this revelation slow her down for a second. "Good. Now let's get you out of there so you can debrief properly. You're close to the shed containing the SUV—you might even be able to hear it idling now."

The camera view of Lashti panned left, then right as he scanned the area. "Not yet. Where to next?"

"Go to the front of the hut you're near right now, then go two more buildings down on your left. The SUV should be behind the second one."

"Affirmative." The operative skulked from hut to hut while Kate kept an eye out for trouble, both of them aware of the glimmers of sunlight brightening the eastern horizon with every passing minute.

"Alpha, freeze right now!" Kate ordered.

Lashti flattened himself against the wall as two men walked out of the hut, dressed in heavy coats against the chill mountain morning. The two men showed up as small moving blue dots on Kate's screen, with tiny red dots for their faces. They turned left, away from Lashti, and walked down the street.

"Give them a few seconds." Kate split her attention between the receding pair of men and the approaching Russians, who were searching the narrow alleys and squat, one-story buildings with precision. "All right, go to the back of the hut. Their SUV is inside the shed. There's one man guarding it, but the others are only about forty yards from your position, so you'll have to take him out silently."

"It's never just as simple as catching a plane out of the country, is it?" Lashti whispered.

Kate sent a quick text message to the hacker. "No, but I think I might have a way to speed this up."

Lashti silently reached the double doors, and both he and Kate could clearly hear the SUV's purring engine. "I'm here. Now I just need a way to get him outside without getting me shot in the process."

"Just wait another few seconds." Kate kept an eye on the two Russians, who were now only twenty yards away and getting closer by the second. The screen flashed as the hacker uploaded a sound file and message to Kate: "I can't guarantee the translation accuracy, but this should do it."

"Alpha, turn the volume on your phone to maximum and set it down in front of the doors and go around the side. Incapacitate your target when he comes out," Kate ordered. She watched Lashti adjust the controls on his lifeline to her and set the phone on the rough, stony ground, then walk around the corner of the shed, his pistol drawn, but held by the slide and barrel instead of the grip.

God, I hope this works, Kate thought as she played the sound file, broadcasting it over the phone. Several excruciating seconds later—even the state-of-the-art satellites could only transmit so fast—the low tones of Alexei Kryukov's voice growled out from the phone's speaker.

"Dmitri, come out here!" The Russian's order was a bit choppy, because the hacker had cut the words from other conversations and strung them together in one file, but it should have been enough to attract the guard's attention. *The only problem is that it might also bring those other two running,* Kate thought.

Nothing happened for several seconds. The door remained firmly shut. Kate sent the wave file again, the lag time just enough that it seemed the person outside had been waiting for a response. The two men were only ten yards away now, and Kate realized they had coordinated their sweep to end up back at the SUV. If the driver didn't bite soon, Lashti would be stuck with the three of them.

She heard a scrape of wood on wood, and one of the doors swung inward. Peering around the corner with her operative, they both saw a man's dark form stroll out, a crooked cigarette dangling from his lips.

"Alexei, where the hell are you?" In the rectangle of light from the shed, he noticed the phone on the ground and walked over to pick it up, his free hand slipping underneath his coat.

With three large, noiseless steps, Lashti crept up and brought the butt of his pistol down hard on the back of the other man's head, smashing him to the street. He picked up his phone, then frisked the unmoving man, coming up with a SIG Sauer 9 mm pistol, which he slipped into his pocket. "Commandeering the SUV now," he whispered.

Kate was struck by a sudden brainstorm. "Alpha, take that man with you."

"Already thought of it, Primary."

Kate watched as he dragged the unconscious body inside the building, which was remarkably exhaust free. Lashti spotted the reason why, and disconnected a hose that vented the exhaust to the outside.

"Get out of there—Kryukov's people are less than ten yards away," Kate said.

Securing the man's hands behind his back with his belt, Lashti shoved him into the back of the SUV, then slipped behind the steering wheel. He eased the vehicle into gear, moving out of the shed slowly. As soon as he was free of the building, he gunned the engine, the wheels slipping on the rocks as they fought for traction. A shout echoed behind him, and Kate saw the two men running after the vehicle, shrinking in the distance as they pursued with guns drawn. They didn't have the chance to shoot, since Lashti had quickly pulled out of range.

"Stinks in here—damn Russians, all of 'em chain-smokers. I'm going to reek like an ashtray by the time I get out of here," Lashti said.

"Worry about the clothes later—you're not safe yet—you still have to make it out of the town and north, across the border. That military base isn't going to look too kindly on you if they spot you trying to leave through Kashmir," Kate said.

"Leave that to me—after this little escapade, getting into China will be the easy part. Thanks for the assist, Primary, I appreciate it."

"Anytime, Alpha. I've downloaded your route to your phone. It should avoid all of the army patrols on both sides of the border. Be careful, and you should be in China by this time tomorrow, if all goes well. Turn over your captive to our operative at the border. I'm sure he'll be able to extract any useful information from him. Report back in when you're clear, or if you discover something. Primary out."

Kate disconnected the call and sent a quick note of thanks to the hacker, telling her to keep monitoring Alpha until he got out safely. She also updated Pai Kun, who promised to have people ready to get Lashti across the border.

Leaning back in her chair, Kate tried to slow her heartbeat. Although her voice had never changed from a calm, modulated tone as she had talked Lashti through his escape, her heart and mind had been racing a mile a minute, always analyzing, planning and discarding several options and variables. Oversight was a part of her job that

Kate simultaneously loved and hated. She loved it for the immediate, real-time access it gave her to the operatives, and hated it for the powerless feeling she got at the same time. Every time she slipped on her headset and Web-viewing glasses or opened those windows on her touch-screen, she couldn't help feeling that although she was a powerful force multiplier for her people, at the same time, she was sitting in plush comfort in her New York City town house while the men and women of Room 59 were out there risking their lives every day. And if they got into inescapable trouble, there was absolutely nothing she could to do to help. She had watched operatives die right in front of her, and had accepted that as part of the job. But she absolutely hated that.

This time, however, was one of the good ones, she thought. With a sigh, Kate peeled herself out of the chair she had been sitting in for hours, took off the headset and went to take a shower, hoping nothing else came up for a while so she could get some rest before conferencing with Denny Talbot about the Texas operation.

16

Nate kept his hat brim pulled low over his face as he drove through the Segundo Barrio in south-central El Paso. Just a hop and skip away from the border, this was the main territory of the Barrio Aztecas, the predominant Hispanic prison gang in the city. Although there were many other places he'd have rather been at one-thirty in the morning, this was the best place to find the information he needed, and right now every minute counted.

Rubbing grainy eyes, Nate drained the last of his rotgut coffee, crushed the paper cup and tossed it on the Bronco's floor. He'd been cruising the streets for several hours, shaking down his contacts and confidential informants for any word about Middle Eastern men crossing the border or any other recent suspicious activity. But for all his questions—and subtle threats when necessary—he had come up completely dry.

Normally he would only come here in the daytime, but he knew the clock was ticking, and he needed something solid to get this potential incident taken seriously. That feeling in his gut was growing stronger—something was going to go down, but without evidence, his hands were tied.

The sidewalks were filled with the usual denizens of the barrio—scattered gang members, streetwalkers, wandering homeless and several low riders cruising the streets. The thump and blare of brassy music echoed off the houses and apartment buildings. He turned left on East Sixth Street, driving toward the north end of Marcos B. Armijo Park, which he would definitely not enter at this time of night. At Ochoa, he turned right and continued down until it ended, with a small cul-de-sac to his right and the street continuing off to his left. Small clusters of Mexicans sat on the porches of several houses along the street, and a few dozen yards away a train rumbled past on tracks running parallel to the border.

Nate took a deep breath and made sure his pistol was near to hand, arranging the tail of his long-sleeved shirt to cover it. The *vatos* had sentries watching out for trouble, be it a rival gang or the police, and he figured he'd been made already, but he knew the leader of the Aztecas did not like trouble of the "shoot first, ask questions later" kind, and would come down hard on any of their sergeants who acted up without permission. If he did get into trouble and had to shoot his way out, there was no way he'd be able to explain it. But there was no way he was going into the house across the street unarmed. He got out of the Bronco and ambled over, the multiple sets of cold eyes staring at him. The conversations among the stoop sitters had hushed at his approach, and Nate was acutely aware of the click of his boot heels on the pavement.

A tattooed, bare-chested group of Mexicans relaxed on the porch of the house, a rambling, two-story, white stucco building with a bare patch of dirt in front of it. The young men, along with a few women, had been passing bottles around and laughing among themselves. Gang tattoos were visible everywhere.

As Nate approached, the group fell completely silent. A barrel-chested Mexican in a tank top and baggy, wide-legged denim shorts and black horns tattooed on his forehead lounged on the front steps. He looked at the lanky Texan as he approached, one eyebrow raised. "*Bolillo,* you better pray you're not lost. *¿Que chingados quieres?*"

Under the circumstances, the last part, "What the fuck do you want?" was as polite a greeting as Nate could have hoped for. "I need to see Lopez. Tell him Nate is outside," he answered in fluent Spanish.

The large Mexican rose from his seat, but instead of sending someone inside, he lumbered toward the border agent, who stood his ground, returning the gangbanger's stare full on. "You should be more careful, *cabrón.* Coming down here by yourself, this time of night, all sorts of bad things can happen to *el rulacho* stickin' his nose where it don't belong." As he spoke, the other gang members slowly formed a loose semicircle around the two men. The worst part was that Nate didn't recognize any of them.

Jesus Christ, just what I need, a guy probably just out of the pen trying to score points, he thought. *If I flash my badge here, I'll never make it out alive.* Nate wiped his nose with the back of his hand, then hooked both thumbs into his jeans, his right hand only inches away from the butt of his pistol. "Just tell Lopez that Nate Spencer is here to see him."

A flash of recognition crossed one of the girl's faces, and she leaned close to the giant Mexican, whispering rapidly. Nate caught the words "Border Patrol" and "in his pocket," or words to that effect.

The man-mountain grunted and waved her into the house. "Hold on," she said.

Nate just stood there, surrounded by members of the most powerful Mexican gang in El Paso. The one overwhelming thought running through his mind was that even though he'd done a lifetime of crazy acts, this had to be the craziest stunt he'd pulled yet. The seconds ticked by with agonizing slowness. At last the screen door slammed, and the girl came back out and whispered in the big guy's ear. He nodded, then slowly moved aside. "Go right in, *pendejo.*"

The others snickered, but Nate didn't rise to the bait, knowing that even though he had permission to pass, disrespecting the guy by insulting him back would just get him beaten or maybe killed. Instead, he pretended that he didn't hear the slur, and walked up to the house, opened the door and entered.

The air inside was thick with blunt smoke and the smell of frying meat. A slow-turning fan in the kitchen did little to clear the haze, just pushed it around. A plump girl was busy at the old stove, and she nodded him toward the next room, where Nate heard the sounds of cursing and laughter, accompanied by the clink of bottles. He strode toward the doorway, steeling himself to take more shit from these lowlifes if it got him the information he was looking for.

A half-dozen men played out a hand of poker around a battered, felt-covered table with a pile of cash and gold jewelry in the middle. There were also two pistols on the green felt, and most likely a half-dozen more were hidden on the various players. Nate swept the table with his gaze, his eyes falling on the man directly across from him. He was covered in tattoos across most of his body, including his entire face, his eyes masked in black. On his bare chest above his heart was a stylized Aztec chief with two feathers in his headdress, signifying his rank—a gang lieutenant.

Everyone else froze when they saw the gringo in the doorway, and the tattooed *indio* frowned when his eyes rose to see Nate across from him. One of the other members moved his hand toward one of the guns on the table, but their leader held up his hand, stilling the movement.

"*Hola, chingado,* you got some balls coming in here. You looking to get shot or what?" Enrique Lopez had risen from a street soldier to a lieutenant in the gang hierarchy after serving most of a dime sentence for armed robbery. Nate had met him while investigating a human-smuggling ring across the border a year earlier, and had cultivated him as an informant on the activity going on among the various gangs in El Paso. Lopez had a brain, and preferred to solve problems without resorting to violence, but he was just as cold-blooded as the rest of his *vatos,* and wouldn't hesitate to cap anyone who crossed him.

"Just need a minute of your time, Lopez, then I'll be outta your hair," Nate said.

The wiry gang leader looked at his cards again, then slapped them on the table. "Shit, cards suck tonight anyway. Deal me outta this round, I'll be right back." He nodded at Nate to accompany him into a narrow hallway.

"You must have a death wish to stroll in here like you owned the place," he snarled as soon as they were out of earshot of the others.

"You know I got better things to do that mess with your business right now." Like most cops, Nate knew cultivating the street was the best way to get the inside score on anything going down. The only problem was that the street always extracted its own price in return.

"*Sí*, that you do. Hey, any news on that injunction getting renewed?"

A few years earlier, the El Paso Police Department had gotten an injunction taken out on the entire Segundo Barrio neighborhood, making it nearly impossible for gang members to meet, conduct business or even be seen together in public. Although it had been successful during its two-year term, it had been allowed to expire, and the gang had reconsolidated its hold over the barrio afterward. However, there was always talk at city hall and in the police department of renewing it, something the Aztecas worried about as much as the rival gangs they were currently fighting.

"I haven't heard anything recently. It's probably stalled in committee right now anyway, so I doubt you got anything to worry about. Look, you hear about that slaughter near the border?" Nate asked.

"Sure, who hasn't? Everyone's talkin' about that mess."

"Anyone owning up to it? You hear about any of the other gangs with itchy trigger fingers?"

"Shit, homes, you know how this works. I do you a favor—you do me a favor."

This was the part Nate hated. "What did you have in mind?" he asked.

"Don't worry, this'll even make you look good. There's a house on the edge of the barrio, corner of Overland and Paisano. It's owned by some Alices, and they're making cheese for the schools right next to us. We want them gone."

Nate knew "cheese" was the latest drug variant to hit the streets, a combination of heroin and over-the-counter cold medicines. Popular among middle-school kids, it was all too prevalent in El Paso and other cities throughout the Southwest. The reference to "Alice" was the Aztecas' derogatory term for the Aryan Brotherhood, a neo-Nazi gang they were fighting with for control of several neighborhoods in the area.

"And you know how it rolls, too—I'll check it out, and if it's confirmed, we'll take them down. Now, what you got for me?"

"Well, I haven't heard about any bangers shooting their mouths or their thumpers off, definitely not any of *chucos* around here. Now the peckerwoods might be a different story, but I don't know nothin' about that."

"Jesus, Lopez, this is what you want me to hit a drugstore for? You gotta do better than that," Nate said.

"All right, but this is some crazy shit, so you gotta raise the stakes a bit. Those same Alices are going to be getting a shipment from down south in six days. Give me a day or so, and I'll get you the location."

Nate smelled a huge rat; this was too easy. "What's in it for you?"

"While you got the cops and border agents swarming all over them, we might be moving some merchandise at the same time, and don't need any interference—know what I'm sayin'?"

Nate took off his hat and ran a hand through his hair. He'd skirted the law to make busts before, like the one yesterday, learned from his contacts in the gang underworld. In return, they were able to conduct their own business unmolested, as long as they kept the violence down. Nate was a realist; he knew the so-called war on drugs would never be won, not with America's insatiable appetites. The best they could ever do was to unofficially regulate it by allying with certain traffickers, and anyone who got out of hand would be taken down, as well. But while he accepted the arrangement as a necessity of the job, he had never liked it, and this blatant overlooking of product entering the U.S.

really rubbed him the wrong way. However, he reminded himself of the consequences of what might happen if they didn't find the nuclear material. *Little fish we let go to catch the big fish,* he thought. "The other shipment better be on the level, or I'll be coming after yours," he said.

"Trust me, you'll be hip deep in *chiva,* no lie."

"We'd better be. So?"

"So my cousin occasionally connects with these homies that run illegals into the U.S, right? I was chillin' with him last week, and he mentions that his crew had gotten a line on some salamis that wanted to sneak into the States, and were willing to pay fifty large to a reliable coyote who could guarantee delivery."

"A reliable coyote? They definitely must have been from out of town," Nate said.

"Yeah, anyway, their cash backed up the story. They were willing to pay anyone who could get the job done. Their only request was they wanted a panel van, said they had some stuff they were bringin' with them. My cuz couldn't take the job, since he had other things goin' down, so he passed it on to a couple of friends of his."

"And?"

"And they're most likely the two dead *vatos* who got taken down in your little bloodbath yesterday, along with the rest of the illegals and your two agents."

Nate jerked as if stung. "How'd you know about that?"

"You ain't the only one who's got people that know people, homes. Anyway, the two bodies are Miguel Santos and Jesus Calaveras."

"That's nothing the crime lab doesn't already know. Come on, Lopez, that's the best you can do?"

"Look, man, that's all I got, unless you wanna know one of these guys was an Elton John fan."

"What are you talking about?"

"My cuz said they was real secretive about the particulars—they wanted to use their own cell phones when they set up the ride. I mean, they sent him a phone to use, then called it. The ringtone on there was that song 'Rocket Man,' you know?"

Nate rubbed his forehead. "I can't believe I came out here at two in the morning for this. If you want that brotherhood taken down a peg, you better come up with something more solid, you hear?"

"Hey, I gave you all I got. What about that cheese factory?"

"I'll look into it. Meanwhile, pass the word you're looking for info on the killings, and let me know what you come up with. Otherwise your competition will be restocking their shelves quicker than you'd like." That last part was a blatant lie. Nate would bust the Aryans in a heartbeat; he actively hated them, whereas he simply disliked the rest of the gangs running around the city. "Get back to me sooner rather than later," he said.

"I'll see what I can do, but you need to move on that real estate first, then maybe I can scare up some details," Lopez said.

Nate shook his head, disgusted at the games he had to play to simply do his job. "Watch the news. I'm gonna head out the back way." He eased around the banger and opened the door, walking out into the darkness and circling around the house.

As he approached his Bronco, he heard snickers from the group out front, and when he got closer, he saw why. They had spray painted a big white 5-0 on the hood and sides of the small SUV.

"Hey, homes, looks like someone came along and redecorated your ride," the big Mexican called out. Nate heard more laughter, along with the distinctive rattle of a spray can.

"Good luck getting out of the neighborhood, *cabrón.*"

Nate smiled thinly and glanced back at the big guy, fixing his face in his mind, which wasn't too difficult. He'd keep an eye out for him in the future. Getting into the Bronco, he started it up, then headed down Ochoa, aiming toward Highway 10. If he could get to the highway unmolested, he should be all right. What'd you expect, calling the SOBs out on their turf? he thought as he navigated the dark streets, not breathing easy until he swung onto the ramp leading to the highway.

17

Hauling her carry-on bag behind her, Tracy was only slightly bleary-eyed as she navigated the El Paso airport. So far, everything had gone relatively well. Her early-morning goodbyes to Paul and Jennifer had been subdued, primarily since Jennifer was still half-asleep. Paul had been grim faced, his lips compressed in a tight line as he had extracted a promise from her to call him every day. The American Airlines flight had been more or less on time, passing her through Houston and into El Paso at 1:50 p.m., only five minutes behind schedule.

She collected her larger suitcase from the luggage carousel, then walked out into the blazing summer heat, hailed a cab and directed the driver to take her to the main U.S. Customs and Border Protection Office. Along the way, she called Paul and let him know she had arrived safely, and would talk to him later that evening. Then she freshened up as best as she could for having gotten five hours sleep in the past twenty-four, all the while trying to quell the butterflies in her stomach at the thought of coming into this place and taking charge of an ongoing investigation. She had the authority and the required documentation to back her up, but actually doing it was another matter entirely.

The cab pulled up in front of the nondescript offices with the Customs and Border Protection sign and the Department of Homeland Security seal out front. She paid the driver, then walked into the air-conditioned building, hauling her luggage behind her. Inside, the building looked like many other properties used for government work—used to the point of shabbiness. The main room was a beehive of activity, with agents working at their desks, making phone calls and handling the constant blizzard of paperwork that accompanied any government job.

Tracy looked around for the chief border agent's office, but was distracted by a tall, weather-beaten man who brushed by her.

"Excuse me, ma'am." He stopped and turned, regarding her from a pair of pale blue eyes set in a tanned face with crow's feet radiating out from the corners. Instead of making him appear old, they gave him an aura of competent experience, something Tracy was very aware she lacked at the moment. "Can I help you?" he asked.

"I'm here to see the chief border agent, Roy Robertson," she said.

"Great, so am I." He nodded toward a door. "Let's get his attention." He knocked on the plate glass.

"Yeah?" came a voice from inside.

The tall agent opened the door. "Roy, it's Nate. I've got your two-thirty here."

"What the—?"

Tracy heard footsteps from inside, and a stocky man, his white shirtsleeves rolled up and rimless reading glasses perched on his head, appeared in the doorway. "Jesus,

Nate, you readin' my mind again? I was gonna call you in here anyway." Noticing Tracy, Robertson nodded. "Agent Wentworth, I presume?"

"Correct. Chief Agent Robertson?"

"Please, come inside. You, too, Nate, since you opened this whole can of worms to begin with."

Tracy couldn't help staring a bit as the agent known as Nate motioned to the door with his hand. "Ma'am. Can I take those for you?"

"I'm fine, thank you." She walked in and chose the sturdier of the two chairs in front of the desk, setting her bags down and sitting next to them. Behind her, Nate closed the door and ambled—there really was no other way to describe it—over to the other chair, folding himself down and crossing his legs, revealing a worn black-and-white cowboy boot that looked as if it had walked through hell and back but was still ready for more. Just like its owner, Tracy thought.

"I just got an e-mail this morning regarding you, Agent Wentworth," Robertson said.

"Then you know why I'm here," Tracy replied.

"Yes, although—and I'm quite apart from Nate on this—I find the scenario you're following up on very hard to believe, or that Washington even sent you here to investigate. The idea that a nuclear device would be brought across this border, especially in this time of heightened surveillance, is simply in the minutest realm of possibility."

Tracy cocked her head. "But that possibility, however unlikely, is exactly why I'm here."

"Hold on a sec." The rangy border agent next to her leaned forward. "Are you both sayin' my e-mail report is what brought you here?"

"Got it in one, Nate. This is Agent Tracy Wentworth,

from the Department of Homeland Security in D.C. Agent Wentworth, this is Customs and Border Protection Agent Nathaniel Spencer, the guy who's responsible for bringing you down here on this wild-goose chase."

"I'll be the judge of that, if you don't mind, Chief Agent," Tracy said.

A peculiar look crossed Robertson's face, as if he had bitten into what he thought was an orange and found a lemon between his lips instead. Tracy figured she might have nicked his law-enforcement officer's pride, but if Agent Spencer was right, the boss would deserve it—the idea of a loose nuke was simply too dangerous to dismiss out of hand. She glanced over to see if Spencer was offended at her jab at his boss since they obviously had a good working relationship. He didn't move a muscle in her direction, just sat back in his chair and ran a hand over his salt-and-pepper mustache.

Robertson cleared his throat. "They've also specifically requested that you serve as the liaison for Agent Wentworth here, and assist her in her investigation in any way possible."

"What about my suspension?" Nate asked, clearly surprised.

Tracy beat Robertson to it this time. "Agent Spencer, I think you'd agree that the threat of a potential nuclear device loose in the El Paso area would certainly trump any internal investigation into an agent's cases, wouldn't you?"

"Absolutely, ma'am."

"Excellent. Chief Agent Robertson, I'll need whatever data your crime lab has procured from the scene, as well as any preliminary reports. Once I've had a chance to review your office's progress, we can discuss follow-up leads and other necessary investigations."

"Sounds good. Of course the resources of our entire department are at your disposal." Robertson's round face turned dark and serious. "I suppose you know those bastards killed two of our men."

"Yes, and on behalf of everyone at the Washington headquarters, you have our deepest sympathies," Tracy said.

"Yeah, I already got the obligatory phone call. What I want, however—especially if these guys are up to what you both seem to think they are—is them stopped, one way or the other."

Tracy looked him straight in the eye. "We'll do everything we can."

"Good." Tracy didn't miss the covert look that was exchanged between the two border agents; the old-boy network rearing its head. Welcome to Texas, sweetheart, she thought.

"Do you have any other questions, Agent Wentworth?" Robertson asked.

She rose, smoothing her suit jacket and picking up her carry-on. Nate had somehow reached around her and snagged the larger case. "Not at this time, sir, but I'll certainly be in touch."

He nodded. "Good luck and good hunting. Nate, you be sure she gets anything she needs."

"Yes, sir." Nate was at the door again, opening it. "After you," he said.

Once outside the office, he paused. "Can you wait here for a moment? I have to go pull that info for you." His gaze strayed across the room to where a serious-looking man in the regulation black slacks, white shirt and tie was typing on a computer.

"Are you sure you don't want me to come with you?" Tracy asked.

"No, there's likely to be some fireworks, and I'm sure you got better things to do with your time. Besides, this will just take a minute." He strolled over to the other man's desk and leaned over him, their low conversation punctuated with the occasional nod. The other man leaned around Nate to look at her, his face darkening with anger. Nate shrugged his shoulders, holding out his hands in an "I don't have a choice" gesture.

"This is total bullshit!" The white-shirted man gathered several file folders and tapped out commands on his computer with forceful stabs of his fingers, then tossed a small flash drive at Nate. Rising from his chair so fast he sent it rolling backward into the wall, the man stalked toward Robertson's door. Nate, who had stayed where he was, nodded at Tracy to meet him at the main entrance. She shouldered her bag and slipped away, leaving the other man banging on the chief border agent's door.

She noticed Nate's grin as they walked out into the bright sunshine. "You enjoyed that, didn't you?"

Slipping on a pair of mirrored aviator sunglasses, he gave her a sidelong glance. "Maybe a little."

Tracy returned the appraising look. "Is there a history between you and the agent formerly in charge of this investigation that I should know about?"

"Travis just likes to be the head bull, that's all."

"Whereas you just blend into the background and do your part, take one for the team, that sort of thing, right?"

He met her gaze, then broke first with a genuine smile. "Something like that. This is my ride." He stopped at a battered black Bronco with what looked like fresh paint on the hood and doors. "Doesn't look like much, but the AC works. I take it you haven't had a chance to check into your hotel yet?"

"What gave me away?" She walked to the back of the SUV and waited for him to open the door. When he did, she saw the pistol grip of what looked like a shotgun sticking out of a sleeve attached to the back of the rear seat. "That doesn't look like regulation," she said.

Nate didn't give it a second look as he set her bags down inside. "I hunt, too." He didn't elaborate, and Tracy didn't ask.

She got into the clean passenger's seat, and when he turned the engine over, true to his word, a blast of cool air wafted from the vents. Nate drove her to the Holiday Inn a few blocks from the Border Patrol offices—nothing but the best for government agents—and waited in the lobby while she dropped off her things. When she came out, he was leaning against the wall.

"Had any lunch yet?" he asked.

"I thought we'd grab something on the way out to the crime scene—I'd like to see it for myself."

"I doubt another hour is going to change anything out there. Come on, I know a great place on the way. They serve up chimichangas as big as your head."

She glanced over at him with a frown. "For someone who was in such a hurry to get some action on this, you're sure laid back now."

"I just thought you'd like a chance to get situated a bit, review the materials we've gathered so far and have a decent meal before we run out into the middle of the desert looking at sand and scrub for several hours. You're a real hard charger, ain'tcha? Most visitors from up north take the travel day off and start fresh the next morning."

"I just don't see the point in wasting daylight, especially if our suspects are on a timeline," she said. Then her stomach rumbled, and Tracy shook her head, grimacing at her traitorous body. "However, a real meal would be good, and you're right, it'll be easier to review all of this without my computer bouncing around on my lap."

"All right, then. And don't worry about me—I'll be sure to keep up with you."

Tracy thought he might have winked at her, but she couldn't be sure with the sunglasses.

Nate drove to Leo's, a local place that was crowded, even at the after-lunch hour. The waitress greeted Nate by name, and showed them to a quiet corner booth. Tracy decided to follow his lead and ordered the chimichanga platter with beans and rice; her only difference was to get the salsa verde sauce instead of the red sauce Nate went with.

Tracy sipped some water. "Now, Agent Spencer, shall we get down to business?"

"Call me Nate, if you don't mind—no need to stand on formality, and calling each other 'Agent' all day always gets on my nerves."

"Fair enough, and I'm Tracy." She flipped open her laptop screen, and Nate remained quiet for several minutes, munching on the complimentary tortilla chips and salsa. Downloading the contents of the drive, she scanned them quickly, comparing them with the written reports. "Not much here so far," she finally said.

"Well, the victims have barely been cold. Usually you all aren't in such a hurry to get down here and poke around."

"Time could be critical. So, what's your take on this?" Tracy asked.

Their meals arrived, the waitress warning them about the hot plates, and Nate waited until she was gone to speak.

"You already know about the e-mail, and when this whole thing happened, it just seemed to match up. What would be worth killing two dozen illegals over? Maybe a shitload of *chiva,* I suppose, but they'd all be carrying it—don't make much sense to off your mules right after the crossing. And they weren't abandoned, like some coyotes do, because the truck was gone. These guys had a plan, and a backup, and when it looked like they were busted, they didn't hesitate to break out the hardware and kill anyone that got in their way."

"So, the question now is, where'd they go? If they've been on the move for the past couple of days, that would give them a range of roughly three thousand miles, give or take a couple hundred. That puts them into any major city on both coasts. We can't alert everywhere—there'd be mass hysteria across the country."

Nate scooped up a forkful of crisp, deep-fried tortilla and spicy shredded beef, chewed and swallowed. "That's good, because I think they're still around here. They came across the border here for a reason. If they had wanted to hit a major city, they wouldn't come in here, then drive it across the country. Too much risk of discovery."

"Okay, if they're still here—and I doubt they're planning on setting it off in El Paso, it's just not central enough, no offense—what's their delivery vehicle, private plane?"

"It'd have to be, wouldn't it? We've already got agents looking into the records of anyone of, ahem, certain nationalities with a private pilot's license in Texas and the surrounding states. I'll say one thing about Travis—that guy I ticked off back in the office—he's an ass, but he is good at his job."

"Okay, so if that's covered, then we try to find the truck. Talk about a needle in a haystack, but I might be able to even the odds a bit. Excuse me." Tracy pulled out the black cell phone and opened it. "Hi, Stephanie?"

The FBI's agent's voice was as clear as if she was sitting across from them. "Hello, Tracy. How's Texas?"

"Hot. Listen, is there any way that you can find out if any satellites were over—" she flipped through the reports until she got the location of the massacre, then used her laptop to translate that into geographic coordinates and gave them to Kate Cochran.

"Great minds think alike. I'm already following that up. I should be in touch with you with whatever we find shortly."

"Good, we're going out to take a look at the actual scene, and I'll call in if anything else comes up."

"All right. Otherwise, I'll be in touch as soon as we have anything of import. Thanks, and good luck."

Tracy closed the phone and turned to the remains of her meal. "Hopefully that'll cut our haystack down to a more manageable size. This was delicious, but I'm more than done. Shall we?"

Nate took care of the bill, and they headed back out to his Bronco. He navigated through the neighborhood to the highway, heading southeast out of town toward the crime scene. Tracy tried not to let her anticipation show by tapping her foot on the floor or her fingers on the armrest, but she couldn't stop the thrill of knowing that she was in the field, doing actual on-site investigation. *Now all I have to do is crack this case before these guys do something horrible, like kill several hundred thousand people,* she thought as the reality of her situation hit her.

The sobering thought dissipated her excitement, and turned the food in her stomach into a leaden lump as Tracy realized the lives of tens of thousands might be in her hands, and if she failed them, each one would be on her conscience for the rest of her life.

18

With an effort, Sepehr al-Kharzi kept his hands from trembling in zealous excitement. The team that was about to insert the nuclear payload into the rocket was performing flawlessly, and he had never been more proud of any operation that he had overseen than this one.

Although there had been many successful insertions of sleeper cells in the U.S. over the past two decades, he was the most impressed with the men that made up this one. They all worked together and lived in an El Paso suburb, spread out enough so as not to attract too much attention, but close enough to stay in contact easily—and to keep an eye on each other, to prevent slip-ups. Sepehr had seen all too many times how promising missions had been busted because of the wrong phrase said in the wrong place, or one member of the cell doing something out of the ordinary, and drawing attention to himself. In that way, the fact that this much larger operation had remained off the government's radar for so long was even more impressive. That was in part due to Joseph's foresight in taking care of his personnel. If there was an immigration problem, his lawyers were available to any employee, day or night. If one of them broke the law, accidentally or otherwise, he got as much help as he needed to take care of the problem. Spaceworks offered generous salaries and benefits packages, as well. The boss understood that religious zealotry and sound business practices could operate alongside each other without too much difficulty.

And now, everything was coming to fruition, praise Allah. The plan was in its final stages, and soon they would wreak the most terrible blow upon this nation that anyone had ever seen.

Over the past several hours, the rocket team had removed the nose cone and brought it inside the building. It had been lined with a thin layer of lead when it had been built years ago, to prevent nosy American satellites from trying to see inside. Because of this, they could handle the nuclear bomb with relative impunity.

Sepehr watched intently as a team of four white-suited, gloved, booted and helmeted men cycled through the airlock and into the room where the nose cone and the device both sat after being cleaned repeatedly, to make sure every part was functioning at optimum capability. They had already attached the altitude timer to the bomb, and, with one man at each corner, they transferred the device into the custom-designed space inside the cone. The team leader ran one final series of tests on it, then turned and gave a thumbs-up to the men in the observation room.

"All that remains is to reattach the cone to the rocket, and the final countdown to launch can begin." Sepehr turned to see Joseph walking toward him. "The cone is also lead lined to prevent any radiation leakage or detection, as well as to defeat any attempt to hack into the rocket's guidance system."

"How will you control its flight, then?" Sepehr asked.

"We have a tight-beam laser guidance system that will transmit any course corrections within one-ten-thousandth of a second, guaranteeing that, if we wanted to, we could put this missile down within one yard of its intended target."

"Truly, my friend, you have thought of everything. While I know that Allah favors our mission, it will also come to pass because of your foresight and planning."

"Allah has seen fit to guide my hand to this place and time. I am only doing as he would have me do for the glory of Islam. I thought you might want to see our various flight plans, perhaps review the primary and secondary ones and the estimated coverage," Joseph said.

"That would be excellent indeed, but I want to see the cone's transfer. Now that we are this close to achieving our goal, I am concerned, even with all of your safeguards in place, that something will go wrong at the last moment," Sepehr said.

"A prudent concern—a wise man is never hasty in accomplishing his ultimate goals."

They both watched as the men loaded the cone into another container, also lead lined, loaded it onto a cart, and wheeled it through the airlock to the loading dock. There they would use a truck to move it back to the rocket, where a crane would lift it to be reattached to the body.

Once it was away, Sepehr followed Joseph into the main workroom, which was still abuzz with activity. The antiseptic smell irritated his nose for several breaths until he got used to the odor. Joseph led him over to one of the plasma screens displaying a map of the United States.

"Watch this simulation of our primary flight plan. I think you will be very pleased with the estimated results,"

Joseph said. He went to a keyboard and hit several keys. On the screen, a small green dot launched from El Paso and arced into the air, soaring up over the Eastern United States, passing over the Mississippi and soaring higher over the Appalachian Mountains. In the corner, a small timer counted the passing seconds. A minute passed, then two. Sepehr realized he was holding his breath, and let it out with a soft whoosh.

The missile reached the apogee of its trajectory, 130 miles above the eastern half of America. Instead of diving down to explode in a city, it detonated in a bright blast of heat and light. A small yellow circle expanded out from the initial burst point, perhaps three inches in all directions.

"That is the initial blast and heat effects, which will be negligible once it reaches the ground. The radiation may have some effect in the atmosphere, but will be dispersed by the prevailing winds rather quickly."

"And the true damage—" Sepehr's words trailed off as a red sphere grew from what had been the missile, expanding out much farther than the original blast radius to encompass the entire eastern half of the United States, enveloping New York, Boston, Washington, D.C., as far west as Chicago, as far south as Miami and New Orleans, and everything in between.

"Our preliminary casualty estimate is three hundred thousand to five hundred thousand people in the first hour, then tens of thousands more in riots and crime once people realize what has happened. No doubt the National Guard will be mobilized, but they are already weakened by America's involvement in overseas conflicts, and perhaps some units will even join the mobs. The government will attempt to declare martial law, but with no way to communicate their orders, it will be paralyzed, and the chaos that will result as fires rage with no power, no water pressure, no lights…it will be glorious."

Sepehr simply nodded, staring at the red circle that represented the electromagnetic pulse that would blanket the entire half of the nation, including a large portion of Canada. The disruptive pulse would short out electronics and communications circuitry in millions of devices across the country, from toasters to airplanes. He imagined the carnage as hundreds of fully loaded jumbo jets fell out of the sky all over the land, crashing into buildings and suburbs in orange-red fireballs. He allowed himself to dream of the Capitol Building going up in flames as a 767 plowed into the dome, collapsing the entire structure.

Cities would grind to a halt as the electrical grid shut down, snarling whatever traffic hadn't already stalled. Thousands of people would be trapped in skyscrapers, crushing each other in the stairwells as they struggled to escape the innocuous workplaces that had suddenly turned into lightless, stifling prisons. As Joseph had said, the infrastructure would collapse almost immediately, with police and fire units not only unable go to where the crimes and accidents would be, but also unable to communicate with each other. Civilization would grind to a complete halt, with hundreds of thousands dying in the violence and looting that followed, and a huge exodus of refugees streaming west over the Mississippi, choking the nearby cities that would be inundated with the seemingly endless stream of panicked people looking to escape to anywhere that still had power.

The one regret that Sepehr had was that he couldn't get the entire country in one blast; the bomb they had simply wasn't powerful enough. Therefore, America would eventually recover, but it would take time, and would never be the same again. And they would bear the scars for decades afterward.

"Are you all right, Sepehr?"

With a start, Sepehr realized that his mind had drifted off into the magnificent daydream of carnage and destruction that he was about to put into motion, a holy storm that would rain invisibly down on the United States, and truly wash away their decadent civilization. He turned to look at Joseph with a beatific smile on his face.

"It will be magnificent, Allah be praised."

Joseph nodded. "Allah be praised."

19

"You've been pretty quiet these last few miles." Nate looked over at Tracy, who seemed lost in thought. "What's on your mind?"

They had left the city several miles back, and were now skirting the edge of the U.S.-Mexico border, sometimes marked with pickets, sometimes with an eight-foot-high steel barrier, sometimes not even marked at all. Once the houses and buildings of El Paso had faded from sight, all that surrounded them was the Chihuahuan Desert, with acres of parched scrubland dotted with various cacti, yucca plants and thin-limbed trees.

His voice seemed to startle her, and her deep brown eyes darted to his face, then looked away just as quickly. "Just taking it all in, I guess. My mother's grandparents lived in Arizona for much of their life. I visited a few times when I was a child, but hadn't been back since they passed away. I guess I'd forgotten how beautiful it can be."

"Don't let it fool you. That desert'll sap the water and life out of you faster than you'd think, and leave you a dried husk in the sand. Every year we find people trying to cross over that ran out of water or got lost, and the desert sucks everything out of 'em and leaves 'em deader than disco. Not a pleasant way to go—from what I understand, as a person dehydrates, their brain basically starts to shrink from lack of fluids, until they go insane before finally dying."

"Thanks for that wonderful image," Tracy said.

"Just thought you'd like to know what people risk to get here."

She regarded him with a curious look on her face. "You mean a slow, agonizing death as compared to being shot and killed quickly?"

"Didn't say either one was a better way to go, just that some folks take the ultimate chance to make what they think is a new life for themselves."

"Unless folks like you and I stop them," Tracy said.

"Yeah, there is that. We're here." Nate pulled the Bronco off to the side of the road. The area where the killings had happened was cordoned off by yellow tape, which was good. Otherwise, it was doubtful he would have found the area again, since it was quickly looking like every other bit of windswept highway out here. The bloodstains had dried in the desert heat, and now were barely marked by slightly darker spots on the road and desert hardpan. White bits of dried plaster marked where Kottke had done his cast work, but the tire marks were also slowly being eradicated by the stealthy desert.

Nate swung out of the SUV and let Tracy go ahead of him, getting the feel of the scene. He kept an eye on her as she examined the site. His first impression was of a confident, capable woman who might be a bit out of her depth here, but was going to do whatever she could to get the job done, which he admired. Whether she could pull it off, well, they'd just have to wait and see.

"Not much to find out here, either. Your team did good work," Tracy said.

Nate raised an eyebrow. "I didn't know there was any other kind."

He had the satisfaction of seeing Tracy flush, and not because of the heat. "I didn't mean it like that—"

"No, but ever since you started looking, I got the impression that you expected to blow in here, look over the files and crime scene, go 'aha' and pull up the perfect bit of evidence that all us local yokels missed. When you're responsible for over 250,000 square miles of territory to cover, with only half the needed staff to do the job, you tend to make damn sure that you don't miss a thing the first time around."

Tracy stared at Nate during his diatribe through her silver-framed sunglasses, then she walked over and held out her hand. "Tracy Wentworth, Department of Homeland Security, pleased to meet you." With her other hand, she brushed off her shoulder. "There, chip's gone. I guess I've gotten so used to relying on the resources back at headquarters—you know, staring at computers for ten hours a day—that I didn't recognize quality crime-scene processing even when it's staring me right in the face."

Nate reached for her hand and shook it once. "All right, then. So, you've read the reports and examined the scene— what's your expert conclusion?"

"I don't suppose the Border Patrol vehicle was equipped with video?" she asked.

"If it was, I would have suggested we review it in the comfort of an air-conditioned room, instead of standing out here in the sun. We're still trying to get the funding approved for those. But even it we had it, it probably wouldn't have done any good, especially after they torched the truck."

Tracy nodded. "Since they didn't leave a sign saying The Terrorists Went This Way, we'll have to see for ourselves where they went." She flipped open the cell phone again. "Stephanie? What have you come up with so far?" She turned up the phone's volume so Nate could hear.

"One of our military satellites recorded the following footage from 0154 hours to 0203 hours on the specified morning."

The small screen on the phone burst into life, showing a grainy picture of a panel truck with two men next to it, moving what looked like bodies to the side of the road. The pair of men kept their heads down as they worked, and the overhead view meant their faces couldn't be seen. When they had finished, they got in the truck and drove away, heading north-northeast.

Tracy frowned. "Away from El Paso? That doesn't match your theory about staying near the city."

Nate held up a finger. "Think about it for a second. These guys just killed two dozen people, and sprayed blood and tissue everywhere, including on the truck they just stole—"

"And they need to hole up somewhere and make sure it's clean—maybe even repaint it—" Tracy continued his line of thought.

"I know an out-of-the-way place that would serve just fine. Come on," Nate said.

Back in the Bronco, he pulled a tight turn and sped off in the same direction the truck had gone, pushing his twenty-year-old SUV down the highway at a shaking eighty miles per hour. The desert sped by in a tan-and-brown blur, dotted with the occasional green cactus piercing the skyline. They traveled for at least half an hour, until Nate pulled off the road before they crested a rise that would have given them a perfect view of the several dozen square miles beyond.

Tracy stared at the large hill. "Why did you stop here?"

Nate grabbed a pair of binoculars from the backseat. "You never know who might be here before you, so it's good to take a look before charging in." He got out and walked up the slope until he could see over the top. As he scanned the old white-walled adobe barn and faded farmhouse, he was aware of Tracy at his side.

The area looked completely deserted. Nate handed the glasses to her. "Tell me what you see."

She lifted them to her eyes and looked down at the buildings for a minute. "There's no dust or sand buildup by the barn doors, which means recent activity—someone's been here within the last couple of days."

"Good eyes. Let's go check it out," Nate said.

They drove down to the supposedly abandoned buildings. Nate pulled the Bronco around to the back. "No sense advertising our presence if anyone does happens along." He took out his pistol and pulled the slide back. "Ready?"

Tracy looked a bit dubious, but followed his example. "Is this really necessary?"

"In the eleven years I've been here, I've seen agents nearly get killed by having their heads bashed in from illegals, coyotes and drug smugglers, and I've seen a helicopter get taken out of the sky by a rock. That's what I hadn't told you yet—the desert may be dangerous, but the men running around out here make it look like an oasis."

She raised a sculpted eyebrow at him. "Hmm, just like in Washington."

"Touché." He slid out of his seat and crept along the side

of the barn, clearing the corner before rounding it to approach the door. Tracy took a position on the opposite side, her pistol steady. "Shouldn't we call for backup?" she whispered.

"What, and wait a half hour for them to get here?" Nate held up three fingers, then counted down to zero. As soon as he did, he grabbed the door handle and yanked it over. "U.S. Border Patrol! Anyone inside, come out with your hands up!" He shouted in Spanish, then repeated the commands in English. Only silence answered him. Nate peeked around the door, then relaxed a bit. "Anything that did go down here, I think we missed it."

The inside of the cavernous barn was empty, with only scattered shafts of afternoon sunlight shining through warped roof boards, illuminating the clouds of dust motes drifting lazily through the still air. Keeping his pistol at his side, Nate stepped into the room, followed by Tracy.

"Smell that?" she asked.

Wrinkling his nose, Nate nodded. "Fresh paint. I wonder if the lab boys can get enough of a sample from anything in here."

Tracy knelt down to examine the floor. "Too hard packed to leave any tread marks or footprints. I think something was stored here in the corner, but I'm not sure what. Painting supplies that they took with them?"

"Most likely, although they might have disposed of them out here, so they wouldn't get caught with them. Might as well bring in a team to go over the area, see if they can pull something up."

Nate walked back outside, where the afternoon heat was only broiling instead of nearly incapacitating, like in the barn. A noticeably wilted Tracy followed, and he went back to the Bronco and got two chilled bottles of water from a small cooler in the back. Going back around the building, he found her on the other side, looking for evidence. "Here."

"Thanks, but I don't feel particularly thirsty. I'm not even sweating."

"I know, that's why you need to drink. Your sweat is evaporating as soon as it hits the air, so you're still losing body moisture—you just don't realize it. Dehydration sneaks up on a person fast—that's why it's so dangerous." He flipped open his cell and dialed headquarters, giving them the location of the barn, directions to it and advising that they would wait for the crime-scene team to arrive.

"They figure about thirty to forty-five minutes, longer if whoever's driving doesn't know these roads. Nothing to do now but wait," he said to Tracy.

Tracy gulped several swallows before Nate shook his head. "Don't drink too fast—you'll get cramps."

"Sorry, it just felt better than I expected." She lowered the bottle and eyed the surrounding landscape. "Do you want to take a look around the area, see if we could find the bury spot?"

"Not without a dozen more men and a full day to do it. Could use a Shadow Wolf out here, too, since they probably left tracks out to it, but—" Nate lifted his head as the sound of a revving engine split the silence.

Tracy listened, as well. "What's that? The forensic team here already?"

"Not likely. Truck engine, coming this way from the south. Get inside."

"You think they're coming here?"

"This place is really the only reason to be out here." Nate hustled her inside and pulled the barn door closed, leaving just a crack open for observation. A few seconds later, another vehicle crested the rise and roared down the hill toward them. It was a bloodred, late-model pickup with an extended cab and dual wheels on the back for hauling heavy trailers. The truck turned into the driveway and approached the barn. Its bed was filled with what looked like illegal immigrants, but as it got closer, Nate saw something that made his blood run cold—automatic weapons in the hands of the two men standing at the front of the cargo bed. "Goddamnit."

"What, more illegals?" Tracy asked.

"Worse." Nate raised his pistol, aware it was about as useful as a flyswatter against the assault rifles roaring toward them. *"Zetas."*

20

Kate's brow furrowed. "What's a zeta?"

Unknown to Nate, he hadn't been talking to only Tracy all this time. The cell phone she had given Tracy was a two-way communication device, even when it was closed. Room 59 often used them to keep tabs on people of interest, or, as in this case, when they were working clandestinely with agents from other departments. The phone could broadcast video when it was out—although in this case, stuck at the bottom of Tracy's purse, Kate saw nothing but blackness—and audio. Even from where it was, they had heard the conversation between the two agents.

Although Kate was well educated in all of the major terrorist groups, this one wasn't familiar to her. The man working alongside her on this operation, however, had a much different reaction.

"Jesus Christ!" Denny Talbot's fingers blurred over the keyboard as the director for North American operations also talked into his headset. "I need CBP backup immediately at the following coordinates, via helicopter if possible. Advise incoming agents that there is a large group of undocumented aliens on-site, heavily armed, I repeat, heavily armed, and may be wearing body armor—approach with extreme caution. There are also two DHS agents at the scene, currently inside the barn. Advise all units in the area to converge on this address immediately."

Kate was busy, as well, sending out an urgent message to all of her hackers asking for whoever could patch into any satellite to get a fix on Tracy's coordinates and patch her in ASAP.

Denny spoke to her from the computer screen, where he was teleconferencing with her on this mission from Washington, D.C. "Kate, your operative should be calling immediately, so as soon as she fills you in, let her know that help is on the way."

As if on cue, Kate's monitor flashed, signaling an incoming call. "This is her, hold on," Kate said to Denny. "Agent Stephanie Cassell," she said to Tracy, employing her cover name.

"Stephanie, it's Tracy. We're at an abandoned ranch about twenty-five miles east of El Paso, and need backup right now. Armed hostiles are outside—dammit, they're coming in!"

"Tracy, sit tight, we are routing all available units to your location."

"Too late, Nate, what are we doin—?" The connection broke off in midsentence.

"Damn, she hung up. What are they facing down there?" If there was one thing Kate didn't like, it was when she wasn't aware of something—especially since that meant she had sent someone into an assignment without the most recent information.

"*Zetas* are highly trained, heavily armed professional soldiers working for the drug cartels in Mexico. Originally they were supposed to be helping the U.S. and Mexico fight the drug wars, but after getting trained in special weapons and tactics, many of them went to the other side and are now one of the largest threats on the border. They are ruthless, efficient and don't take any prisoners," Denny said.

"You mean that if some help doesn't get down there immediately, those two operatives are dead," Kate said.

"Yeah, that's about the size of it."

"Dammit, these *zetas,* whoever they are, weren't supposed to be there."

Denny gave her a wry look. "Kate, you know that's the nature of any mission. As much as we try, we cannot foresee every complication."

"That simply isn't good enough. At the very least, we should have been able to warn them of potential incoming threats," Kate said.

"May I remind you that these agents aren't ours, and have their own protocols to follow? It would look pretty unusual for either the DHS or the FBI to be *that* efficient. Like it or not, we have to work within certain parameters, especially when masquerading as someone else."

"Unfortunately." Although Kate grudgingly agreed with Denny, she certainly didn't like it. That was one of the reasons that Room 59 had been created in the first place—to circumvent the often cumbersome bureaucracy that bound more traditional intelligence agencies, and successfully complete the jobs that needed doing before disaster could strike. However, even working through their back channels and direct links, sometimes Kate still found herself in a situation like this—where she could do nothing but wait, listen and hope her operative came out alive.

21 ▐▐ ▐▐▐65 ▐▐ ▐ ▮ ▐ 59▐▐ ▐▐ ▮▐ ▐▐ ▮

"Nate, what should we do?" Tracy slipped the cell phone into her pocket and raised her pistol. "Is there a back way out of here?"

Outside, she heard what sounded like some sort of disagreement between some of the men in the truck, with at least two raised voices, but couldn't make out what they were saying.

Nate stared through the crack in the barn door. "I count at least four, all with automatic weapons. Running would be suicide—they'd take us out with the rifles. Only one thing to do, and that's catch them by surprise. If we get them off balance, we can take them."

"Are you nuts?" she hissed. "Shouldn't we wait for backup?"

Tracy now saw one of the men set his rifle down, jump off the truck and walk toward the barn. Her suddenly slick fingers gripped her pistol as she watched the man come closer. This was something she'd never thought she'd be in the middle of, and now she was only a few yards away from smugglers armed with automatic weapons. *If I get out of this alive, I'll be glad to go back home and tell Paul he was right,* she told herself.

"We wait any longer, and they're only gonna find two dead agents out here. We go now! Follow my lead." With that, Nate shoved the door back and leaped outside, aiming at the approaching man and shouting, "United States Border Patrol, nobody move!" He spoke first in Spanish, then in English.

Tracy followed, aiming her pistol at the men in the truck. She smelled harsh exhaust from the vehicle, and the thrum of its revving engine vibrated through her head, setting her teeth on edge. She called out, "Raise your hands, and no one move!"

For a moment the men and illegals packed into the truck stared in total surprise. Then everything went straight to hell. The man walking toward the door charged at Nate, covering the distance to him faster than Tracy thought possible. Nate fired, but his aim was off, and the *zeta* barreled into him, knocking him to the ground, his hands scrabbling for the pistol. The shot made the other men and women in the cargo bed scramble out any which way they could, leaping over the side walls and out the back of the vehicle.

The second man in the back leveled his assault rifle. Tracy swallowed around a golf-ball-size lump in her throat, but aimed at him, knowing if she didn't shoot first, they were both dead. "Freeze!" she shouted.

Instead, he sighted in, and she squeezed the trigger, the gun bucking in her hand. The man lurched back just as the truck's engine revved, and it zoomed forward, heading for Tracy.

Aiming at the windshield, she got one shot off, spiderwebbing it, but the truck still kept coming, and her instincts took over. She dived out of the way, scraping her hands and knees on the sandy ground as the pickup roared past, smashing through the barn door in a crash of wood and metal. The truck revved again, and Tracy rose to see a large off-road tire in front of her. She put two bullets into it, but then the vehicle reversed out of the barn in a shower of broken boards, and she saw the passenger holding a small submachine gun as he popped out of the open window.

A shadow fell over her, and Tracy jerked her pistol up, only to see it grabbed and levered up at the sky.

"Are you crazy, woman! Let's get the hell out of here!"

Tracy looked up to see Nate, who grabbed her hand and yanked her to her feet as he fired several rounds at the truck, which had been coming around for another attempted ram. She ran with him around the corner of the barn just as someone opened fire behind them, chewing boards apart in a hail of bullets. Running to the back, they rounded the corner to see several men trying to get into the Bronco, with one smashing the driver's-side window with a large rock.

Nate fired into the air, scattering the illegals, but not before the window shattered. Tracy felt keys pressed into her free hand. "Drive!"

Too shocked to argue, Tracy ran for the door, unlocked it and brushed glass chips off the seat before climbing in. "What are you doing?" she shouted.

Nate had jerked open the SUV's tailgate and slid in the back. Grabbing the shotgun out of its holster, he racked the pump action. "Just get us to the road. I'll keep 'em from following us out!"

Tracy jammed the key into the ignition, twisted it, slammed the clutch down and shifted into Reverse. She stomped on the gas and the Bronco shot out from behind the barn, Tracy spinning the steering wheel as they shot toward the highway. Just as they cleared the front of the building, the other truck flew out from the other side and slammed into the Bronco. Tracy screamed and fought the wheel as the SUV slewed from side to side, but regained control and kept going.

"Jesus, watch it up there, will you!" In the back, she saw Nate get back onto his knees and rack the shotgun, then duck down again. "Get down!"

Tracy did her best to hunch down while trying to keep the wheel straight—she knew if they hit the ditch instead of the driveway, their miraculous escape would end quickly. The chatter of an AK-47 sounded right next to her, and the back window exploded in a shower of glass, followed by the roar of Nate's shotgun.

The truck swerved away for a moment, and Tracy let up on the gas long enough to shove the gearshift into third. The driveway seemed endless now, the distant road looking as if it were hundreds of yards away. *And even if we reach it, there's no guarantee they'll stop—it's not like we'll be safe there,* she thought.

"They're coming back—make sure they don't hit the engine!" Nate racked the shotgun again and shot at the truck's cab, shattering the driver's-side window.

"Hell, I'll do better than that." Tracy swung the wheel, feeling the Bronco lean as it lurched over and crunched into the side of the truck, making the driver fight for control of his vehicle. One of the riflemen triggered a long burst, but the bullets kicked up dirt to the left of the SUV. The pickup's wheelman regained control, however, and nudged his heavier truck over against the Bronco, trying to send it off the driveway and into the ditch. They were only about thirty yards away, and closing on the narrow entrance fast. Tracy hauled on the wheel, but couldn't force the truck over. In a straight power contest, the other vehicle had the edge. Metal shrieked as the two vehicles rubbed together in a fight for dominance.

"Goddammit, punch it and get ahead of them!" Nate shouted.

"No time!" The driveway was only a few yards away, and Tracy spun the wheel in the opposite direction and slammed on the brakes, wrenching the SUV into a shuddering bootleg turn. Taken by surprise, the pursuing pickup raced out the driveway, onto the road and into the ditch on the other side. Tracy gunned the engine, running on the desert hardpan parallel to the road, leaving the *zetas* behind.

Stray shots from the automatic rifles pinged around them, and then they were out of range.

"Thank God that's over." Tracy slumped in the driver's seat, the hot desert wind parching her face. She slowed down automatically, aware that she was running over scrub brush and other things that wouldn't be good for the Bronco's undercarriage.

"Hey, hey, keep an eye on where you're going, all right? We blow a tire or break an axle out here, and it's a long walk—oh, shit."

"What?" Tracy's eyes strayed to the rearview mirror again, and widened in disbelief.

The truck was growing larger in the mirror as it came after them, its front end caked in dirt and its fender crumpled, but otherwise no worse for wear.

"Guess they weren't as stuck as we thought. We either need to head into the desert or get onto the road," Nate said.

"Hold on!" Tracy had spotted a flatter stretch ahead, and gunned the engine to make sure she had the forward velocity to make the switch. She edged closer to the ditch, then tweaked the wheel again, aware that the slightest wrong move could send them rolling over.

"Where are you—Jesus, I thought you were gonna head into the desert!"

Tracy didn't reply, but steered the Bronco into the wide wash carved out by long-ago flash floods. She saw a grade that she thought they could make, and turned into it before she could think twice, flooring the gas pedal. "Grab something back there and stay low!" she shouted.

The Bronco spun its way out of the wash as its front end launched up into the air and crashed down on the road with a bone-jarring impact, the heavy-duty off-road tires and shocks absorbing most of the landing. Tracy feathered the wheel as she kept the SUV moving in generally the same direction the road was going, although she did come close to the ditch on the other side for a heart-stopping second.

Nate fired several rounds at the approaching truck, hitting the windshield again, and making steam plume from the grille. The pickup's engine revved as it tried to keep up, but the buckshot had hit something vital, for they were pulling away.

Nate climbed over the seat back and practically fell onto the cushion. "Jesus, Mary and Joseph, where in the hell did you learn to drive like that, Beltway rush hour?"

"Growing up with three brothers obsessed with the stock car circuit. It was either play with them or play alone, so I learned a few things along the way," Tracy said.

"I'll say. You can be my wheelman anytime." Nate leaned back in the seat just as the flashing cherries and blueberries of the Border Patrol, sheriff's department, El Paso police and even a fire truck appeared out of the hazy desert, barreling straight toward them.

22

Nate surveyed the damage to his Bronco with a doleful expression. The entire passenger's side, from the engine to the back bumper, was crushed and dented, with the front quarter panel bent down to within an inch of the tire. The right rear window was gone, matching the missing windows from both doors and the back. Bullet holes pocked the cab and the side, as well. "I knew I shoulda signed out a truck. It's gonna take forever and a Sunday to get all this fixed," he said.

Once the cavalry had arrived, he and Tracy had gone back to the barn, where the rest of the Border Patrol had immediately starting rounding up the rest of the immigrants before they got hopelessly lost in the desert. Overhead, a helicopter swept the area, herding scattered groups into the waiting arms of the patrol. They had found the shot-up truck, abandoned about a mile from the farm with tracks leading away, but when Nate let the rest of his people know they were *zetas,* they let them go, as per standard operating procedure.

Tracy, however, was less than pleased by this turn of events. "What do you mean, you're letting them go? They did just try to kill us, or have you already forgotten?"

Nate jerked a thumb back at the battered Bronco. "That seems to be pretty good evidence to back up your story." He took her aside. "Look, I'm gonna be in enough shit as it is about this—it's bad enough we had a run-and-gun in the first place, not to mention me using an unauthorized weapon. Rules of engagement say we're not supposed to engage armed illegals out here, but are supposed to let them go whenever possible."

"So instead, you deliberately put us in danger by confronting them? Are you insane? We came this close to being killed!" Tracy was aware of the attention she was drawing from the other Border Patrol members, but at the moment she didn't care.

Nate whirled on her, his voice low. "We were already in danger the moment that truck appeared. If we hadn't done something, our backup would have come out here and found two dead bodies—ours. Or maybe they would have taken you with them so you could have been gang-raped before being killed. Get this straight—this isn't a comfortable office in Washington where you get to sift through evidence at your leisure before sending a report to your boss. This is the border, and out here you either make a decision and follow it or else you die. There's no room for error, and no second-guessing yourself after the fact. You need to stop analyzing everything to death and start acting on what you know."

Tracy scowled, even as a part of her knew he might be right. "None of that excuses your behavior, Agent Spencer. We could have held them off from inside the barn until help arrived. Let me remind you who's in charge here."

"In that case, it'll be a wonder if either of us survives the day," Nate said angrily.

Stung, Tracy was about to really lay into him when a shout came from the barn.

"Hey, Nate, you might want to come take a look at this," a man called.

Nate immediately turned and walked, followed by Tracy, to a trio of men in a corner of the barn clustered around a strange-looking handheld metal machine that rested on three small legs.

"We were doing our usual sweeps when Jason took out the CryoFree radiation detector and took a pass. He found an unusual concentration of residual radiation in this corner—not enough to be a threat to our safety, but certainly more than should be here. If, at some point in the last day or so, something radioactive was here, it apparently was leaking a bit."

Jason, the far-too-young-looking hazmat tech, beamed with pride as he held his new toy. "We just got this a month ago. First time I ever got to use it, and got a hit, too." His expression sobered. "Come to think of it, that isn't a very good thing, I mean, that means I just registered radioactive material coming through here."

Nate exchanged a knowing glance with Tracy, who spoke up first. "Let's keep this to ourselves right now, gentlemen. That's the Model 25, right? Is there enough here to find out what kind it is or where it might have come from?"

"It was doing the type analysis when y'all came over." Jason checked the readout again. "Son of a gun—says it's plutonium 239."

"That clinches that." Nate straightened up and looked at the open doors where the illegals had gathered. "Did you find a guy near here when you cleared the barn?"

"It was empty, but we found blood spatter over there." The agent pointed toward the front door where Nate had wrestled with one of the *zetas*. "You lookin' for anyone in particular?"

"Yeah, the guy I head-butted in the nose."

"All of the illegals are being held near the house until we can transport them to process."

Nate headed toward the open doors. "Come on, let's go see if they caught him," he said to Tracy.

"Just a minute, Nate." Tracy still faced the three crime-scene techs, and showed her identification. "Gentlemen, I remind you that this investigation is a joint effort between the Department of Homeland Security and the FBI. Therefore, I must tell you to treat this information as confidential and not to disclose it to anyone else. The only people who should receive your final report are myself, Agent Spencer or Agent Robertson. Failure to comply with this order will result in charges of obstruction of justice being filed. Is that clear?"

The expressions on the three mens' faces had been relaxed, almost condescending, but by the time Tracy had finished speaking, all three men had stiffened almost to attention, and Nate thought Jason was on the verge of saluting her. They all nodded and answered affirmatively.

"All right, get as many soil samples as you need from the area and go over them as quickly and as thoroughly as you can. I want a full workup and report by tomorrow morning." With that, Tracy turned on her heel and caught up with Nate.

"A bit officious, don't you think?" he asked.

"We don't need this mission compromised because one of your boys decided to share this with one of his drinking buddies, and the next time we hear about it is on the nightly news."

"Fair enough." Nate led the way to the cluster of illegals waiting for transport to a processing and holding center. Everyone there, about a dozen people, stared back silently. He scanned the crowd, looking for the guy he'd tangled with earlier.

"See him?" Tracy asked.

"Oh, yeah." Nate circled around to where a man with his head hanging down stood on the outskirts, trying to stay as far apart from the group as possible, yet still remain within the main cluster. Whereas most of the other men wore either T-shirts or had the sleeves of their flannel shirts rolled up in the heat, he had his sleeves down and collar buttoned up, but couldn't hide the dark bloodstain on his shirtfront. Nate grabbed his arm and yanked him out of the group.

"*¡Hola!* Remember me, *cholo?*" Nate's grin was mirthless.

The man kept his eyes on the ground. *"No habla inglés."*

Grabbing his chin, Nate wrenched the man's head up, revealing a swollen broken nose. "Sure, you do. Now take off that shirt."

"¿Que?"

"I said—" Nate hooked two fingers in the man's nose and lifted, making him stand on his tiptoes and grunt in pain, tears filling his eyes "—take off the goddamn shirt, or else I make you strip bucknaked out here."

"Nate—" Tracy began, but was stopped by his curt head shake.

The *zeta* waved his arms helplessly. *"Sí, sí.* Just stop!"

Nate set him back down, wiped his fingers on the man's shirtsleeve.

The *zeta* stared at him now, his dark eyes filled with hatred. *"¡Pinche cabrón!"*

"Yeah, yeah, let's go, show that skin."

The man slowly took off his shirt, revealing a wealth of tattoos, including the one Nate had been looking for—the Aztec warrior head, this one with no feathers—etched on his chest, above his heart. "All right, Montezuma, you can put it back on." He was about to find someone and commandeer their ride when Tracy cocked her head and looked over at the abandoned house.

"Did you hear that?"

23

Nate frowned as he stared at her. "I didn't hear anything. Come on, we need to get back."

Tracy, however, ignored him, walking to the agent watching over the group. "Was the back of the house cleared?"

"Yes, ma'am."

"Just a sec, Nate." She trotted toward the side of the house, listening intently for the noise she swore she had heard. As she approached, she heard it again—the whimper of a child.

"Nate, I've got someone back here." She ran around to the back, but didn't see anything but overgrown scrub brush. "*Hola,* where are you?" she called out.

The whimpering continued, and Tracy homed in on the noise, spotting a thin, crushed trail of brown grass near the corner of the house. Kneeling, she peered into what looked like a narrow crawl space under the house, where the noises were coming from.

"*¿Hola, chica, quien es?*" Tracy moved closer to the black hole, trying to see inside.

The face of a small girl, maybe about Jennifer's age, appeared in the opening, tears running down her cheeks as she answered Tracy in Spanish. "My mama…she told me to hide in here…now she won't wake up."

"Okay, sweetheart, we'll take care of her. What's your name?"

"Julia."

"Hi, Julia. My name is Tracy, and I'm going to help both of you. But first, can you come out of there?"

The girl drew back into the darkness. "I won't leave her!"

"All right, then, if you don't come out, I'll have to come in." Tracy got down on her hands and knees just as Nate rounded the corner.

"What in the hell are you doing?"

"There's a girl in here, and her mother has passed out, probably from heatstroke."

"For God's sake, hold on. There might be rattlesnakes or scorpions under there, or who knows what. Jesus, I'll be right back." Nate took off around the house.

"Just stay where you are, sweetheart, we're coming." Tracy stayed by the opening until Nate returned with a large flashlight. He shone the beam inside, revealing a stick-thin girl crouched over the still form of her mother, lying on the ground facing away from them.

"Don't see any rattlers, and I don't hear any, either, but let's get 'em both out of there right away." He squatted down and moved toward the entrance, but the girl shrieked, a high, piercing sound that cut right through Tracy's ears, and scurried away from him.

"Nate, maybe you'd better let me handle this. I'll get the girl out, and once we're clear, you get the mother." Tracy edged him aside and got on her hands and knees.

"Keep that light on me." She crawled into the space, gasping at the intense heat.

Julia edged farther away, torn between her urge to hide and her desire to protect her mother. Tracy tried to calm her down by speaking in Spanish. "Shh, sweetheart, it's all right. Can you come over to me?"

"Help my mother, please."

Tracy held out her arms. "If you can come over here, then we can get out of here. The other agent can get your mother out of here, but we have to get out of the way first." She nodded back at Nate, bent over at the entrance and smiled. "He's too big, so we have to leave before he can come in."

The girl peered past her at the opening. "Promise he won't hurt her?"

"Cross my heart."

"And hope to die?"

"Let's hope it doesn't come to that. Come on, sweetie, you must be thirsty."

The girl hesitated a moment longer, then scrambled into Tracy's arms, who hugged her tightly, feeling her ribs underneath the soiled shirt, and her hammering heart underneath. Her skin was hot and dry, and Tracy was sure the poor thing was dehydrated, too. Still holding her, she crawled backward on her knees, uncaring of the dirt being ground into her slacks. When she got outside, the air felt at least twenty degrees cooler.

"Here." Nate passed her a chilled bottle of water. "Slow sips, not too much, or she'll get sick. I'll get her mom." He disappeared under the house, leaving Tracy to cradle Julia on her lap and dole out small swallows of water. A few seconds later, he reappeared, moving slowly as he dragged the mother out from the blackness. "She's in bad shape. We need to get her to a hospital right away."

As soon as she was clear, he scooped her up in his arms. "Come on."

"Hold on to me, honey." Tracy picked up Julia, shocked at how small and light she was, and followed Nate out to the rest of the agents.

"Hey, I need to get this woman into a hospital ASAP, so I'm borrowing your truck. Got any liquids inside?" Nate grabbed the keys that were tossed to him and opened the back door, laying her on the bench seat. "Sit next to her and keep a blanket handy. If you can, try to get her to take some water. Once her temperature starts to come down—"

"She may go into shock, yes, I know the symptoms," Tracy said.

"Good." He slid into the driver's seat, cranked the air conditioner up to regulate the temperature, turned the truck around and kicked up dirt as he headed down to the road. Once there, he got to the nearest highway that led back to El Paso, then headed for the south side of the city.

In the back, Tracy alternated between giving Julia sips of water and trying to get some liquid into her mother. When the girl began to shiver from the temperature change, she had Nate turn down the air conditioner, and wrapped her in the blanket.

Twenty minutes later, they pulled into the emergency entrance of Providence Memorial. The SUV had barely stopped when Nate got out and was pulling the mother out of the backseat, carrying her through the double doors.

"Got an undocumented alien with heatstroke and dehydration, suggest IV fluids and observation," he said.

Tracy noticed that the nurse who took charge of the patient, a chunky bottle blonde, looked startled when Nate came in, but covered her surprise under a professional mask and got a gurney ready to take her into a room. Nate and Tracy followed, and got information from Julia to fill out the necessary forms to admit her mother to the hospital. When that was done, the nurse—she introduced herself as Sharon—asked to examine Julia in the back, leaving Nate and Tracy in the crowded waiting room.

"How long are we going to wait here?" Tracy asked.

"Well, we'll make sure she's all right—I imagine they'll want to watch her overnight—and then tomorrow both she and her daughter will have to be collected, processed and returned to wherever they came from."

"Isn't there any way to keep them here? I'm sure they don't have a lot to look forward to going back."

Nate turned to look at her, his face neutral. "Look, I know this is your first hands-on experience with this, but we're going to follow procedure just like every other UA we apprehend, whether they've got one child or a dozen. Like as not, as soon as she gets back, she's gonna turn right around and head north again, and keep tryin' until she either makes it across or dies in the attempt, just like tens of thousands of others every year."

Tracy couldn't believe her ears. "Jesus, you sound like you're herding cattle. These are human beings you're so casually dismissing."

"Yeah, human beings that are breaking our laws to enter this country." He waved at the people in the waiting room, more than half of whom were Hispanic. "How many of these people do you think are here legally? When they get medical care—care they're not entitled to and have no way to pay for—the hospitals have to eat that cost. There's no reimbursement from the government or anyone. There are medical centers all over Texas and throughout the Southwest going broke because they can't keep up with the flood of illegal immigrants coming through their doors. When they close, they don't just stop treating illegals—they stop treating the surrounding communities, too."

Nate glanced around again, but Tracy wasn't sure if he was checking to see if anyone heard him, or if anyone was going to challenge him. "UAs get their forged papers and green cards, get jobs here with companies willing to hire them without doing the proper checks, and have their kids educated—also paid for by the state and federal governments—and most of the money they earn goes back to their family in Mexico. A good cause, sure, but every dollar sent comes out of our economic system. And I haven't even mentioned the criminals that flee to America to commit more crimes against our citizens, or the ever popular and increasing drug trade that flows across our border, as well."

Tracy brushed a lank lock of hair out of her face, more aware by the minute that she hadn't had a shower since early that morning. "I know the issues the Customs and Border Protection faces down here, Nate—"

Nate rubbed a hand over his eyes, which came away coated in dust and sweat. "Spoken like a true bureaucrat. Maybe that's the real difference between us and you. Up there you call them *issues*. Down here we call them *problems,* and they're gettin' larger every single day."

"Well, of course we can't have criminals coming here, but still, the INS system should be corrected—it's ridiculous to make people wait for six or eight or ten years to immigrate to America."

"I agree, but that isn't my problem—sorry, my *issue*—down here, but something for you folks in Washington to chew on. However, if you come up with a quick, easy, foolproof way to solve the immigration process, I'm sure INS would love to hear it. My only problem at the moment, along with the rest of the CBP, is to find a way to locate and detain anyone crossing the border into America who doesn't have the right to be here, and if we could, to figure out a way to make them stay on their side of the river until they can come here legally."

Tracy gritted her teeth, trying to rein in her temper. "You keep saying 'you' and 'I' like we're two different groups. Last I checked, we were still on the same side."

Nate shook his head. "Maybe so, but not in the way you and I see those issues of yours." He looked around her. "Nurse's comin' back."

Sharon walked over to them. "Mrs. Martinez is resting and taking intravenous liquids, so she should be all right for now. We'll monitor her overnight, just in case."

"Good, we'll check on her tomorrow, and someone from the agency will be by to pick her and her daughter up later, assuming she's ready to travel," Nate said.

"Call about midmorning—we'll know more then." The nurse looked as if she wanted to say more, but didn't.

Nate nodded. "Thanks. Someone will be in touch later." He turned on his heel and headed for the doors, leaving Tracy behind.

"Are you his partner?" the nurse asked, her expression neutral, although her seemingly nonchalant tone was anything but.

As soon as she heard the question, Tracy figured out what was going on between the two of them, but was too tired to blush at the inference the nurse had drawn. "Just temporarily. I'm from out of town, here on assignment. Besides, I'm not sure I could handle being his partner for more than a few days." She offered a wry grin, and got a small one in return.

"Yeah." Sharon's eyes hadn't left the doors Nate had walked through. "Is that why you're still standing here?"

"Maybe. Maybe I just like pissing him off." Something slammed against the glass, and Tracy looked back to see Nate standing there with a "what the hell are you doing?" look on his face. "Duty calls. Thanks for looking after them," she said.

"Oh, sure, at Providence the revolving door is always open." Sharon shook her head. "They'll be all right—until the next time they try to cross."

Tracy watched her walk away, then she turned to catch up with Nate before he decided to really leave her at the hospital.

"You girls have a good time catching up?" Nate said snarkily.

Tracy considered teasing him about the nurse, but stole a look at his face that told her it wasn't a good idea. Instead, she dug the phone out of her purse. "I'd better check in." She waited until they got back into the truck before flipping it open, bracing herself against the door as Nate tore out of the hospital driveway on squealing tires.

24

Kate looked as if she was sleeping in her chair, tilted back with her eyes closed. In reality she was deep in thought, letting all of the sketchy data she had flow through her mind while she brainstormed. She was searching for a logical connection that might give them a lead, anything to go on.

The problem was that the trail was already cold when Kryukov got the bomb—well, what he thought was the bomb. They had researched the arms dealer's extensive list of associates, searching for the missing link between him and al-Kharzi. Although they had connected him with several other terrorist groups, they hadn't come up with anything connecting the two men.

Of course, it's not like I could just log on to www.terrorist.com and find whatever I'm looking for, she thought. Although the various U.S. intelligence agencies had made some very good strides, they still had a long way to go. Getting accurate, timely data was still difficult at best.

With the 9/11 attacks, there hadn't been any excuse for intelligence agencies dropping the ball—there had been a clear, definitive chain of ignored or passed-over evidence. But if a day ever came where a terrorist group managed to stay off America's radar until they struck, then she didn't want to see what would happen in the aftermath. *That's one of the reasons I'm in this job in the first place, and supposed to be good at it. But all I've got is three men, a truck and a nuke to go on…a truck…*

Something about the truck bothered her, but before Kate could grasp it, her computer chirped, signaling an incoming call. *Let's see, who am I this time?* she wondered. It was from Robert Lashti. *Hmm, I hope this is interesting.* Kate tilted her chair forward and slipped on her wireless headset. "This is Primary."

"Primary, this is Alpha. I've got some information on that switched package you'll find interesting."

"Go ahead, Alpha."

"The acquaintance I made recently was very informative. He said that one of Kryukov's men had run a side deal with a man claiming to be with a group known as the Fist of Allah. The buyer paid Kryukov's man at least two million for the suitcase and its contents. They mentioned a ship going to Mexico in front of the seller, not knowing that he spoke Arabic."

"Mexico? He's sure of that, Alpha?"

"If you've ever watched the Chinese interrogate someone, you wouldn't ask that question, Primary. Mexico is confirmed as the suitcase's destination. He didn't know anything beyond that."

"Great work, Alpha. Time to come on home."

"With pleasure, Primary. Just one thing—when Kryukov pops up on our radar again, I want a shot at him."

"I can't guarantee that, but we'll see what we can do. Primary out."

As Kate disconnected, her computer chirped again. It was Tracy. That girl must be psychic, she thought.

"Agent Stephanie Cassell," Kate said.

"Stephanie, it's Tracy."

"It's good to hear from you. Are you all right?" Kate already knew the answer—although from what they had heard during the chase, she and Denny had had their doubts until it was over—but she couldn't mention that at the moment.

"Yes, apparently I got a less-than-traditional border welcome here."

Kate heard a noise that sounded suspiciously like a snort or guffaw in the background, and a quick check of the camera revealed that they were in a truck of some kind. "What did you find out?" she asked.

Tracy took a few moments to fill her in on what they had discovered, which wasn't much. "The best thing we can say is that there was definitely something radioactive in that barn in the last two days, but that's it. I've got the team staying up all night analyzing the soil if they have to, but it's doubtful they'll come up with anything useful in the next twelve hours."

"Okay. I'm pleased to let you know we've confirmed that the device was delivered to Mexico, but after the killings in the desert, the trail goes cold. We've been crunching data here, as well, but haven't come up with anything else. We've been concentrating on nontraditional vectors, but there's way too many of them to evaluate quickly, even just in the area. What about your partner, does he have any ideas?" Kate asked.

"Oh, he's got ideas, all right. It's just that he's a bit reluctant to share them."

"Well, now isn't the time to be holding out. Shall I talk to him?"

"I don't know if that will do any good, but…" Kate heard muffled voices in the background.

"Yes, Special Agent Cassell, how may I help you?"

The file Kate had reviewed on Nate Spencer had indicated that he was a cowboy, in law-enforcement parlance— a guy who got the job done, but who took unacceptable risks compared to the results. He was a good agent, but one that chafed under authority. Kate could relate. Figuring the quickest way to get through to him would be with brute power, she didn't mince words.

"Agent Spencer, are you confident that you are doing everything in your power to assist in this investigation?"

"Yes, ma'am, we are pursuing every approved lead we've uncovered. In fact, we're heading to a new source of information at this moment, but I'm afraid that I cannot say any more than that at this time."

"I understand. Have there been any issues with Agent Wentworth that you wish to discuss?"

"She has performed her job superbly in all regards and is a pleasure to work with."

"Very well. Then I'll let you get back to it. Thank you, Agent Spencer, and good luck."

"I never believe luck has anything to do with it, ma'am."

"Well said. Keep us informed as to any new developments." Kate disconnected just as an e-mail popped up on her screen from NiteMaster, another of Room 59's hackers.

Hey boss,
Here's the list. Keep in mind that this does not bear any relation to that distasteful law-enforcement practice known as racial profiling, and I will deny any implication as such. Hope it helps.
NM

Kate grinned. The list was a summary of the racial backgrounds of the employees of all the various transportation and other companies that might have the capability to deliver such a weapon within a hundred miles of El Paso. The problem was a suitcase nuke could be easily hidden so every freight company, truck and rental-car agency, small-airplane service, cab company, train line, courier service, import-export company and pretty much any that worked with boxes or vehicles had been tagged.

In clear violation of several federal laws, NiteMaster had cross-referenced the ethnic backgrounds of each company's employee roster, looking for a certain percentage of Middle Eastern or Indian workers. The prevailing logic was that the cell most likely worked together, perhaps at the same company, or in similar lines of work. However, even that list had more than one hundred companies on it.

With a weary sigh, Kate split the list into two parts, sending the *A-M* section to Denny, and keeping the *N-Z* for herself. She added a note:

Denny,
I don't care if you parcel this out or handle it yourself, but I need the ten most likely candidates for our loose nuke from your list by 0800 hours tomorrow. Have fun—
I know I will.
Kate

She looked at the first company on her list. "All right, let's see what's cooking at the Nabcon Waste Removal Company. Oh, yeah, another night of glamorous data crunching."

25

Tracy thought she had reined in her temper fairly well at the hospital, but Nate's actions since then had put her on a slow boil, and now she felt her anger building like steam—white and scalding hot.

After he had hung up with Stephanie, he handed the phone back to her and didn't say a word as they drove back to headquarters. He signed out what was obviously an undercover vehicle, a late-nineties Chevrolet Silverado with tinted windows. He didn't say anything as they got in and headed back to the south side of El Paso. They pulled into a cul-de-sac as the sun began to sink below the horizon. He parked about a block and a half away from a two-story stucco house hosting a loud party. Every light was on, and loud music was blasting from a sound system as figures clad in baggy shorts and jerseys or tank tops wandered in and out, drinking, smoking and talking.

Nate took his binoculars out and scanned the house, looking at the partygoers for several minutes.

Finally, Tracy couldn't stand it any longer. "All right,

I'll bite. Are you going to tell me what we're doing here, or do I get the silent treatment until the bomb goes off, and we have to explain to our superiors how, when the terrorists were blowing up the city, we were sitting on our asses watching gangbangers?"

Nate lowered the glasses and handed them to her. "Take a look out there and tell me what you see."

"I am getting really tired of this." Tracy raised the field glasses to her eyes and watched the scene for a minute. "Typical Mexican street gang, operating out of a neighborhood headquarters. I'm surprised that the police force hasn't taken them out yet."

"They've got juice with the local police. From what I can tell, it's a sort of a you-scratch-my-back-I-scratch-yours situation," Nate said.

"Also quite illegal. Do you know any of the people in that house?" Tracy asked.

"As far as I know, they're all American citizens. Our paths have crossed in regards to a relative or two once in a while."

Tracy lowered the glasses. "Which begs the question again, why are we here?"

Nate turned to look at her. "How far are you willing to go to find that device?"

"I'm willing to pursue all legal angles to get the information we need," Tracy said.

"What if there isn't time for that?"

"Get to the goddamn point already, would you, please?"

Instead of erupting at her outburst, Nate smiled. "All right. During the course of my investigation, I have learned that a person in that house has material information relating to our case. However, to go through the usual channels will mean a delay of a couple of hours, maybe even a few days. If you and I are both right—and I think we are—

every hour we waste is one more hour they have to do whatever it is they're planning. So, if we were to break a law or two regarding entry, search and seizure and interrogating a suspect without a warrant, how would you feel about that, knowing that to not act may be putting the lives of tens, maybe hundreds of thousands of people at risk?"

Tracy had blanched during Nate's speech, and grew even paler as he laid out the scenario. "So you want to break the law to go in, get this guy and get him to talk about what he knows? Just throw due process, innocent until proved guilty, Miranda rights, all that out the window?"

"If we want to catch a break in this case, yes. Look, we could haul him downtown for unpaid parking tickets or some other bullshit charge, but he ain't gonna break in the interrogation room. Besides, we can't even follow an evidence chain, because we don't have one, so any questions or answers we might get will probably not even be admissible."

"Nate, you know there's a right way and a wrong way to do this. We can't afford to screw up on this case. You know the press is just waiting to jump on any mistakes we make."

"Yeah, I guess I'd much rather see the headline, Border Agent Loses Job Over Violation of Suspect's Rights than Mushroom Cloud Blows Over Dallas, Texas. Never mind, I should have known a data cruncher wouldn't have the stones for the real job."

"Jesus Christ, you can be a real asshole. You must be divorced—I don't know any sane woman who would put up with you for longer than a day," Tracy snapped.

Nate recoiled, and for a second, Tracy feared she had gone too far. He pointed a rock-steady finger at her. "My personal life and my professional one are completely separate. You remember that or we're done, right here, right now, and I'll get that bastard myself."

Tracy took a deep breath. "I'm sorry, Nate, that was uncalled-for."

She looked away and regarded the house. Two men had stumbled out and were wrestling on the barren front lawn. There were lights on in several neighboring houses, but no people on the porches and no children playing in the street. She saw evidence of kids in the neighborhood, a small tricycle in one driveway, and a leaning swing set visible in the yard next to it. She imagined those toys, that house, the entire neighborhood suddenly vaporized in a white-hot flash of light, followed by the devastating shock wave that came right after, flattening anything in its path. If not here, where? Fort Worth, Dallas, like Nate said, Washington D.C.—?

Jennifer. Tracy banished the vision of that angelic face melting in the blast.

"Speaking purely hypothetically, what did you have in mind?" she asked quietly.

Nate told her what he knew about the gang and their leader, then outlined his plan. By the time he was done, Tracy found herself nodding in agreement. It was simple and practically guaranteed to flush out whoever was associated with al-Kharzi and the nuke—assuming they were still in town. It also involved breaking at least a half-dozen laws and bending several others.

"You think you can convince your nurse friend to go along with this? It could mean her job along with yours," Tracy said.

"You let me worry about that. What I need to know is, are you in or out?"

"Give me a little time to think about it, will you?"

"The clock's ticking, Tracy."

"I know…I know."

"We have to do this tonight, if we're going to at all."

"But not immediately, right?"

"No, we need to give them some time to get good and hammered first. It's always easier to get in and out when they're sleeping it off," Nate said.

"All right, then I want to go back to my room, take a long shower and think about this. Whatever I decide, even if I turn you down, I won't tell anyone else."

"Thanks, I appreciate that. Let's get you cleaned up, and I got a mountain of paperwork to take care of after this afternoon."

Tracy frowned as they pulled away from the house. "How are you going to explain the shotgun?"

He smiled. "I'll come up with something. Folks owe me a favor or two here and there. You just think about what might happen in the next few hours, and let me know what you decide."

"Fair enough."

The ride back was as quiet as the ride over, but for a very different reason.

Two hours later, the sun sank below the horizon, letting the south Texas night steal across the landscape. In her hotel room, washed, changed and fed, Tracy paced back and forth and tried to decide which way to go.

After her shower, she had called Paul. While hearing his voice was a welcome link to normalcy, she didn't want to tell him what she had gotten mixed up in down in Texas. She told him everything was fine, that it was a complex but safe job that required on-site analysis, which was true from a certain point of view. She complained good-naturedly about the dry heat and said she missed him and Jennifer, which was very, very true.

Paul had put Jennifer on and Tracy kept her tone light and upbeat. She promised the girl that when she came back they would all go to the beach for an entire week. Even though she had no idea how she would manage that much time off, it was worth it to hear Jennifer's squeal of delight.

When the call was over, her problems still remained. The plan made sense to her—go in, get the bad guys and get the information they needed, instead of crunching reams of information to create a report that could be squashed by any one of a number of bosses for whatever reason he thought best.

Nate's words to her out in the desert echoed through her head. *Am I too analytical? Am I not cut out for the field?* She thought she had acquitted herself well enough in the debacle at the barn, but at the same time, she had also lacked Nate's reflexes and instincts to seize that moment and use the element of surprise to get the drop on their adversaries. In fact, she had almost blown it, and then covered for her mistake—and it was a mistake, she realized—by taking it out on Nate in front of his team. Not the smartest thing to do to a partner you just met. *But that doesn't mean I owe him anything, and I'm damn sure not going to jump into this out of any sense of obligation, or to prove myself— I'll do it only because I think it's the right thing to do.*

She considered the issue staring her in the face—the loose nuke. It was simple enough on the surface. Break several laws, circumvent the rules and save hundreds of thousands of people, or do it by the book and take the chance that they could catch the terrorists—whom they still hadn't identified—before they could detonate the nuclear device that had been smuggled into the U.S.

Nate, even after she had scolded him like an errant child, apparently still thought enough of her to include her in his plan. Of course, you could also be a convenient scapegoat if it all goes wrong, she thought. But that didn't seem to be Nate's style. He was direct, abrasive and perhaps working on a hair-trigger, but she hadn't sensed any sort of machinations when he had made the offer, just an honest desire for her help. From what she'd seen in the short time they had been working together, he truly thought this would be the best way to move the case forward.

That was one factor. The other was her own instinct in terms of analyzing the data she had and reaching a conclusion. She sat down on the bed and quickly ran through everything she knew so far, from when she had first received this case to what they had discovered at the barn. Everything she knew pointed to one very real fact—there was a nuclear device loose in America, and it was going to be used soon. The longer the terrorists had it, the more likely they would be caught, so they would only bring it in when their plan was nearing its final stages. If it was still in El Paso, then they had a chance of stopping it. If it wasn't, they had to find out where it had gone as soon as possible. And if it was headed east, toward the White House…

Tracy shook her head, reaching for the phone, then actively restraining herself from calling Paul and telling him to take Jennifer and leave the city. She had no way of knowing that was their final target. Instead, she dialed another number.

"Customs and Border Protection, Agent Spencer speaking."

"It's Tracy. I'm in," she said.

"Good. Everything's arranged at the hospital, so all we need to do it pick up our source."

"You set this up already? You knew I was going to agree?"

"Let's just say I played a strong hunch. You're smart, aggressive, and I can tell you don't like to lose. And if we go through the normal channels on this, we are going to lose—I guarantee it."

"Pick me up as soon as possible," she said.

"I'm already on my way."

Tracy snapped her cell phone shut and sat on the edge of her bed, hoping she wasn't about to flush her career down the toilet.

26

Nate's stomach twisted into knots as he drove though El Paso's south side, working his way toward the Barrio Aztecas hangout. For a wild moment, he considered calling the whole operation off, but knew that was impossible. They had one shot at a solid lead on whoever had the nuke, and he was going to take it, even if it meant risking everything.

As he headed south on Kansas Street, deeper into the heart of the Segundo Barrio, his gaze passed over Tracy, who was dressed in black sweatpants, a black, long-sleeved T-shirt and black running shoes. His outfit was the same, except he wore steel-toed combat boots. Neither of them had any identification, no badges, not even wallets. If it went wrong, they didn't want the gangbangers to know who they were.

"You all right? Last chance to back out," he said as they approached their destination.

Tracy mustered a game smile. "What, and leave you to

go in and get shot by yourself? You know the stakes are too high to risk all on this one person. You go—I go."

"All right, then." He turned off the ignition and held out the keys. "Take these. If you leave and I don't, there'll be a damn good reason for it. And no last-minute heroics, either—if I tell you to get out, you better go like your ass is on fire and your hair's catching. Get to the truck, get the hell out of here, turn left at the intersection, turn right at the next one, and that road will take you to the highway. That should get you clear. Say it back to me."

Tracy repeated his directions in a clear, steady voice, then said, "Let's get on with it."

Nate nodded. There was nothing left to do but finish their prep and go. He got out, checked his pistol and made sure it was accessible in its holster on his hip. He casually scanned the area, which he had chosen for its lack of nearby housing.

On the other side, Tracy was making her final preparations, including pulling a black knit mask over her face, then securing a strap around her head. Nate did the same, then took a small night-vision monocular from his pocket. Standing on the running board of the Silverado, he put it to his eye and studied the route they would take to the house. The streetlights in the area worked intermittently at best, which was good, since there were no trees for cover, only the sides of houses. Nate checked the windows for signs of observers, a moving curtain on this breezeless night, a shadow passing in front of a living-room or bedroom window or anything else that tripped his stakeout senses. He saw nothing. So far, so good, he told himself.

With Nate leading the way, they crossed a small median, then entered the block containing the gang house. On one side, one of the single-story homes had suffered a fire and looked abandoned, with empty, gaping window frames yawning wide in smoke-blackened walls. The other house was either deserted, or the occupants were asleep.

Nate crept down the narrow space between the two homes, trying to look everywhere at once, expecting a gangbanger to pop out from the shadow. He reached the end of the space, and peeked out at the gang house, only a few yards away. Putting the monocular to his eye, he scanned the back of the house carefully, finding what he was looking for on the flat roof. A guard had nodded off, apparently exhausted from keeping watch over all the partiers during the evening.

Nate pointed at Tracy, held up his hand to indicate she should stay put, pointed at himself, then at the back door. After her nod of understanding, and steeling himself for the impact of a bullet out of nowhere, he walked slowly toward the door, every sense alert for the slightest indication they'd been made. When he reached the door, he took up a position beside it, then waved Tracy forward.

When she reached the side of the house, he removed night-vision goggles from a hard-shell container on his left hip and clicked them into place on the hands-free mount on his forehead. After checking to see that Tracy had done the same, he turned them on, and the world around him flared into sharp, brilliant, green-and-black life. They were too powerful to use on the street, where the light from the lamps would have blinded him, but in the dark backyard, they were perfect. Every detail of the squalid area around him was visible as if it were high noon. With the goggles in place over her eyes, as well, Tracy flashed him a thumbs-up, indicating she was ready to go.

Nate extracted a lock pick and torsion wrench from his

kit and went to work on the back door while Tracy kept an eye out for anyone. Minutes ticked by, until he finally engaged the last tumbler and was rewarded by the lock opening with a soft click. Nate froze, but when no one showed up after another minute, he put his picks away, drew his pistol and gently eased open the door.

The inside of the house was stifling, with a pall of marijuana smoke hanging over the rooms in a thick haze. Tracy muffled a slight cough as she came inside, drawing a glare from Nate. The hallway ran two-thirds of the length of the house, terminating in the living room he had been in yesterday. Next to the hallway was a staircase that went up to the second floor. Nate pointed up, where he could hear the far-off rattle of a window air conditioner. Pistol aimed at the second-floor landing, he cautiously stepped on the first stair, near the wall, so it wouldn't creak. Partway up, he reached over and unscrewed the single bare light bulb from the hallway fixture. He then proceeded up the rest of the stairs, sweeping and clearing the second-floor hallway before motioning Tracy up after him.

This hall had five doors set in its walls, but Nate had eyes for the far one, the only one that was completely closed. Sweat soaked his mask, but he couldn't wipe his face. The harsh smoke burned his lungs, as well, but he ignored the discomfort as best as he could while he watched the hallway.

Tracy stood next to him after creeping up the stairs as quietly as he had. Nate motioned for her to follow, and they headed for the end door. Without being told, she took up a position on the far side, pistol at the ready.

The sudden crash of the pull-down staircase as it dropped to the floor behind him made Nate's heart race. He stepped over to Tracy, who looked as if she was preparing to take out whoever was coming down. Putting a finger to her lips, he pushed her into the shadowed corner as the wooden staircase creaked under someone's every step. Nate half twisted and looked back to see the big man who had given him crap yesterday step on the floor with a thump that shook the entire landing.

Muttering to himself, the hulking Latino lumbered down the hall to the stairs. Nate's free hand held his pistol, ready to fire if necessary, but he let his hunch play out first, hardly daring to breathe. He felt Tracy's body against his own, tense as a taut steel cable, her breathing light and rapid.

Without looking up, the bruiser rumbled downstairs. As he had hoped, covered from head to toe in their black clothes and masks, Nate and Tracy blended perfectly with the thick darkness. They waited until the heavy thuds faded away on the first floor, then Nate was back at the door, warning Tracy to watch the stairs as he tried the knob again.

Turning it very slowly, he made sure it was rotated all the way before pushing inward. The door didn't move. Nate pushed harder, leaning his body into the wood and pushing as carefully as he could. It flexed a bit, but he knew from the resistance near the jamb that there was some kind of dead bolt or hasp lock holding it shut from the inside.

Releasing the knob, he went back to Tracy. "Locked from the inside," he whispered.

"We need to abort," she said.

"Hell, no, we're too far in now. Let's—"

The thump of approaching feet silenced Nate. He listened as the big gangbanger approached. "Stay here," he whispered in Tracy's ear. "Get your flashlight ready, and flip your goggles up when the door opens. Move only if he takes me down."

Nate crept back along the hallway, stopping only to push the attic staircase back into the ceiling. Stealing to the farthest door, he held his breath and pushed it open, slipping inside just as the man-mountain hit the first step below.

A quick scan of the room revealed a slumbering form underneath a crumpled sheet on a queen-size bed. A slow-turning ceiling fan moved the hot air around. Nate closed the door most of the way, leaving a thin sliver to see through. While he waited, he found the inside lock button on the door and pushed it.

The man reached the top of the stairs and stood there sweating for a moment, a bulging burrito in his fist. He took a huge bite, chewing noisily, then ambled down the hall. At the stairs, he looked up at the pull cord, then looked around at the other doors, for the practical joker who had pushed up his stairs. Seeing no one, he reached up for the knotted cord.

Easing the door open, Nate slipped out, making sure to close it behind him. As soon as it clicked, he charged full speed ahead, his booted feet pounding the thin carpet. Even with only about five yards between him and his target, Nate got up a good head of steam before he lowered his shoulder, knowing he had to make this count.

The gangbanger had just started to turn at the noise behind him when Nate plowed into his back. Already off balance from reaching for the cord, the massive gang member staggered, aided by Nate shoving him forward with all his might. The burrito went flying, disappearing down the hall as the hulk crashed into the locked door with every one of his 350 pounds moving at an unstoppable velocity.

The door broke under the impact with a splintering crack, as Nate rode the big guy down to the floor.

"Lights!" he hissed, flipping up his goggles and switching on his flashlight. Scrambling to his feet, he ran at the bed in the center of the room, shining the blinding beam into Lopez's groggy face. Nate was aware of at least two women, one fumbling to cover herself with a sheet, the other lying motionless, dead to the world. But he only had eyes for the man in front of him.

"What the hell—?" Lopez threw up an arm, squinting at the harsh glare. His chest was covered with tattoos, and as the sheet flew off him, stolen by the woman, it revealed that he was dressed only in red satin boxers. His other arm reached under his pillow, withdrawing a pistol just as Nate brought the butt of his own gun down on the man's shoulder. The collarbone cracked under the blow. Lopez's shout of pain was cut off by Nate sticking the barrel of his gun in the Mexican's mouth as he knocked the pistol—a cheap Smith & Wesson knockoff—out of the punk's hand.

Sweeping his flashlight over the dirty nightstand, Nate spotted Lopez's cell phone. He dropped the light and swept the phone into his pocket.

"Get up if you want to keep breathing." Using the gun as a prod, he guided Lopez out of bed and over the unconscious man he had used as a battering ram.

In the hallway, Tracy covered the doorways with her flashlight, making sure no one poked his head out. Nate removed his gun and whipped his arm around Lopez's neck. "Tell your homies to stay put—otherwise, we shoot the first face we see." He nodded at Tracy to check the stairs, and she slipped by them to cover the landing.

Lopez relayed Nate's instructions, more loudly than Nate would have liked. "Whoever you are, you're a dead man, *pendejo*. I'll hold your fucking heart in my hand before this is over," he growled.

"Move it," Nate said. Keeping the pistol jammed into the gang leader's neck, he moved past the doors, making sure to keep the man between him and other rooms at all times. Tracy was halfway down the stairs when she seemed to slip just as a flash and boom roared from the living room, chopping the banister to kindling and making her grunt in pain.

"Out the back, now!" Nate shouted. He forced Lopez down the stairway, catching up to his partner. "You all right?"

"Caught some pellets—in my vest. I'll be fine," Tracy said, wincing.

"Watch our backs." Nate tightened his hold on the wiry man's throat. "Tell them to drop their guns and slide 'em over, or I'll redecorate the hallway with your brains," he told Lopez.

Lopez issued rapid orders in Spanish, and moments later a short-barreled shotgun and two pistols came clattering down the hallway.

"Let's go." Nate kept Lopez in the hallway, blocking the other gang members' views of him and Tracy. "Get the door."

Keeping her right arm near her side, Tracy went to the door and cracked it open, leading with her pistol before opening it all the way. "We're clear."

Nate kicked all three guns out into the yard. He turned to Lopez. "All right, we get outside, and you run like hell with us. If you don't, I blow your elbow out, and you still run like hell. Got it?"

Lopez hesitated, then nodded once. Nate looked at Tracy, who nodded.

"Go!"

Tracy took off into the darkness. Nate gave her three steps, then shoved Lopez out and followed right behind him, keeping a tight hold on the gangbanger as they ran.

The backyard was only about ten yards from the door to the other house, but it felt like the longest distance Nate had ever covered in his life. Even though they had taken out the roof guard, and the guys in the hall would have to fumble around to find their weapons, the gang would not take this lying down. And as he expected, just as they hit the alley between the two houses, gunshots exploded in the night. Nate hunched instinctively, expecting to feel the impact of a bullet in his back at any second. Adrenaline-charged blood pounded in his ears, making it difficult to pinpoint where the shots were coming from. He saw Tracy racing for the truck, and followed her as fast as he could, propelling Lopez in front of him with hard prods of his pistol.

They burst out from between the two houses and headed for the vehicle, their shoes slapping against the pavement. Lopez stumbled and went down hard, shouting in pain as he skidded across the pavement, almost taking Nate with him.

"Get up right now!" Nate grabbed his shoulder, trying to get his prisoner off the street.

"Fuck you, asshole. I think I broke my ankle!" Lopez rolled back and forth, clutching his lower left leg. Nate glanced back to see lights and motion in the alleyway. The truck roared to life a few yards away. Leveling his pistol at the alleyway, he squeezed off several shots, making the approaching gangbangers duck and cover.

The truck roared as it powered over the curb to skid to a stop next to him. Tracy rolled the passenger window down. "For Christ's sake, get him in here and let's go!"

Nate was already moving. Wrenching open the back

door, he hauled Lopez up and threw him into the backseat, then scrambled in himself. "Go!"

Tracy slammed the gas and spun the steering wheel, making the Silverado buck and sway as it ran over the curb again.

"Take the second street on your right!" Nate said while prying Lopez's hand away from his ankle and raising it to where he could handcuff him to a restraining bar set in the ceiling. The truck skidded as she took the turn a bit too fast, making Nate fall into Lopez as the big vehicle rocked back and forth. Behind them, they heard the loud pop of gunfire, but no bullets struck them.

"Go up two blocks and turn left on Seventh!" Nate began patting Tracy down, his hands roaming over her sides, back and chest.

"What the hell are you doing?" She tried to shrug him off as she whipped the wheel to the left.

"Seeing how badly you got shot, dammit!" Under her legs, his probing fingers found something soft and mushy. "Shit, did that hurt?"

"No, but it feels kinda wet and warm. Why, what'd you find?" Tracy, while still breathing hard, had slowed the vehicle down to a respectable speed while keeping an eye open for police cruisers.

"I don't know—it's too thick to be blood." Nate held his fingers up to his nose. "Refried beans—what the hell?"

He felt Tracy's body shake in her seat, and for a panicked moment he thought she was going into shock. But as she drew breath, he realized she was laughing—tinged with just a hint of hysteria, but laughing all the same. "Must have been that huge burrito. I slipped on it when I went down the stairs. Just as the shotgun went off. Damn thing saved my life."

Already strung out by their narrow escape, Nate sat back and guffawed at the ludicrous thought. "Saved by Mexican food. Who'd have thunk it?"

Tracy's mirth had subsided and she looked back at Nate. "I think I'm all right—we can check later. I've got a T-intersection coming up—which way?"

Shaking his head, Nate pointed. "Hang a right on Oregon, and we'll head up to Missouri, where we can get on the highway." Still chuckling, he kept a close watch behind them as they sped through the dimly lit streets with their prize.

27

Holy shit, it's a good thing Paul can't see me now, Tracy thought as she drove the Silverado through the neighborhoods of north El Paso. *He'd probably think I've gone completely insane.*

She blinked rapidly, trying to slow her racing pulse. Her senses were on input overload. Everything around her — from the flashing traffic lights to the oncoming cars to the hum of the off-road tires as they propelled the truck down the streets—seemed preternaturally sharp and bright and loud. She took a deep breath, held it for a second, then let it whoosh out of her lungs. She took another one, and felt her pulse begin to slow.

She had lost count of the laws they had broken. She concentrated on their goal of getting the information they needed to make sure that nuke didn't go off. She told herself if that meant busting the chops of some low-life gang members who were already breaking half a dozen laws when they got out of bed every morning, that was a trade-off she could live with.

Besides, the rush she had gotten when they had infiltrated the house and pulled Lopez out had given her a jolt that no amount of DHS training could. She had gone through the basic firearms training at the Federal Law Enforcement Training Center, and she shot at the range at least twice a month to stay current, but that couldn't compare to creeping through the pitch-black house using only night vision, but still feeling completely in control of the situation. Even when it had started to go bad, she hadn't freaked out, but had stayed focused on the mission. She hadn't held them up during their withdrawal. *Maybe it's time to consider a different assignment when I get back, something more field oriented.*

But first we've got to find out what this scumbag knows. Checking the rearview mirror, she saw Nate keeping an eye on Lopez, who was hunched over as best he could with his arm restrained, his head leaning against the window. "He all right? He might be going into shock," she said.

"Hey, Lopez, you gonna make it?" Nate reached out and grabbed the Latino's chin to see his face, then yanked his hand back as the gang member snapped at him with his teeth. "Oh, he's still got some fight left in him, don'tcha, bucko?"

"I swear, my people are gonna track you both down, stake you out in the desert and leave you for the ants and the coyotes." Lopez's cold gaze flicked from Nate to Tracy and back again. "You and your *puta* are walking dead—you just don't know it yet."

"I'd be more worried about you making it through the night yourself first, tough guy. After all, it'll be hard for your buddies to do anything if they never find you again." Nate leaned close to him, putting his face right next to the other man's. "And you won't be giving any orders from a shallow grave, *pendejo.*"

Tracy swallowed hard in the driver's seat. She knew they were going to interrogate him, which meant they might have to resort to less-than-legal methods to get what they needed, but from the tone of Nate's voice, she could have sworn that he planned to kill the man afterward, no matter what. The line between the necessary means and the ends, already blurred by what they had just done, stretched out in her mind. Was torturing a suspect to get information okay? Was killing him? She squared her shoulders and concentrated on driving. Once they got to the desert, she'd pull Nate aside and find out exactly what he planned to do.

They left the city behind, and Tracy followed Nate's terse directions as they headed into the rough Texas plains just south of New Mexico. As the lights of El Paso dimmed, the dark desert seemed to expand all around them until Tracy felt as if she were traveling through a dark alien landscape with the insignificant glow of the high beams illuminating only a tiny portion of it. She slowed down to turn off the main highway onto a two-lane paved road, then turned off several miles later onto a rough dirt road, where she slowed even further to navigate the winding, narrow lane. Lopez had ceased issuing threats and now hunched in sullen silence behind her. Nate sat across from him, his eyes never leaving the gangbanger.

Tracy drove for at least another dozen miles, until they were in the middle of nowhere.

Suddenly Nate leaned forward. "Stop here."

She pulled the Silverado over as he unlocked the handcuff from the bar, but not from Lopez's wrist. "Ow, man, that fuckin' hurts!"

Nate yanked the cuffs hard. "That was the point. You're getting out here, and I don't want any bullshit from you. Otherwise, I'll drag you out by the cuff, *comprende?*"

Lopez nodded. "Don't worry, I ain't going anywhere with this busted leg, in case you forgot."

"Cover him while he leaves. I'll meet you around the other side," Nate said to Tracy. He slid out of his seat and came around the front of the vehicle. He gave Tracy a look that she recognized immediately, as she had been on the receiving end of it from Gilliam several times during her tenure at DHS—follow my lead, and don't ask any questions.

She nodded once, but her overriding thought as she turned the engine off, leaving the headlights on, was *I'll go along—for now.* She kept her pistol out and trained on Lopez as he hopped out of the Silverado. He almost lost his balance, but managed to stay upright by leaning against the vehicle's side. Out here, Tracy was surprised how chilly it was, the desert having rapidly lost the heat it had soaked up all day long. She shivered, glad for the long-sleeved shirt as she realized the other reason Nate had brought Lopez all the way out there.

"All right, hobble your way out there in front of the lights and turn around so we can get a good look at your sorry ass," Nate ordered.

Lopez seemed to finally realize the seriousness of his situation. "Look, whatever you want—drugs, money, women, children—I'm sure we can work something out."

Nate drew his pistol and pulled the slide back. "Go."

Lopez hopped out in front of the lights, his satin boxers rustling in the breeze as he tried to maneuver on the hard-packed dirt without falling over.

"That's far enough," Nate said.

Lopez managed to turn around and stood in the glare of the headlights, shielding his eyes with one hand. "All right, you made your point. Now what the fuck do you want?"

"I always knew you were a businessman at heart, Lopez." Nate holstered his pistol and walked out in front of the lights. "Now I've got a deal for you." He reached up and took off the black knit mask, eliciting a snort of disbelief from the Mexican.

"Spencer? *You* broke into my house, dragged me all the way out here and broke my fuckin' arm and leg? Do you know how dead I'm gonna make you?"

Tracy didn't know who was more surprised, her or the gang leader. They knew each other—and had for a while, apparently. She snapped her mouth closed and focused back on the conversation.

Nate tossed the cell phone into the dirt near Lopez. "I'll be fine, and so will you. I ran into one of your boys near the border, running illegals across the border with a couple of *zetas* earlier today. When I saw his tattoo, I knew you'd lied to me about what we'd discussed yesterday."

Lopez tried to cross his arms, but only winced when a stab of pain reminded him of his broken collarbone. "So one of my boys is running wetbacks into the U.S. What's that got to do with this?"

Nate shook his head. "Don't shine me on, not now, and definitely not out here. The Barrio Aztecas are involved in everything that comes through El Paso, especially from the south. You knew about the Middle Easterners and that they were carrying something, but you didn't want to give me any more information than necessary. You told me what you thought I needed to know, including the dead end of your two boys, then sent me on my way, didn't you?"

Lopez looked as if he was going to plead ignorance again, then shrugged. "Hey, man, when word of the job came my way, I had no idea it would get so out of hand. But once it did, we were gonna take care of it our way, you know?"

"I figured as much—you were also way too cool about your two *vatos* getting killed. But I'm gonna do you a favor. With your help, I'm gonna take these guys down for you."

Lopez frowned and shivered in the cool air. "Really? You can't even find these guys, but now you're gonna take care of 'em for me?"

"Yup. After you get on that phone and tell whoever your contact is that one of the illegals survived the slaughter in the desert, and is at Providence Memorial Hospital, in room 305—and get that number right—I don't need an innocent getting killed over this."

Lopez nodded as he reached down and picked up the phone. "And you're gonna set out the welcome mat and see who comes to call, right?" He flipped the phone open, his finger poised to dial. "Huh, can't believe I get a signal out here."

"Yeah, it's as far out as we could get to have this little talk and still have you reach whoever you need to reach. And just in case you get any ideas about sending a few of your boys over to Providence to wait and see who shows up, remember where you are right now, and who's your only ride out of here at the moment."

Lopez paused just long enough for Tracy to realize that's exactly what he had been thinking about doing.

After making the call, Lopez flipped the phone closed. "He'll get the word out, but I'd get your welcome party set up sooner rather than later. My boy wasn't too keen on not being in on the action himself. I managed to keep him out of the way for you—for now."

"Good, 'cause I'd hate to have to run him in on obstructing justice and attempted-murder charges," Nate said.

"Yeah, like bustin' into my house and dragging me out

into the middle of the desert is approved procedure."
Lopez's entire body was shaking, and he kept his balance
with an obvious effort. "Could we at least finish this in the
car. I'm freezin' my cojones off."

"In a minute."

"Goddammit, I made the fuckin' call—what more do
you want! You're really pushing me, Spencer." Lopez's
face grew sly as he thought it through. "Or is that what
you're anglin' for, huh? You doing me this favor so I owe
you one, is that it?" He looked down at his limp arm and
oddly bent leg. "After all this shit you did to me, we're not
even by a long shot, *rulacho,* and I ain't gonna forget it."

Nate walked over to stand in front of him. "After all this
shit I did to you, I'm gonna drive you back to town, and
you're gonna call your homies and they'll come pick you
up, and you're not gonna to do anything to me, her or
anyone else. I'm not doing this for you—I'm doing it for
a bigger reason than you can even begin to comprehend.
And after I drop you off, and you tell your boys whatever
bullshit story you want to tell them, we're through. No
more deals, no more looking the other way, no more
scratching each other's back. I'm done with you—I'm out."

Tracy watched the exchange as she tried to mask the
shell-shocked look on her face. In the past three minutes,
her entire perception of Nate had been wiped away as if it
had never existed. *"Paths crossed a couple of times,"* my
ass. *Jesus, I fell for his story hook, line and sinker. And if
he was withholding on that, what else hasn't he told me?*
she wondered, her mind reeling.

"Just like that?" Lopez's face had run the gamut from
patronizing to incredulous to furious while Nate had
been talking. "Listen, asshole, you aren't walkin' away
from me that—"

Faster than Tracy could follow, Nate drew his pistol and placed the barrel against Lopez's temple. "Yeah, it is that easy. The way I see it, you got two choices. Either you agree to what I just laid out right now, or you don't, and hop yourself right into a shallow grave. Now what's it gonna be?"

Lopez's eyes flicked over to the barrel of the pistol resting against his skin, then back to Nate's cool blue gaze. He was silent for a few seconds. Tracy feared he was going to do something stupid, but finally he replied, "All right, when we get back to the city, you and I are done. But know this, done means done. You get in my way on the streets tomorrow, and I will take you down without thinking twice."

Nate withdrew the pistol from the gang leader's head. "Fair enough, 'cause I'm gonna do the exact same thing if you cross my path."

"As long as we understand each other. Too bad—for a pig cop, you were all right. Now get me back into that truck before my dick freezes off."

"I always knew you were a smart man, Lopez." Nate didn't help the other man, but didn't hinder him, either. The gangbanger hobbled to the back door and climbed in.

Nate walked past Tracy as she stared daggers at him. "I'll explain on the way to Providence. Let's go," he said.

28

"Jesus, Kate, you been holding out on me? This guy's got balls the size of grapefruit, and he knows how to get things done, that's for damn sure. Where the hell did he come from, and why haven't we poached him yet?"

Denny had checked in with Kate after attending a party thrown by a consortium of energy lobbyists in Washington. He attended several of these events each a year, so he could get the scuttlebutt about what was going down on Capitol Hill. He also kept an ear open for potential trouble spots around the world. Denny had attended in his international-businessman persona. He had run a multinational Fortune 500 company for more than a decade before covertly joining Room 59.

After the party had wound down, he had logged on to report his findings to Kate, who had been engrossed in listening to the events that had been going down in Texas. After giving him a summary, she sipped iced lemon tea and shook her head.

"I'm not surprised that you'd like this guy once you

heard this. I don't have to remind you that we're not looking for cowboys here, remember?"

Denny shook his head, which was still perfectly groomed at five in the morning. "No, we're looking for guys exactly like this one, men—or women, for that matter—who can evaluate a situation quickly and take whatever steps are necessary to solve it. Hell, once he knew what was on the line, he barely hesitated when he had to step outside the law to get what he needed."

Kate raised her glass to hide the quick smile on her lips; Denny had walked into her subtle trap. "Right, so what would happen if we brought him in and gave him less rules and even more control? Yes, he's effective, but he's too much of a loose cannon. I thought Tracy might be able to control him, but instead he seems to have brought her over to his side, which surprises me a bit."

"Does it, Kate? You know what's at stake here, and I think your analysis put together the two people best suited to find this nuke outside one of our own operatives." Denny leaned forward in his leather chair. "I think they're doing exactly what you want them to do, the law and their careers be damned in the bargain if necessary."

Kate bristled at the insinuation. "You have one too many at that Georgetown mansion? No one made them break the law to get that information. They know full well the risks they're taking. What they're doing, in their eyes, is the right thing—putting the end result ahead of the means. That's what we do here every day, so watch that sanctimonious tone."

"Now who's been staring at their computer monitor a little too long? I didn't say I disapproved. Shoot, you know some of the things I've done in the name of God and country, and thankfully it was to people who deserved it.

And it's one thing to send in one of our boys or girls to do a job we know needs doing. It's just that sometimes I find it a bit unnerving to deal with people who don't know who's really pulling the strings to make them dance, people who are on our side, too. Yet we expect the exact same results from them."

Kate slumped in her chair and took a breath. Denny's words had hit a nerve, one she preferred not to show. "Yes, but we're only so large, and even with our resources, we can do only so much ourselves. But if we wait for the bureaucrats to get off their keisters and actually act instead of just endlessly discussing the threat, who knows how many might suffer or die in the meantime? If the American intelligence community is a huge, often indiscriminately wielded club, I like to think of us as the scalpel that excises the dangerous cells before they destroy the entire body. Sometimes there can be a bit of collateral damage—unfortunate but necessary, I'm afraid. And as an ex-SEAL, you must have run into the same thing more than once."

Denny had, in fact, commanded a team of the elite military force for several years. "Yeah, and I was never fond of it back then and still am not. These two are certainly competent, and I'd like to see them both come out of this in one piece," he said.

"You and me both, so let's see if we can't give them some help. How you coming on that list of potential launch points?"

"I put some of our brightest on this, with dinner for two at the D.C. Capital Grill on the line as a reward for their analysis within eight hours."

"Really? What happens if your winner lives outside the area?"

Denny smiled. "I fly them in and put them up at no cost—but they don't know that yet. By the way, why are you so sure that a company is involved—why not just a few guys who rent a truck and drive it into a metropolitan area to set it off?"

Along with the screen she was using to talk to Denny, Kate had her own data-mining screen open, as well as a window with all of the available information on their ultimate quarry, Sepehr al-Kharzi. "That's a good question, but the answer is quite simple—al-Kharzi doesn't think that way. His psychological profile indicates a fervent belief in his cause, jihad, of course, but also a grandiose way of thinking. His last attempt on America involved the largest amount of explosives that would have been used in the U.S. since the Oklahoma City bombing. He aspires to be the next bin Laden—a megaterrorist whose name would strike fear into our hearts, and strengthen his allies. The suitcase nuke would cause death and destruction in any city it was detonated in, but that's only striking at one head of the hydra he thinks America is. His ego wants more than that, which is why we think he's trying to execute something on a much higher scale. For all the low-profile living he's been doing, he wants to take a swing at us that will send America reeling, and that means outdoing 9/11, which is a tall order indeed."

Denny frowned. "Yeah, which makes it even more unlikely that he or his people haven't popped up on someone's radar yet."

"No one ever said that the terrorists haven't learned from their mistakes. For every ill-conceived plot to attack an isolated fuel pipeline at JFK, there's an as-yet-undetected sleeper cell working very hard to contaminate the water supply of a major city. They're becoming smarter, more capable of exploiting the holes in our security net, which, as you well know, are pretty large in places—like the border," Kate said.

"Yeah, yeah, no need to remind me. We've got a couple marked as highly probable. One's a trucking outfit that regularly makes runs back and forth across the border, with the target percentage of Middle Eastern employees. It would be easy enough to blackmail or even take out a driver and replace him with a cell member, and roll the nuke straight through the checkpoint. They're supposed to be searched, and the cargo highways are monitored, but a heavily shielded box could still could get through. It's one of our strongest leads. A second one is a small commuter airline based near El Paso. They might try an aerial detonation to disperse the radiation, not to mention the EMP could disable most of a city if the bomb goes off at ten thousand feet—"

"What was that?" Kate had been scrolling through her own list, looking at her own narrowed list of possibilities, which still numbered at least a dozen, and she had barely cracked the *T*s.

"The Electro-Magnetic Pulse is the disruptive radioactive energy wave created by an electromagnetic bomb, or it can also be a byproduct of a nuclear detonation. Supposed to damage transistors, components of electronic devices, that sort of thing. Tests have shown the damage varies depending on the type of circuit used, but with so many electronics in America, if one of those was set off, it would probably knock out a lot more than just thousands of toasters and radios."

For a moment, Kate didn't hear him, as all her attention was focused on her computer screen, where a single name had caught her attention—Spaceworks, Inc.

A quick tap on the screen brought up all of the information NiteMaster had acquired, including their Web site, which showed them to be a research-and-development facility that constructed rockets for businesses to use in commercial space ventures.

Her own words replayed in her mind—*He aspires to be the next bin Laden.*

Could he have managed to put something this complex into place? She brought up everything they knew about the company. Its owners, history, roster of employees, everything she could find. Once the picture of the grinning owner, Joseph Allen, appeared on her monitor, along with his completely clean background, Kate's gut feeling solidified into something more—the certainty that this was the vehicle al-Kharzi planned to use to carry out his attack against the U.S.

"Earth to Kate. Hello, Kate, you got something?"

"Yeah, Denny, I think I do." Kate gritted her teeth as she scrolled through the data. She discovered Joseph's father had been a radical Muslim thirty years earlier. "The son follows in the footsteps of the father," she muttered under her breath.

"What was that?"

"Nothing, Denny. We need to scramble a hacker team—pull the best ones we have ready right now. They need to work on infiltrating this company's network ASAP. Tag one of them to get satellite time over the compound so we can get an idea of what we might be facing. Also, get me the dossiers on whoever's up in the midnight-team rotation. If there's enough time, we can send them in to take out the facility. Finally, we need to figure out how to stop them before they fire, and if they manage to get it launched, how to stop the rocket before detonation—"

"Whoa, whoa, Kate, why don't you bring me up to speed first on what you've got there?"

She linked him to the Spaceworks site, and he whistled. "How do you know you're right about this?"

"It fits al-Kharzi's profile. The head of the company is a fifth-generation Muslim born in the U.S. His father immigrated from Syria back in the 1960s, and had connections to terrorist groups that fought in Lebanon. It seems that he left for the U.S., and found an even bigger enemy. Joseph has kept his nose scrupulously clean, but that's just what a sleeper agent does now, isn't it? If I'm right, he could cripple the entire eastern or western seaboard with the right missile, the suitcase and the EMP blast. I've got to let Tracy and Nate know—I think we've found our sleeper cell."

Denny held up his hand. "Before you do that, you need to know that the rocket has to be taken out before it launches. Once it's airborne, there is no contingency plan to stop it by shooting it down."

Kate's smile was grim as she dialed. "Then I guess we'd better make sure it doesn't get launched."

29

Sepehr took a deep, steadying breath, and stared straight into the small digital videocamera, preparing to record the message that would be broadcast throughout America and the world. He was taking complete responsibility for what he would wreak in the next few hours. His message would emphasize that he had accomplished this from inside the United States itself, serving as a clarion call to the rest of the holy warriors around the world that, for all its vaunted might, the imperialist superpower was vulnerable, filled with weak, morally corrupt people who deserved to be destroyed by the cleansing blast he would unleash, the first, he hoped, of many.

He was about to to start recording when there was a knock on the small studio's door. Sepehr glanced up at the interruption, his angry expression turning more so when he saw Joseph Allen standing outside, worry etched on his face. Rising, he stood and walked to the door. He wanted to be alone when he made his message to the world, but it seemed creating his victory message would have to wait. "What?" he asked.

"I'm sorry to bother you, but we may have a problem."

"Yes?"

"One of my people got a call from the infidels that were part of the group that were supposed to bring our men and their cargo into the States. They say that they've received word there was a survivor from among the illegal immigrants in the desert. Apparently she's being kept at Providence Hospital, in room 305, under guard."

Sepehr remained quiet, digesting the information. "We are approximately two hours from launch, correct?"

"Yes."

"What possible threat could this person be to us? They know nothing of our plan, and they cannot possibly know where we are. The chances that they could impart some bit of information about us are infinitesimal. Bring Rais and Antarah to me immediately."

The two men who had served as part of the three-man team charged with escorting the bomb arrived at the door in less than a minute. By that time, Sepehr had made his decision. "There is one task that remains to insure that our strike against this nation of infidels will be successful. One of the infidels that you were supposed to have killed is still alive, and is at this address." He handed them a slip of paper. "Take an unmarked car and finish what you started. If you are caught or trapped, you know what to do. May Allah watch over you both and reward your efforts this day. Now go."

The two men nodded and headed for the main doors. Joseph's brow furrowed as he waited to speak until the men left. "I don't mean to question your decision, but are you sure you're not overreacting to this? You said yourself that there was no possible way they could know about our mission or where we are. How can we be sure it is not a trap by the American authorities?"

Sepehr shook his head. "If the Americans knew where we were, they wouldn't hesitate to beat down our doors at this very moment. If they are fishing, our men will either kill them or die in the process, and either way, that trail will be closed. It was a seemingly insignificant thing—like what we have just learned—that brought down my previous operation against the United States, and forced me into hiding. Even as close as we are to success, I will not take that chance again."

"Of course. Just the same, I will notify all of our guards to be extra alert and to report anything suspicious, no matter how insignificant it may seem. Do you think there is any cause to issue anything larger than the pistols the guards are currently carrying?"

Sepehr clucked his tongue. "Now who is being paranoid? As I expect you have done already, just make sure that the heavier weapons are available to the men. Although wise men do not go looking for trouble, they would be fools indeed not to expect it."

Joseph turned to go, but stopped at the door when he heard Sepehr's voice.

"Joseph—if something were to happen, and we needed to launch sooner than the countdown allowed for, could we?"

"The countdown is for optimal safety, to make sure that all parts of the rocket are in working order, but we have run the tests on all systems several times, so if we need to go to ignition for launch ahead of schedule, we could do so within two minutes of receiving the order."

"Very good. Please carry on." After Joseph had left, Sepehr turned to the camera and sat in front of it again. He closed his eyes and calmed himself, wanting to appear as the epitome of a man in control, then hit the remote, waited for the green light to come on at the top of the camera, and began speaking the words he had waited to say for many, many years.

"People of the world, my name is Sepehr al-Kharzi, and in the name of Allah and his people, I am sending this message to claim responsibility for the attack that has crippled the nation of infidels, the United States of America...."

30

What the hell have I gotten myself into? Tracy wondered for about the hundredth time as she lay under a light blue sheet on a hospital bed in Providence Memorial Hospital, her head covered in a hastily wrapped bandage. Although she appeared to be dressed in the regulation hospital gown, underneath she was fully clothed, including a Level II ballistic vest. Her pistol was tucked under her right leg, and Sharon had hooked her left finger up to a simple heart monitor, which displayed her heart rate and pulse readout.

After they had dropped Lopez off on the outskirts of town, Nate had cut through the heart of El Paso to get back to Providence Memorial as fast as he could. When they arrived, he flashed his badge at the night-shift supervisor and let him know they had reason to believe that the immigrant they had brought in earlier could be in danger from local gang members. He said they wanted to isolate her and set up a sting operation to catch anyone who might try to hurt her. The supervisor, a kid who barely looked thirty, was overwhelmed by Nate's no-nonsense demeanor and authority, and quickly agreed to let them set up in the Mexican illegal's former room, 305. He'd also offered the loan of their security officers. Nate politely declined, saying that too many visible guards might scare the suspects away. He left instructions that the men should be directed to the proper room, and they would take care of the rest.

Now Tracy found herself lying on the hospital bed in near darkness, waiting for two or three potential assassins to come through the door. They had set up Sharon as the night nurse on duty in the quiet hall, and Nate was poised and ready in the bathroom, with the outer door open just enough for him to see the rest of the room. All they could do was wait. Nate had given Sharon explicit instructions to let any visitors through, even though normal visiting hours wouldn't start for another two hours.

Tracy stared at the ceiling and tried to stay calm, aware that her every heartbeat was actually visible on the monitor. It was tough to do—her nerves were already jangled from the night's events, and every noise in the hospital seemed amplified. Every squeal of a wheel on a cart as it came down the hall and every rubber-soled footstep could herald the approach of men who were coming to cut her down. She had been lying there for about forty-five minutes, but it had seemed like forty-five hours.

The squeak of shoes on the linoleum made Tracy grip the butt of her pistol tighter. She moved her head on the pillow so she could see the door, which was half-open. A white-uniformed nurse appeared, framed in the light of the doorway, and Tracy, letting out a sigh of relief, recognized Sharon.

"What the hell are you doing in here?" Nate snarled from the bathroom, raising his pistol from where he had almost taken aim at her.

"Sorry, Nate, but Tracy's phone keeps vibrating, and I thought it might be important. No one's come by in the past fifteen minutes, so I thought I'd bring it in on my rounds." The nurse held out the phone that Stephanie Cassell had given the DHS agent. Tracy had left it with Sharon, not wanting it to distract her at a crucial moment or to startle whoever came to call.

"If the FBI keeps calling, maybe they've found something. Let me see." Tracy flipped the phone open, but no one was one the other end. Instead a text message appeared.

Tracy,
Contact me ASAP. Have a lead on group that may be involved in plot. Check out a local company called Spaceworks—

As Tracy read, she heard the chime of the arriving elevator. Sharon looked out in the hall. "A Middle Eastern-looking man just came out. He's wearing a doctor's coat. Let me see what's going on."

"All right, but be careful. This might be them. Tracy, wrap it up." Nate shrank back into the bathroom.

Tracy flipped the phone shut, shoved it in her pocket, then leaned back and feigned sleep again, slipping her right hand back under the sheet. She heard the mutter of voices at the nurses' station, then the soft pad of footsteps. Sharon's instructions had been to direct the men to the room, then to leave the station immediately. Dread gripped Tracy's stomach as she realized they might kill the nurse outright to eliminate witnesses.

The footsteps stopped outside the room, and Tracy heard an indistinct noise that might have been a whisper or two, then the gasp of someone drawing a startled breath. What's going on out there? she wondered.

Another shadow appeared in the doorway, but something was wrong. Through her slitted eyes, Tracy saw that the shape was too big to be one person. She grasped the butt of her pistol and inched it up to the top of her leg.

Sharon edged into the room bit by bit, forced inside by the man standing behind her, his white-clad arm wrapped around her throat. Tracy couldn't see a weapon, but assumed that he had one. She kept perfectly still, waiting for the right moment.

"See, I told you there are no guards in here." Sharon's voice quavered, but she remained calm as she stood stock-still in his grasp. "They were called out about a half-hour ago—"

"Shut up, bitch!" The man's voice was low and guttural, definitely accented. "If you remain still and do as I say, you might live to see the morning." The man, who was barely taller than Sharon, remained in the doorway, peering into the darkness.

Tracy's gaze flicked over at the bathroom door, which was still ajar. Nate hadn't moved, but that made sense, since he couldn't see his target yet. She couldn't risk taking a shot, since the man was standing behind Sharon, with only his head and arm visible.

"Take two steps forward and stop," the man said.

Sharon grunted as the man pushed her forward, but she stepped far enough inside so that she was even with the bathroom door. Tracy thought she heard the thick door squeak just a bit, but didn't see it move. She returned her attention to the assassin and his hostage.

"Walk to the foot of the bed." The man punctuated his command with the thrust of the pistol that Tracy now saw was jammed into Sharon's lower back. But then the killer moved around her so that he was protected again.

My only chance is to fire when he raises the pistol to shoot me, she thought, hoping he would aim for her chest. But she'd have to throw back the sheet; otherwise, there was too much risk she'd hit Sharon. Jesus, what would Nate do in this situation? she wondered.

The answer came a split second later. The assassin, still keeping his arm clamped around Sharon, raised his pistol to aim at Tracy's cloth-covered form. The moment the barrel wasn't pointed at either woman, the bathroom door burst open as Nate lunged for the man. Startled by the sudden movement, the lab-coated killer instinctively swung his gun toward his attacker, but Nate grabbed his wrist and wrenched it up before the intruder could draw a bead. The sound-suppressed semiautomatic pistol coughed once, and Tracy heard a bullet smack plaster as it burrowed into the wall.

The assassin shoved Sharon toward the bed and used his suddenly free hand to try to force the gun back down toward Nate. The two men struggled for an advantage, while Tracy kicked off the sheet and leveled her pistol, shouting, "Homeland Security, don't move!"

The gunman's only response was to twist around, putting Nate directly into Tracy's line of fire. She raised her weapon and started to climb out of the bed to assist, but Nate apparently had other ideas. With a growl, he shoved the smaller man back toward the doorway, building up steam as he did so. The shorter man tried to resist, but the tall, rangy Texan's leverage made it impossible for him to keep his position. With his shoes slipping on the waxed floor, the intruder was forced back toward the hallway.

"Antarah!" The strange call was punctuated by the man suddenly reversing direction and falling, taking a surprised Nate with him. As soon as the two men fell into the hallway, a burst of gunfire echoed through the hall.

"Nate!" Tracy scrambled off the bed and rushed to the doorway, just ahead of Sharon. She put her arms out to block the other woman from rushing out. "Hold up!" Grabbing her arm, she yanked the nurse out of the doorway just as three shots whizzed past, shattering the window on the far wall. They were followed by a metallic ping, then something small, round and smoking rolled into the room to stop under the bed.

Grenade! Tracy's thought hadn't even fully formed before she pulled Sharon into the bathroom and slammed the heavy door closed. "Cover your ears!" she said, dropping her pistol to do the same and closing her eyes.

"What's happening—?" Sharon had just clapped her hands to her head when a deafening explosion erupted in the outer room. The fire alarm and the sprinkler system went off. The cool water soothed the pounding ache in Tracy's head, and she grabbed her gun, pulled open the smoking door and stepped out, leading with the pistol.

The room was a shambles. The bed had taken the brunt of the blast, and now lay on its side in a tangle of steel frame and smoldering mattress. Pieces of it had been blown around the room, with several rods embedded in the walls. The rest of the broken window had been obliterated by the explosion, and every wall and the ceiling was scorched and blackened. Water poured down from the sprinklers, soaking everything.

"Nate?" Tracy shouted over the earsplitting din of the fire alarm. When she didn't hear a reply, she scrambled out to the hallway and came upon the sodden body of the imposter doctor. Large red splotches covered his upper chest. The hallway was wet from the sprinklers, and Tracy looked around for Nate through the downpour, her hair plastered to her face and the dripping hospital gown molding itself to her body until she peeled it off and tossed it aside. Noticing a strange bulge in the gunman's left coat pocket, she patted it down and came up with another grenade. She stuffed in her pocket.

"Tracy! Come on!" Nate had to shout at the top of his lungs to get her attention. He stood at the stairway, trying to hold the door against a sudden tide of people being evacuated from the floor.

Tracy turned back to Sharon, who was standing, staring at the body, her face pale with the knowledge of how close she had come to death.

"Sharon?" The nurse looked up at her. "The patients need you now. He doesn't."

Sharon nodded and walked down the hall, calling for the patients to evacuate in an orderly fashion. Tracy followed in her wake until they reached the stairway, then Nate took the lead. Rushing past frightened gown-clad patients as they made their way down the steps, helping when they could but always moving toward the bottom level, they were aware their remaining suspect was closer to escape with each passing second.

They reached the main floor just in time to hear screams and gunfire. Nate drew his pistol, eliciting gasps from several patients.

"Department of Homeland Security, please clear the way and stay back!" he shouted. He jerked the door open and swept the outside corridor with his pistol, then glanced back at Tracy. "You ready?"

She nodded, and Nate held the door open and covered

the right side while she stepped out and used the door for cover to sweep and clear the left. They crouched to stay under the wire-mesh-covered glass window.

Nate ran toward the main doors, and Tracy rose and followed. Along the way they saw several dozen patients crouched or huddled on the ground, apparently cowed by the fleeing terrorist. "I am a federal agent with the Department of Homeland Security! Everyone get up now and move in an orderly fashion toward the nearest exit! This is not a drill!" Nate's voice shocked many out of their paralysis, and they started streaming toward the doors. Two paramedics were working on a downed security guard, one pumping up and down on his chest, the other performing mouth-to-mouth. Tracy's lips tightened as she watched them, knowing that she and Nate were responsible.

A few steps before reaching the double doors, she stopped and stared in shock. In front of her was the Mexican woman she had saved at the farm the day before. She was sitting in a wheelchair, and her small daughter was trying to push her toward the door. She looked around for an orderly or nurse, but they were all helping more critical patients.

"Come on, Tracy, we're gonna lose him!" Nate hadn't broken stride.

"Help me, just for a second." Tracy swept Julia up in her arms while Nate ran back and grabbed the wheelchair's handles, maneuvering it through the doors and off to one side. "Stay with your mama, little one," Tracy said as she deposited her by the chair. She ran after Nate, who was already in the staff parking lot, where he'd parked the Silverado.

As he ran, a dark blue sedan roared straight toward him. Nate leveled his pistol, but ended up diving out of the way as the car flew past, the driver spraying bullets out of his side window as he tore out of the driveway. The car didn't stop, but ran straight through a red light, clipping a sub-compact and sending it spinning across the road, where it stopped by slamming into a light post.

"Jesus!" Rising from where she had ducked behind a car, Tracy looked back, checking for injuries. The gunman had been aiming high. Although the front of the building was pockmarked with bullet holes, and two more windows were broken, no one seemed to be hurt.

"Let's go!" Nate had backed the Silverado out of its place and gunned it right to her. Tracy leaped in, and barely had time to get her seat belt on before he laid rubber out of the parking lot. They both heard the distant whine of sirens as they hit Rim Road, then turned north on Oregon, following the trail of honking horns and stopped cars the terrorist was leaving in his wake.

"Get on the phone to your FBI buddy and see if they can set up a roadblock in the next mile. I'm calling in re-inforcements!" Nate snatched the radio mike from its stand as Tracy flipped open her phone.

"Dammit, this shouldn't be that difficult." Kate paced back and forth in front of her screen, monitoring the chaos at the hospital, along with the status of the midnight team en route to Texas and their hackers' attempts to break into the network for Spaceworks, Inc.

While the security of the rocket company network was top-notch, Born2Slyde hadn't thought it meant anything out of the ordinary at first.

"They're in a high-tech field, probably lots of corporate espionage," B2S had typed as she continued her exploratory foray. "Nothing too spooky here yet."

"Good, then accessing it shouldn't be an issue—I want you inside as soon as possible," Kate said.

"Okay, but I'll need mainframe access for this if you want it ASAP," the hacker typed.

"You got it." Kate opened a screen to the DHS mainframe system in Washington and gave her limited access. "Just get access to their rocket telemetry systems—nothing else."

"Yes, Mom."

Kate's screen flashed, signaling an incoming call. The ID said it was Tracy Wentworth. "Finally." Kate hit her earpiece. "Agent Stephanie Cassell."

Tracy's voice was faster than normal, but still in control. "Stephanie, Nate and I set a trap at the hospital to try and lure one of the terrorists, but they blew up a hospital room, and almost got me with it. We took one out and are chasing—watch that minivan, Nate!—the other north-northwest. We're trying to set up a roadblock to stop him in the next mile."

"How close are you to him?" Kate asked.

"About twenty yards behind."

"Okay, press star-nine-star-five-star-one on your phone. Do it right now."

Kate heard the beeps, and on her satellite map of the chase, the pursuing truck was now the centerpoint of a red circle that moved with it, enveloping the fleeing car in the crimson field, along with several others that they passed.

"What did that do?" Tracy asked.

"You've just jammed his cell communications, along with everyone else's in a fifty-yard radius—we don't want him alerting his bosses that we're on to him."

"My phone just did that? But mine still works—"

"Yes. Tell Nate he needs to take this guy out now," Kate said.

Tracy relayed the message and heard a furious Texas drawl in the background. "What in the hell does she think I'm doing, playing tag with him?"

Kate smiled grimly at the border agent's tone. "Hardly. Look, we've uncovered a company that we think may be involved in the plot. Spaceworks, Incorporated. Do you think he's headed back there?"

"If he's got half a brain in his head, he won't lead us back to his HQ—oh, good, we've got two cops behind us. Nate, let them know who we are."

"Already on it—whoa!"

Kate heard the screech of tires, then the loud bang of plastic and metal impacting. She looked up to see the sedan they had been chasing had stopped in the middle of the lane, and Nate's truck had almost plowed through it, but just ended up smacking it instead. The police cars swerved to avoid the pile-up, but the sedan was already moving again.

"Tracy? Are you all right?" Kate asked.

"Nate, get down!" she heard in her ear, along with the distinctive sound of a submachine gun firing.

"Goddammit, this ain't happening again!" Nate shouted. The truck leaped forward, whizzing past other cars, the rise and fall of police sirens accompanying them. "There's a clear patch coming up. Hold on, I'm gonna give him a little tap."

"That might not be such a good—shit!" Tracy screamed.

Kate heard the screech of tires again, followed by a loud thud and the roar of a revving engine. On-screen, she watched as the truck approached to the right rear of the sedan, then swerved, hitting it on the left rear body panel. The sedan spun wildly, tires screeching as the driver fought for control. Still spinning, he roared down an embankment and stopped at the bottom.

"Suspect's car has stopped. All units, approach with caution, subject is heavily armed and may be carrying explosives on his person." Nate's voice carried loud and clear, then Kate heard the sound of a car door opening, and traffic rushing by.

"Department of Homeland Security. Come out with

your hands up!" Kate heard his voice, electronically modified as if he were speaking through a bullhorn. In the distance, she heard a faint cry.

"Allahu Akb—!"

The shout was cut off by an explosion that made Kate snatch her earpiece off her head, gasping in shock. As she watched the satellite image, the sedan erupted in a glowing, gold ball of flame forcing everyone to retreat. Kate inserted the earpiece again. "Tracy? Tracy, are you there?"

"Yeah, Stephanie—yeah, I'm here. Jesus, he just blew himself up. Must have been a grenade or a bomb or something, I don't know. But he's gone and he took any evidence we might have found with him."

"Listen, you have to get over to Spaceworks—they're a rocket company. We think al-Kharzi is planning a low-earth-orbit strike to spread an EMP wave over the eastern United States."

"Could these guys have come from there?"

"Right now it's our strongest hunch. Did you manage to get a look at the car's license plate?"

"There wasn't time, but the camera in the Silverado probably got it. Nate, we need to get out of here."

"I'm downloading the address and directions from your location now. Try to coordinate the Border Patrol and any other DHS agents in the area if you can, but go in quietly—we can't tip them off, or they might launch early. Brief everyone there on keeping the press out of this for now—we don't want to cause a panic."

"Got it. Nate, let's roll!"

"Oh, one more thing," Kate said.

"Yeah."

"Reverse that code, one-five-nine, to turn off the cell-jamming program."

"Thanks, Stephanie, we'll be in touch once we're at Spaceworks."

"We'll be watching over you," Kate said.

Before Kate hung up, she heard Nate say, "Hey, that isn't too far from here, maybe about fifteen minutes southwest."

I hope that's quick enough, she thought, turning her attention to crafting a message that would bring every law-enforcement officer in the area running, and hoping to God that she wouldn't have to broadcast it.

32

Nate kept his eyes on the road while Tracy skimmed through the camera data, searching for the license plate. "Here it is. Call the plate number in," she said.

He read off the plate number to the DHS office and requested a priority response. A few minutes later it came back as a personal vehicle belonging to Zakariya Malik Jasfari. "Where does this guy work?" Nate asked. He heard keystrokes in the background. "Okay, that's everything we need. Thanks very much," he said. He turned to Tracy and said, "Bingo!"

He switched channels while he punched up the address for Spaceworks, Inc. "All units in the area, I need immediate backup at the following address on a code thirteen. I repeat, this is a code thirteen." Nate used the common law-enforcement code to refer to a possible disaster situation. "Request hazmat team respond, as well. All units converge at the junction road that leads to the target area." He replaced the mike and nodded to Tracy. "At least these guys are in the middle of the desert, and not right in town.

I'd get on the horn with your feebee buddy and get us a search warrant for the entire premises, if she can."

Tracy was already dialing. "Shouldn't be a problem, especially since we only have to mention the *nuke* word." She connected in a few seconds. "Stephanie? We're following up on the Spaceworks lead, and our fleeing terrorist apparently worked for them…. Yes, a search warrant—you're already working on it? Great, fax it to the El Paso DHS office, and we'll have someone run it out here…Will be in touch as soon as we've secured the area." She disconnected.

"Okay, we're almost there." Nate scanned the barren desert on both sides, looking for the dirt road driveway. "Come on, where the hell are you?"

"Right there." Tracy pointed at a narrow road to their right, which barely looked like anything special compared to the rest of the stark landscape.

"Hmm, not even a sign pointing out the road to anyone coming out here. Not a very effective way to advertise your company, is it?"

Tracy looked at the dirt road that climbed a hill and disappeared over the crest. The glow of bright lights could be seen in the distance. She glanced back at Nate. "I hope you don't want to handle this like the illegals back at the farm."

"Well, if we're only a couple of miles away from an organized terrorist cell, perhaps a more measured approach might be in order. We'll drive parallel to the road close to the top of that rise and see what we can see. Once the cavalry arrives, then we can go in full bore and shut them down."

Tracy nodded. "Works for me."

Turning off the headlights, Nate put his night-vision goggles on and drove onto the driveway just long enough

to get off the main road, Then he turned into the desert
itself, powering up the rise until they were only about
twenty yards from the crest. He stopped the truck and
checked his pistol. "Close enough. Ready?"

"After what we did earlier, I'm ready for just about
anything." Tracy made sure her pistol was locked and
loaded, and slipped out of the truck. Nate waited for her
to join him, his shotgun slung over his back, and they
began creeping up the rise.

33 ⅠⅠ ⅠⅠ65 ⅠⅠ Ⅰ ■ Ⅰ 59ⅠⅠ ⅠⅠ ■Ⅰ ⅠⅠ Ⅰ ■

Surely Allah will not let this transgression happen—not when we are so close.

Sepehr could scarcely believe that the events of the past half hour had even occurred, much less that they had resulted in what he was watching at the moment.

It had all started with Joseph coming back into the sound booth after Sepehr had recorded his triumphant message to the world. Instead of his neat attire and hair from yesterday, the owner of Spaceworks was now haggard and unshaved, dressed in rumpled clothes, with dark circles under his eyes from staying up for over twenty-four hours. "Sepehr, you must see this!"

He turned on the television mounted on the wall, and a local television station showed footage of the Providence Memorial Hospital, followed by the burning remains of a destroyed car. Joseph turned up the volume, letting the news anchor fill them in.

"Witnesses reported hearing gunfire on the third floor of the hospital, followed by a loud explosion. One of the two men suspected to have caused the blast was killed at the scene, while the other fled, pursued by law-enforcement officers until he was driven off the road, where his car exploded. Police and fire crew are on the scene. Police are not releasing any further details at this time, but we expect a press conference to be called about this incident later this morning—"

"We had not received any calls from either man before their deaths, correct?" Sepehr asked.

"I'm afraid not."

"Then we do not know if they were successful in completing their mission."

"But the blast—that surely must have come from a grenade," Joseph said.

"It is not confirmation that the woman—if there even was one in the first place—is dead. However, that does not matter now, when we are so close to launch—" Sepehr stopped when he saw the look on Joseph's face. "What?"

"That was what I was coming in to tell you before I saw the news report. We're having a slight problem with the gimbal nozzle control system. If it's not working perfectly, we will not be able to control the direction of the rocket."

Sepehr took a deep breath. "How long until it is fixed?"

"It should not be long—ten, perhaps fifteen minutes at the most."

"Very well. Once that is solved, I want you to move to launch immediately. We do not know if we have been compromised by the trap the Americans laid for us."

Joseph's cell phone rang, a harsh, jarring tone that made him look down in surprise. "That's a priority security alert. Come on!"

Sepehr was already moving before the other man stopped talking, running past Joseph to push the door open and head for the main lobby. Once there, he swiped his ID card through and ran to the station, where the night guard was watching a bank of monitors inset into the console.

"Sirs, one of the thermal cameras has detected intruders approximately one mile from the outside perimeter. They are observing the base. They appear to be using night-vision equipment, and are armed with handguns."

Sepehr's fingers curled into fists as he resisted the urge to shove the man out of the way. "Show me," he said.

"On this screen."

He stared at the pair, showing up in stark red, yellow and orange against the blacks and dark blues of the surrounding desert. One of them watched the compound through binoculars. The other lay beside him, just looking down at the compound.

Surely we are being tested. Before our ultimate victory, we must face all manner of obstacles in our path, he thought. Sepehr's head snapped up. "Joseph, order your men to fix the problem with the rocket as soon as possible. Launch the moment you are ready." He turned to the security man. "Send a team out in the hybrid to eliminate these two. Prepare the sniper teams on the roof, but do not let them take their positions until these two are dead. If the Americans want to sniff around our door like dogs, then we must be prepared to welcome them."

"So far everything looks normal. Here, take a look."

Tracy took the binoculars from Nate and focused on the object that most interested her—the rocket. About three stories tall, it certainly looked as if it could roar up and spread electromagnetic chaos across the land with ease. She panned across the rest of the compound, looking for security points and any weaknesses.

"I see the guard post with two men inside, a steel arm gate and, behind that, what looks like a pop-up barrier to stop anything heavy from entering the perimeter. Pretty elaborate for a private company. Looks like the guard at the main gate is reporting in—security isn't lax, that's for sure. Not much other activity. I'd have thought there would be people around the rocket, checking it out and such."

Nate ducked down behind the hill. "Maybe they aren't launching tonight, which would be great—we could take them out without worrying about that thing taking off. Hey, did you hear something?"

Tracy lowered the field glasses and glanced around them. "Something like what?"

"I don't know, some kind of hum. The desert plays a lot of tricks on your senses, messes with the direction you hear things coming from, that sort of thing. I just thought I heard a low humming noise, like some kind of generator."

"It might have been from down there," Tracy said.

"Yeah, but it didn't sound like it came from down there. It sounded like it came from—"

Behind them, the Silverado's hood suddenly buckled and popped up, and Tracy heard the metallic noise of bullets hitting the engine and windshield. Ducking down behind the slope, she looked back to see the driver's-side tires blow out, making the truck lean to one side. But she didn't hear the loud report of an automatic rifle, nor did she see the flash of the weapon. She scooted farther down the rise. "Where's it coming from?"

Nate had pulled out his shotgun, which he clutched in helpless anger. "Looks like about ten o'clock, somewhere over there. They've flanked us, they got our range, and now our wheels are gone, so we're stuck until the reinforcements arrive."

The firing had stopped for the moment, and Tracy risked a quick peek in that direction. "Even with the night vision it's tough to see—wait a minute, I got someone. Looks like a three-man team, driver, spotter and shooter, all in a four-wheel-drive. I think the bastards are playing with us."

"They might as well. We can't use the other side of the hill as cover, and it seems that they have either night vision or thermal, too. We're pinned down here. We need some kind of diversion."

"Like an explosion?" Tracy held out the fragmentation grenade she had taken from the dead terrorist at the hospital.

Nate grabbed it out of her hand. "That'll do. I'll hurl this as far as I can over there. When it goes off, run for the truck. We should be able to hold them off from there. Give it a two-count after the blast so you don't get hit by shrapnel. Ready?"

Nate pulled the pin, reared up on his knees and threw the grenade overhand toward the shooter. He hit the dirt and covered his ears. A few seconds later, the detonation kicked up a plume of dirt and dust. Hands over her ears, Tracy counted silently in her head—one…two…go!

She ran for the hulk of the disabled Silverado. Nate's long legs pounded the dirt as he sprinted for cover beside her. She reached the truck a second after him, her chest heaving with the exertion. Pistol gripped tightly, she took up a position at the back and ducked out for a quick peek at their attackers.

"I got nothing back here. How about you?"

Nate's reply was cut off by the impact of high-velocity bullets against the Silverado, making them both hit the dirt as lead punched through the body panels of the truck above their heads.

Tracy spit dust from her mouth. "You sure this was the best idea?"

"Better than staying trapped on the open desert to be cut down. At least here, under some cover, we've got a chance. All we have to do now is wait for backup," Nate said.

"And if they come in to get us?"

"Then we take out as many as we can. If they really want us dead, they have to come over here to do it."

"That's a comforting thought." The firing had stopped and Tracy sat up with her back against the wheel, waiting for the next assault to begin. Instead of automatic-rifle fire, she heard tires crunching on the dirt, but no engine noise. As she started to turn to look under the truck to see what was coming, a small four-wheel-drive with an open top raced out of the darkness at the Silverado. A man in the back was leveling a long-barreled assault rifle at her.

"Down!" Tracy shouted and rolled back as the 7.62 mm bullets ripped through the back of the vehicle, shattering the windows and sending glass cascading down on her. Prone, she raised her pistol and fired four shots in the terrorists' direction, more out of the need to mount some kind of defense than hoping to actually hit something. She heard a loud roar next to her, and figured Nate must have let loose, as well. The oddly quiet vehicle veered off to the right, back into the desert, moving out of range in seconds.

"Dammit, where's that backup?" Nate thumbed more rounds into his smoking shotgun as he looked in all directions—whether for other Border Patrol agents or their attackers, Tracy wasn't sure.

She strained her ears for the sound of the vehicle, but heard nothing. "We have to do something or else they're going to chop us to pieces here," she said.

"I'm open to suggestions at this point," Nate said.

Tracy sniffed the air, inhaling a familiar acrid odor. "They hit the gas tank. The next time we'd have shot, we'd blow up with it."

Nate produced a lighter and a cheroot. "Then let's help it along."

Tracy glanced under the truck and saw a steady trickle of gas leaking from the tank. She dug a furrow in the dirt to make the gas flow toward them, improvising a fuse. Crawling backward, she extended the small trench as far as she could, with Nate covering her until the quiet sound of the approaching off-roader reached her ears, followed by the unnerving noise of more bullets tearing apart the truck.

Tracy saw the other vehicle slowly approaching the truck while the gunner on top chewed it up with short bursts from his rifle. She saw the driver was wearing night-vision goggles similar to hers. "Let's see how you like watching this. Now, Nate!"

Nate flicked his lighter and touched the flame to the trail of gas, then they both scooted away from the booby-trapped vehicle as fast as they could without drawing attention to themselves. The flare of the gas showed up white-hot in her night-vision goggles, and Tracy flipped them up at the last minute and looked away, shielding her face and head with her arms.

The truck's gas tank ignited with a dull whoomp and blew out the back of the cargo bed, flames licking all around the remains of the vehicle. Tracy felt the patter of shrapnel on her back and legs, and twisted around, making sure no burning debris had hit her.

"Come on, get up!"

She looked up to see Nate standing and ready to charge in.

"You go left, I'll go right. Shoot as soon as you have a target!"

And with that he was gone, circling around the burning wreck. Goddamn cowboy, she thought, but got up and, holding her pistol low, trotted the other way, using the flames for cover as she tried to see around the inferno. She took another step out, and saw the hood of the four-wheel drive. One more step and she spotted the driver rubbing his eyes with one hand while trying to maneuver the stubby SUV away from the blazing vehicle. The gunner had apparently been more alert. He wasn't wearing his night-vision goggles and spotted Tracy at the same time she saw him. With a shout, he leveled his rifle at her as she brought her pistol up, knowing that she was about to die but wanting to take this bastard out if she could—

A shotgun blast boomed, and the rifleman jerked in his harness, the rifle barrel wavering as he triggered his weapon, sending a burst of bullets into the dust about three yards from where Tracy stood. She lined up the SIG Sauer's sights on his upper chest, squeezed the trigger twice and was rewarded with another jerk from the gunman. Shifting her pistol down a few inches, she put three bullets into the driver's side of the windshield, making the four-wheel-drive vehicle slowly drift away as the driver slumped over the wheel. The passenger's door popped open, and a third man staggered out, holding a short-barreled submachine gun. Blood flowed down the side of his face, looking dark in the firelight.

"Homeland Security. Drop the weapon and raise your hands!" Tracy shouted, aiming right at him. Hearing her voice, he stepped up to the hood of his vehicle and aimed the subgun at her.

Tracy's pistol and Nate's shotgun roared at the same instant, and the terrorist stiffened under the impact of the bullet and buckshot, the pellets tearing at his face. He slid from sight behind the vehicle.

"Cover me!" Tracy ran to the front of the off-roader, then, keeping her pistol trained on the man, moved up and kicked the subgun out of his hands. It was unnecessary, however—he was already dead.

"Other two are gone, as well." Nate came around the side. "You better reload—we're not done here by a long shot."

He pointed back down the slope toward the road, and Tracy glanced back to see a procession of police, CBP vehicles and a SWAT team van, all with their lights off, coming toward them.

She looked back at Nate, covered in dust and sweat, and sighed. "About goddamn time."

35

"I'm telling you, Kate, if these two make it out of this in one piece, I'm recruiting both of them. Improvisational skills, dead shots, able to think and react on their feet— they're both naturals."

Denny had logged in to assist with the coordination of what was suddenly turning into a major U.S. government field operation, and had watched in admiration as the two agents had taken out the Spaceworks security team.

The Room 59 hackers had grabbed a row of geosynchronous satellites that would be passing over or near the area, and set up a chain of surveillance to keep an eye on the situation.

"Shut that dangling jaw of yours and let's keep our eyes on the prize. There's still a loose nuke on that site, and if we're not careful, they might just set it off to make sure they destroy something," Kate said.

"You don't really think he'd do it, do you?" Denny asked as he tapped keys at his office in D.C.

"No, not unless he had no other choice. While impressive, it's still in the desert, far enough away from the city proper that there wouldn't be that many casualties, and they could most likely evacuate the closest neighborhoods without too much difficulty. If he was crazy enough to actually come here to see that rocket off, my guess is he's not going to immolate himself in the blast. No, he wants to set that sucker off above D.C. or New York City, or both if he can manage it."

Denny nodded. "I agree, which means he's probably got an escape route planned. I better put one of our boys on finding that—oops, gotta go, my federal judge is calling on line two. I'll let you know how it goes." He turned to another screen, but not before Kate heard him greet the man on the other end of the line, affecting a slight Texas twang as he did. "Marty, how the hell are ya? Sorry to bother you this early in the morning, but we got a bit of a situation in your neck of the woods—"

Whether it's tax cuts to Democrats or welfare programs to Republicans, Denny can sell damn near anything to anyone. Kate smiled as she touched the screen linking her to B2S, secure in the knowledge that the federal search warrant was as good as signed.

"How's it going?" she asked. The words transcribed into text on her screen.

"Better if my boss wasn't breathing down my neck." The reply brought Kate up short—B2S usually wasn't that curt.

"Give me a sitrep."

"That 128-bit encryption was taking too long to hack, so I thought I'd do a back door—find out who programmed the system, and break their sysop code for instant access."

"And?" Kate asked.

"I haven't found anything yet. Whoever did this was

good enough to find and eliminate the normal programmer back doors. Their own are very, very well hidden. I'm still working on the front door, and have been searching for the back way in—there's gotta be one, but it's a riddle wrapped in a mystery wrapped in an enigma."

Kate felt the first pang of doubt spike her stomach with a needle-sharp sting. "Are you telling me you can't break it?"

"I can, but I can't give you a good estimate of how long it will take. Might be five minutes, might be thirty—"

"That's about twenty-five more than we have. Keep at it, and you let me know the instant you're in," Kate said.

"Okay. Want the rocket dxed once I'm there?"

Even though she was concerned about the lack of progress, Kate couldn't help smiling at B2S's logical leap. "Negative. Establish operational control, but do not get caught, and if it launches, let it proceed as planned."

"Got ya. I'll let you know when I'm in."

"Right." Kate let the young woman work and rubbed her temples for a moment. It wasn't that B2S wouldn't gain access—there wasn't a system made yet that she couldn't break, but it was how long she might take to do it that could be the problem. Kate touched the screen again, and the night sky appeared in the window, along with an airspeed reading, longitude and latitude and digital compass pointing southwest. Kate split the screen and brought up a topographical map of the route that her midnight team, currently in a modified Lockheed C-130J Super Hercules, was traveling. At the moment, the GPS locator put them on the border between Oklahoma and Arkansas.

She opened a channel. "Midnight Rider One, this is Primary."

There was a brief pop of static, then the pilot replied.

"Copy that, Primary. This is MR-1, go ahead." Even with the sound baffles in the headset, Kate heard the roar of the four massive jet engines propelling the huge aircraft forward.

"Estimated time of arrival at drop point, MR-1?"

"ETA to drop point approximately ninety-four minutes, over."

"Copy that. Secondary cargo is on board and ready?"

There was a brief pause, then the pilot answered. "Affirmative, secondary cargo is on board." He paused again. "Are you issuing a target-elimination order, over?"

"Negative, MR-1. I say again, negative. I'm just checking over all of my options. Continue on your flight plan and await further instructions. Primary out."

"Roger that. MR-1 out."

Kate rubbed her hands together. The secondary cargo was a pair of GBU-32 smart bombs, each carrying a two-thousand-pound warhead. Guided by GPS coordinates and satellite tracking, one of those would be enough to flatten the main building of the Spaceworks compound, or destroy the rocket, although she would not call for a strike on the missile unless absolutely necessary, due to the high possibility of a nuclear-materials leak.

She turned her attention back to the cluster of vehicles and men that had gathered around her two floaters. They seemed to be planning their next steps. As if on cue, Kate's screen flashed, telling her that Tracy was calling.

"Agent Cassell."

"Stephanie, this is Tracy. We're at Spaceworks. We were attacked by their security forces, forcing us to defend ourselves. Our backup has arrived, and we're currently organizing the assault on the compound to arrest all suspects on the premises."

"Very well. Is there anything I can do on this end?"

"Yes, mobilize any other law-enforcement officers or agents that have not been informed of the situation. Also, get me plans of the site and each building here."

"More reinforcements are on the way." Kate had already sent out a radio call for all available law-enforcement personnel in the area to report to the site. "Believe me, soon you'll have more people there than you'll know what to do with. Remember, you're the agent in charge at the scene, and don't let anyone bulldoze you. Also, check your phone once we're off this call. The plans will be there, and you'll be able to download them wirelessly to any computer you wish."

"Believe me, that isn't going to happen here. I'll report in once we've secured the area."

"Good luck and good hunting." Kate signed off and sat down, her eyes glued to the Spaceworks site, the ever-increasing number of police, Customs and Border Protection and FBI vehicles arriving, and the rocket with its deadly payload, still sitting quietly on the tarmac, waiting to be launched.

36

Sepehr was livid as he watched the infidels kill his security team, but he kept his voice and fists under control. "Not as weak as I had first thought," he said under his breath.

Beside him, Joseph paced back and forth. "What are we going to do? This wasn't how it was supposed to happen!"

"Patience, my friend. The Americans will want a peaceful resolution. They will try to negotiate first, to resolve this without violence. They may even think this is a misunderstanding that can be resolved by talking with us. However, any attempt will be met with weapons. You've told me the defenses you have out there."

"Sepehr, do you see what I see out there?" Joseph pointed at the screens, which showed a large and ever-growing contingent of federal and local law-enforcement officers setting up a mobile headquarters. They heard the beat of rotor blades as a helicopter passed overhead. "They're not going to wait this out like Waco or Ruby Ridge. They're coming in here, and they will kill all of us!"

"Then we will die in the service of Allah, if he has

willed it, and when we open our eyes next, we will be in Paradise." Sepehr's eyes narrowed. "I am sure that every man here is willing to give his life for our cause. Are you telling me that you have doubts about our mission?"

"No, of course not. It's just that I didn't think we would be discovered before we'd had the chance to launch. Now they may stop the whole thing," Joseph said.

"No, that will not happen." Sepehr turned to the guard manning the console. "Deploy the sniper teams on the roof, with orders to destroy anything that approaches the outer perimeter. It doesn't matter who they are, local police, FBI, Border Patrol—anyone is a target now. The guards at the front gate are also authorized to use whatever means necessary to repel the infidels."

He turned to Joseph. "Get me an update of the repairs to the rocket. We must launch as soon as possible." He grabbed the other man's arm, halting his aimless pacing. "Do not lose heart now. We are so close to achieving everything we have worked for, what you have labored your entire life to create. I need you to believe for only a few more minutes, then we are done."

Joseph stared into Sepehr's burning brown eyes, then, as if gathering strength from his will, nodded. "My belief in the jihad is infinite, brother. We will show the infidels the glory of Islamic might this day."

"Good." Sepehr leaned close and spoke his next words into Joseph's ear. "Make sure the tunnel is prepared, in the event we will need to leave quickly."

"Everything is ready. We just need that damn rocket to be ready, and we will strike a blow against America that they will never forget," Joseph said.

"Inshallah," Sepehr replied. "As Allah wills, so shall it be."

37

Tracy snapped her phone closed and walked over, with Nate in tow, to a group of SWAT team members who had just exited their van. Behind them, a smaller armored truck pulled up. "Who's in charge of your unit?" Tracy asked.

A Latino man a few years younger than Nate stepped forward, dressed in the usual SWAT uniform of black fatigues with a bulletproof tactical vest, elbow and knee pads, a submachine gun slung over his shoulder, a pistol at his side and a Kevlar helmet on his head. "Sergeant Jose Elidondo. And you are?" His tone wasn't confrontational, merely neutral.

Tracy held out her identification. "Special Agent Tracy Wentworth, Department of Homeland Security, and ranking agent in charge of this operation."

Although Tracy saw a few eye-rolls from the other team members, Elidondo absorbed this information without a pause. "What's the situation?"

"There are anywhere from a half-dozen to thirty armed and barricaded terrorists in this compound that need to be neutralized. There is also the strong possibility of hazardous materials on site."

"Chemical?" the sergeant asked.

"Radioactive," Tracy replied.

That got a reaction out of the previously unflappable SWAT leader. His eyebrows rose. "Confirmed?"

Tracy barely hesitated, then nodded at the wreckage of their truck. "That's their security team's handiwork. They fired on us without provocation—it's why you're out here now."

The sergeant glanced over the smoldering remains. "Okay, call the ball."

"Sergeant, I don't want to tell you how to do your job, but I need the people inside that fence captured or eliminated as soon as possible. However you choose to accomplish that is fine with me. There is one stipulation, however." She gave him a photo. "If this man is seen on the premises, take all care to capture him alive."

Tracy heard surprised muttering from the rest of the team. One tall man said, "Someone from DHS is actually gonna let us do our jobs? What alternate universe is this?"

They were quieted by a look from their superior before he turned back to Tracy. "You're sure this is the way you want to go? You don't want to try and negotiate?"

"We cannot afford to give them any more time. Even now, they may very well be on the way to putting their plan into action." She pointed to the nose of the rocket, jutting up above the hill.

"Holy shit." Elidondo's eyes widened. "Take out everyone inside except your guy—got it. What about the rocket?"

"We've already got people working on that," Tracy said.

"Okay, what can you tell us about the site?"

"I have detailed files. You boys got a laptop or patrol

computer? What I can't tell you is the level of weapons or any after-construction security details that may have been added."

"Right this way, Agent Wentworth." Briggs, the tall man who had scoffed at her, opened the back door of the van and pointed to a console built into the wall behind the passenger seat. He gave her a USB cable to hook into. Tracy used the touch screen on her phone to send the files to the SWAT computer, then got out of the way as they all clustered around the screen. Elidondo printed copies, distributed them and outlined the insertion with swift strokes, creating a three-pronged assault in a few minutes. He led his squad out and joined a half-dozen more men. All of them gathered around as the plan was reviewed and copies of the building's schematics were distributed. Four got into a small armored truck and drove back out into the desert. The helicopter that had been circling overhead was directed to land on the other side of the road. Three snipers, each carrying a Remington M700 rifle with telescopic sights, headed out to the rise with their spotters, giving the smoking remains of Nate's truck a wide berth.

"You know some of these boys ain't gonna come back." Nate stood beside her, his arms folded, as they watched the teams prep for the assault.

"I'm trying not to dwell on that at the moment. If necessary, I'm prepared to sacrifice all of them to get the job done. They knew the risks when they signed up. If they pull this off, they'll have saved hundreds of thousands of lives." Tracy's words were strong, but they belied the hollow feeling inside at sending those men off to perhaps die in the next few minutes. "What I need is a way to watch what's happening."

"Ma'am, you can follow our teams on the internal monitors here." Briggs must have overheard her remark.

"Deal, but only if you never call me that again. 'Tracy' will be fine."

"Yes, ma— Agent Wentworth."

With a shrug, Tracy climbed into the back of the SWAT van, which was equipped with more than the standard bench seats and storage lockers. Next to the lockers were three small monitors, each corresponding to one of the teams that were about to make their move.

"I can't recall the last time we had to use all three of these," the tall officer said as he adjusted one of them for a cleared picture. "Team Alpha, you are online. Team Bravo, you are online. Team Charlie, you are online. All copy."

A chorus of affirmatives answered the ops officer, then they heard Elidondo, who had taken a position in the armored truck that was going to breach the front gate. "All teams assume your positions and commence operation on my mark."

There was a moment of silence, and Tracy heard the roar of the truck as it powered up the rise.

"Briggs, let your sergeant know that they have a pop-up barrier at the main entrance."

"Thank you, Agent, that was already noted on the plans you provided. They'll be accessing the grounds through the cyclone fence after eliminating the guard post."

"I thought you weren't going to tell them how to do their job," Nate muttered, but Tracy was too intent on the images unfolding before her to take the bait.

The helicopter had picked up the members who would assault from the roof, and now waited for the word to swoop down and disgorge its heavily armed passengers to seize the high ground. The truck was waiting to roar in to breach the fence near the front gate, while the third team would enter at the rear of the compound and access the main building, sweeping forward to catch the occupants by surprise and overwhelm them with superior forces and firepower.

Sergeant Elidondo radioed all the teams one last time, making sure they were in position, then gave the order. "Execute, execute, execute!"

The truck lunged over the dune, heading off-road to ram a portion of the fence. Immediately they began taking fire from the guardhouse. What looked like blasts from assault rifles ricocheted off the front armor and bulletproof glass of the truck. "Goddamn, they put out the welcome mat for us!" Tracy heard the driver exclaim. She heard the SWAT snipers on another channel, and as she watched, one of the riflemen was taken out with a well-placed shot into the viewport.

"Be advised, be advised, there are gunmen on the roof. Repeat, gunmen on the roof, Team Bravo," the ops officer radioed.

"Roger that—see three emplacements, two front, one back. Will disembark between all three—they'll never know what hit 'em."

The truck screamed down the hill, but when it was about thirty yards from the fence, Tracy heard a loud explosion, followed by a column of dirt and flame erupting under the truck's front tire. The vehicle tilted on two wheels, and for a moment it looked as if the driver might have been able to bring it back down upright, but then it rolled over on its side, crashing to the ground with an earthshaking impact and skidding to a stop.

Tracy heard everything as it went down.

"Team Alpha, Team Alpha, what is your status? Can anyone hear me in there, over?"

"Tag Team One to Base, have eliminated one guard in the gate post, over."

"This is Air One. We are in initial descent—what the hell was that, over? Jesus Christ! They've got heavy weapons up here. Repeat, heavy weapons, possibly .50-caliber rifles."

A huge report echoed over the small valley and the helicopter pilot yelled into his mike, "Base, this is Air One. We are taking fire from heavy weapons on the roof. Repeat, taking heavy fire—" A scream came from the helicopter, and the steady pitch of the rotors became labored and whining. "Air One to Base, Air One to Base. Mayday, Mayday, we are going down. Repeat, we are going down! Return fire, dammit, return fire!"

Throughout it all, Briggs remained as calm as anyone Tracy had ever seen. "Roger that, Air One. Can you make it outside the perimeter and regroup with Team Charlie, over?"

Tracy tore her gaze away from the monitors and looked out the front window to see bright flashes flare on the roof, followed by a series of concussive reports that overpowered everything else in the area. The helicopter, its rotors laboring to keep it aloft, sideslipped and lumbered away from the roof of the building, smoke trailing from its lower fuselage, no longer the swift, powerful bird of war it had been only a few seconds ago.

"Flash-bangs to cover their withdrawal. Good idea." Nate shielded his eyes as he watched the debacle unfold. They didn't hear a crash or see an explosion, which made Tracy dare to believe the pilot had put the bird down safely.

"TacCom, this is Alpha. We are pinned down approximately thirty yards from the gate. Lofgrend is injured and cannot move—oh, shit. RPG, there is an RPG at the main gate!"

"I'm on it." This came from one of the snipers, followed by a single gunshot a few moments later. "RPG is down."

"…Thanks, Tag Team. We still need evac ASAP…."

Tracy shielded her eyes from the glow of the firefight and tried to make sense out of everything that was happening. The well-thought-out plan was disintegrating before her eyes. The terrorists were dug in, and it might be hours, perhaps days until they could get a force inside, giving their adversaries plenty of time to get that rocket off the ground. They needed to do something immediately. But what?

"This is bulllshit!" Nate got up and stalked to the back doors of the truck. Tracy followed, only dimly aware of the SWAT officer trying to regroup the remaining men.

"All Border Patrol, on me! Form up right here." In less than thirty seconds Nate had a dozen men and women around him. "All right, this is what we've been expecting ever since 9/11. We've got terrorists back on our home soil, and we're gonna take 'em out. Everyone wearing vests, raise your hands." A half-dozen arms shot up. "All right, you're with me in the insertion team. Everyone else, you'll follow behind and extract the SWAT team in the truck."

"Hey, who says you get to be the hero here?" Billy Travis shouldered his way to the front of the group.

"I don't have time to bulldog you, Travis. Either you got a vest and you're with me, or you don't and you're on second team. That's the way it is."

Travis thumped his chest, revealing the bulky outline of a vest under his shirt. "I never come to a party unprepared," he said.

"Well, get these boys into an SUV and wait for my signal. All right, people, mount up. Use channel 26 for our comm. Move out in thirty seconds."

"Whoa, whoa." Tracy grabbed Nate's arm. "What are you going to do?"

"Try to turn this cluster-fucked op around before it's too late." Nate headed back to the large SWAT van. "You can sit this one out back here—it's liable to get real nasty down there," he said.

Frowning at the suggestion, Tracy thumped her chest, too. "In case you didn't notice, I raised my hand back there. Let's go."

Nate ran to the driver's side of the SWAT van and jumped up into the seat, twisting the ignition key. Briggs looked over in surprise. "What in the hell are you doing?"

"Officer, I'm commandeering this vehicle in the name of the United States government," Tracy said as she slapped a fresh magazine in her SIG Sauer and pulled the slide back. "You can stay on or get off—the choice is yours."

The lanky officer grabbed a lethal-looking HK MP-5N, rammed a 30-round stick magazine into the receiver and cocked the weapon. "Those are my people dying out there. Let's hit it."

Tracy nodded, and turned back to Nate. "Go!"

"Briggs, tell your back-door team to make their entrance in thirty seconds if they haven't done so already. And give me covering fire from all your snipers—I need those snipers on the roof to keep their heads down for a minute!" Nate bellowed.

"You got it!" Briggs began issuing orders to the rest of the SWAT teams on the perimeter.

"Extraction team, ready! Insertion team, ready! Go, go go!"

With that, Nate floored the gas pedal, making the huge van lurch up the rise between two of the sniper teams, who were firing steadily at the roof of the compound. The tall, black, armored behemoth reached the crest of the hill and seemed to pause a moment before plunging down into the valley of hellfire. As soon as it did, bullets began ricocheting off the windshield from several directions.

"What happens if a .50-caliber round comes at us?" Tracy asked the SWAT officer, who had buckled a helmet on. He grabbed a spare and quickly adjusted the inner webbing, then held it out to her.

"If it does, don't worry about it—you'll probably be dead before you even know what hit you."

"Glad I asked." Grabbing the Kevlar helmet, Tracy jammed it on her head and hunkered down behind Nate's seat, all too aware that it would be little protection. She braced herself for the impact of a huge bullet, but it didn't come—apparently the snipers were doing their job.

"Extraction team, as soon as I pass the truck, get to it and get them out of there!"

"Copy that, Nate."

"Insertion team, on me. Follow me through the hole."

Travis's voice came over the radio. "What hole? I don't see any hole!"

"The one I'm about to make, goddammit!" Nate goosed another burst of speed out of the van, pushing it to more than fifty-five miles per hour. Tracy and Briggs swayed back and forth as the vehicle lurched forward even faster. "Hang on back there!" Nate shouted.

Tracy saw the guard post looming dead ahead in the windshield. She ducked back and wedged herself into the corner of the cargo area. Across from her, Briggs had done the same thing, folding himself into a surprisingly compact ball. Their eyes met, and he actually dropped her a wink. "Here we go—"

The armored SWAT van hit the fortified guard post in a shriek of tortured metal and exploding concrete—the ultimate unstoppable force meeting an immovable object. Tracy was thrown hard into the back of the driver's chair, the breath driven out of her with the impact. Incredibly, the van was still moving forward. Peeking out, she saw a scratched and battered windshield, and the Spaceworks compound stretched out before them. Nate had plowed the guard post completely off its foundation. He lolled in the driver's seat, stunned by the impact.

"Order Team Charlie in!" Tracy said as she got up to check Nate, grabbing the radio mike at the same time. "Insertion team, the front door is open. Repeat, the front door is open."

"We're right behind you."

Briggs had recovered his earpiece from where it had been knocked out, and Tracy heard him order the backdoor team to make their way inside. Tracy checked Nate's body as gently as she could. "At least you wore your seat belt." She unbuckled him and held him up as he leaned forward, coughing for a moment.

"Wha's—did we do it?"

"Yes, you dumb son of a bitch, we certainly did," she replied.

Nate came more awake at her words, then his eyes cleared, and he looked around. "We're not done yet." He started to get up out of the seat, but groaned and folded his arms across his ribs.

"*We* aren't, but *you* are, buddy. You've got at least two cracked ribs, maybe a broken one. Time for you to hold the fort here, and we'll go in and wrap this up," Tracy said.

"Aw, hell, no. I started this, and I'm sure gonna finish it." Nate leaned back to find Briggs. "Hey, buddy, you

SWAT guys must have something to rev me up a bit, don't you?"

The officer went to a small backpack and opened a side pouch. "Lucky you snagged the medic, as well." He shook out two small blue pills and held them out. "Take these— they'll keep you going until this is over."

Nate picked them up and tossed both into his mouth, then stood with an effort and grabbed his shotgun from where he'd stored it beside the seat. "Let's go hunt us some terrorists."

38

"Sir, the roof teams report they have driven off the infidels' helicopter, but the front gate has been breached, and the enemy is inside the fence!"

The young man's voice was tight with fear, but he remained at his post on the security console, watching the assault unfold. Sepehr could hear the faint, sharp chatter of automatic rifle fire, punctuated by the deafening booms of the Barrett sniper rifles the three terrorists had smuggled into the country along with the nuclear weapon. He scanned the monitors, looking for the infidels. "Where are the biggest concentrations of Americans?"

"Team Three reports a large group of intruders at the rear fence, and the front guard station has just been destroyed by a vehicle that rammed into it. The Americans are crazy! What should we do?"

Sepehr glanced at Joseph, who seemed to be coming unhinged at the idea that his company was being invaded. He looked back at the young man, whose name he couldn't remember—Mamood, or something like that. "Order all of the men to fire at will on any infidel they see. They must keep the Americans away from the rocket at all costs."

He ran to Joseph and grabbed the other man by his shirt. The once-proud scientist was mumbling under his breath. "I can talk to them…explain that this was all a mistake…they'll listen to me…."

"Joseph—Joseph!" The other man stared at him dully. "What is the status of the guidance system?"

"Last I checked, they were almost done—just a couple more minutes—"

"And they have their orders to launch once the repairs are complete, yes?" Sepehr asked.

"Of course." Joseph flinched as another explosion shook the walls around them.

Sepehr turned back to the guard. "Mamood, do you truly believe in the glory of Islam and the righteousness of Allah?"

"With my very last breath."

"Good, I am entrusting you with this most sacred mission." Sepehr snatched a short-barreled AKS-74U from its clips under the table and thrust it at the man. "You must protect this room with everything you possess—above all else, the enemies of Islam must not be allowed past this point. Do this, and the highest respect and honors will be yours." He decided against adding "in Paradise." This one might be naive enough to believe that he could come through the onslaught outside in one piece. "I must get Joseph to safety, but I will radio you when the time comes to leave, all right?"

"Yes, sir." The young man took the weapon and checked the load, then hunkered down behind the console to await the coming invaders. Meanwhile, Sepehr took Joseph's elbow and steered him out of the room, making sure the security door closed behind him. Once inside, he smashed the key card panel with the butt of his pistol until it was completely destroyed.

Joseph stared at him in shock. "What—what are you doing?"

"I am sorry, my friend, but precautions have to be taken to insure that we are able to complete our divine mission." They heard the chatter of rifle fire from outside, then another explosion that made the hallway tremble. "Your man out there will be in the hands of Allah soon enough, and the rewards of Paradise will far outweigh any pleasures he might have known in his life here. You said the tunnel is ready?"

"Of course, this way." Joseph took the lead, and Sepehr followed him past the main workroom to a small supply closet. Producing a different key card, he swiped it through the reader, making the red light turn to green. Opening the door revealed a small, empty space with a patterned metal floor and a hatch in the middle. Joseph bent down to open it, while Sepehr made sure no one was around.

"All right, everything is ready. I've even set the trap on the door—once we go through, we cannot go back." Joseph turned back to him. "We must leave now."

"Contact your team once more," Sepehr urged. "To ensure that they have finished their task."

Joseph raised his cell phone and hit the walkie-talkie feature. "Guidance control?"

"Yes, sir?"

"Give me a status report on repairs to the nozzle guidance system."

"Sir, the fix has been made, and the entire system is functioning perfectly. The rocket will go to full launch status in the next sixty seconds."

"You have done well. As soon as the launch status is

confirmed, initiate ignition cycle, I repeat, initiate ignition cycle as soon as you have confirmed launch status. Once done, you will take up arms and fight the infidels as long as possible. The rocket must take off unmolested."

"Yes, sir."

Joseph flipped the phone closed. "You see, we have done it. Now, let us get out of here before it is too late."

Sepehr motioned at the square of darkness in front of them. "After you."

As Joseph turned to descend, Sepehr raised his pistol and fired point-blank into the back of Joseph's head. The founder of Spaceworks, Inc., died instantly, collapsing to the ground in a limp heap.

Sepehr dragged the body out into the hallway. "You see, my friend, precautions have to be taken, and leaving you here is the best way of insuring that no one comes looking for me." He walked back inside the room, closed the door behind him and climbed through the hatch, pulling it shut above him once he was completely inside the narrow tunnel.

39

Every step sent a stab of pain shooting through Nate's side, but he didn't slow down as they ran across the compound to the front door. Made of heavy steel, he thought, it looked damn near impregnable. Reaching it first, he took up a position on the left side, and looked for a keypad or card slot or any other way of getting in. He was joined by Tracy, Briggs, Travis and four other Border Patrol agents. Around them, the battle raged as the snipers on the roof exchanged fire with the riflemen on the perimeter.

"Okay, hotshot, you got us this far. Now how are we opening this sucker?" Travis asked.

"Can't exactly take a SWAT door knocker to it." Briggs rapped on the door, getting only the heavy, distant echo of thick metal. "I doubt the Barretts could get through this."

"No, but I know someone who can." Tracy grabbed her cell phone and turned to Nate. "Send someone up to take out those emplacements. If—"

"We come at them from the side, we should be able to get the drop on them. I'm on it," Nate said.

Travis gestured for two other agents to follow him, but was stopped by Nate's hand on his shoulder.

"That hero bug better not be catching. I expect to see you back down here in one piece," Nate said.

"Don't worry, old man, someone's gotta look good at the press conferences. Come on, boys." The cocky Border Patrol agent led his small team around the corner and into the darkness.

Nate turned back to Tracy, waving at her with a "hurry up" motion. She was on the phone.

"No, the rocket is still on the ground, but we need access to the main door. Haven't your people accessed their security yet? Look, we don't have a few more seconds—just run the override on the door's maintenance program—"

Shouts and automatic-weapons fire made everyone duck, and Nate, Tracy and Briggs all scanned around, looking for the threat. "Come on, come on," Tracy muttered, keeping the phone glued to her ear. "I know the government is slow, but they have to get something done sometime."

Over their radios, they heard, "Front door, this is Team Charlie. We have accessed the back door, and are on-site, over."

Nate keyed his radio. "Roger, sweep forward, and we'll come to you from the front and meet in the main control room, over." Just when he was about to suggest trying to find another way in, the main door jerked up several inches, then stopped, then rose another three feet before grinding to a halt.

"Good enough, Stephanie, thanks." Tracy put her phone away while Briggs handed Nate a flash-bang grenade.

"Just pull and throw it inside. Ready?"

Nate nodded, and the two men pulled the pins and tossed the grenades into the room, ducking and covering before detonation. The million-candlepower flashes lit up the area like a miniature supernova, their deafening blasts echoing in the enclosed space.

Nate took his hands away from his ears and whistled. "Damn, that's gotta fuck up your whole day. Let's see who's inside. Briggs, you go left. I'll go right. Tracy, come in behind us and cover the middle. Take out anyone you deem to be a threat."

He ducked under the door, leading with his shotgun. The recessed halogen lights in the room flickered on and off, lending a surreal look to the area, now wreathed in smoke from the flash-bangs. A security console stood on one side of the main doors, and next to it was another formidable-looking metal door. Nate swept and cleared his side of the room, confident that Briggs was doing his part on the right and that Tracy had the middle covered, as well. "Clear left!" he called out.

"Clear right!" Briggs responded.

"Moving to—" Tracy froze as a flash of motion from the floor console alerted them that they weren't alone.

Nate swiveled his gun over just in time to see a swarthy, bearded man bringing up a stubby assault rifle, aimed at Tracy, and spitting fire and bullets in Tracy's direction. Without thinking, he aimed from the hip at the shooter's upper chest and squeezed the trigger. He cycled the slide and let the man have another, his shotgun's boom overwhelming the popping sound of the AK-variant weapon. The man staggered backward, his chest erupting in bloody spatter as buckshot caved in his ribs and pulped his lungs and heart. He fired the last few bullets of his magazine into the air, then fell on his back and died.

Briggs, his pistol smoking, ran to Tracy. "Jesus, are you all right?"

She stood with her own pistol out and smoke curling from the barrel. "I—I think so. I don't think I was hit. How is that possible?"

Nate pointed at the wall above her head, where a cluster of bullet holes provided testimony as to what had just happened. "Jumpy on the trigger—brought the gun up and let the burst go too late. The muzzle climb sent the bullets into the wall. Happens to inexperienced shooters all the time." He motioned them forward, not wanting her to think about it too much. "Let's clear that console of any more surprises."

"Yeah." Tracy shook off the near miss and strode forward, flanked by Nate and Briggs. Nate made a mental note to keep an eye on her as they went. He knew when an agent started overthinking something like that, he or she ceased to be effective in a combat situation.

They paused at the side of the console nearest to them, then all three moved at once, Nate over the top, Tracy to the left and Briggs to the right. The console was empty.

Nate walked over to the large door. "Great, another friggin' security door. I don't suppose that guy's ID or key card survived, did it?"

Briggs knelt by the body, holding up a small shard of plastic. "I think this might have been part of it. Now what?"

"Tracy, get on the horn to your FBI buddy. Surely they can pop this one, too." While he waited, Nate keyed his radio. "Travis, how's it going up there?"

"We have secured the roof, and reinforcements are on the way. Four enemies killed, two wounded. We lost one, with one wounded."

"Good work. We're sweeping the rest of the building. Will radio when it's cleared. Send the others in as soon as they've swept the rest of the buildings. We don't want any ambushes. We're heading in to shut down the rocket guys. Spencer out."

"Roger that, and good hunting. Travis out."

"How's that door coming, Tracy?" Nate asked.

"Just open all of them—that should eliminate the problem." Tracy's tone could have cut through steel by itself, but it wasn't doing the trick this time. The door stayed closed. "We gotta get to those other guys right now," she said.

Nate took a closer look at the heavy doors. "These look like they slide into the wall."

"Yeah, so?" Tracy asked.

"Over, under, around or through." Nate rapped on the wall next to the door, hearing a hollow echo under his knuckles. "Get behind that console—just in case I'm wrong." He brought up his shotgun and fired a round to the left of the door, the double-aught pellets punching through the thin metal of the framing mechanism and out the other side. "I think we just found our way in." He racked the gun again and fired until his magazine was dry, enlarging the hole until it was big enough to climb through. Nate waved the others in as he reloaded.

Tracy and Briggs scrambled through the ragged hole, with Nate bringing up the rear. Just as they did, the security doors ground open with a whine, almost catching the border agent's leg. Nate snorted. "That's government work for you—always a day late and a dollar short."

"What's that say about you, buddy?" Briggs said over his shoulder as they went down the hallway, clearing each opened door as they went.

"Hell, I'm a subcontractor—"

"Shh!" The urgent whisper silenced both men instantly. Nate peered around. "What you got, Tracy?"

"A body." Tracy knelt by the outstretched form of a man with a round, bloody hole in the back of his head. She rolled him over to reveal a once-handsome man, his eyes glazed and sightless in death.

"This is Joseph Allen, the founder of Spaceworks." Tracy looked up at the nearest door, which was closed. She waited until Nate and Briggs had taken covering positions, then pulled the door open, revealing a small, empty room with a hatch in the floor. "A falling-out among terrorists, perhaps?" she said.

"Who knows, but I'll bet my next month's pay I know which way al-Kharzi went." Nate ran to the hatch. "You guys stop the launch. I'm going after him."

"Not alone you're not!" Tracy started to walk toward him, but Nate was already lifting the metal hatch. She heard a click before the world exploded around her. Tracy heard a deep thunderous roar from somewhere far away, echoing through the hallway and shaking the floor.

Oh, shit, she thought as she sank into darkness, *the rocket's launching. We're too late.*

40

"Preliminary data indicates that the SWAT team has taken control of the main control room, but they also reported that the rocket completed its launch cycle and lifted off twenty-three seconds ago. If its intended target is the Washington, D.C.–New York corridor, we have approximately eight minutes before optimal altitude and geographic coordinates are reached. Here's the projected flight path."

A radar screen popped up on Kate's monitor. It showed a red line arcing out from El Paso on a direct route over the Midwest toward the East Coast. A three-year-old could have drawn a line indicating where it was going to end up.

Denny sounded as stressed as Kate had ever heard him—which wasn't much, as the military-man-turned-businessman had seen too much in his lifetime to really be fazed by anything anymore. "I hope you stocked up on bottled water, because if this thing does go off, it'll make the '03 power outage look like a flicker."

"What about a self-destruct? Doesn't every rocket have one, in case it goes out of control?" Kate asked.

"Sure, if it's a government-backed one. Private companies are supposed to, but since we're dealing with terrorists posing as rocket scientists, who the hell knows? The SWAT guys said the scientists have locked down the computers, and they aren't giving up the password."

"Well, where's our two cowboys? After everything they've done, sweating the access out of an engineer geek should be a walk in the park for them," Kate said.

Denny bent over his own monitor, keeping track of three camera feeds and a half-dozen audio streams at once. "Radio chatter says they heard a secondary blast right after they secured the room, but before the rocket launched. They're investigating right now."

"Get every hacker on duty targeting that rocket with anything they've got to bring it down, preferably in an unpopulated area. I'll take any idea anyone's got—self-destruct, laser beams, sun spots, anything. I've got one last ace up my sleeve, and it better be enough."

She opened her window to B2S. "What's your status?"

"Still working on it. I noticed a big spike in data transmission. Don't tell me—"

"Got it in one, the rocket has launched. Your window of opportunity just shrank to six minutes and counting." As she spoke, Kate brought up another window that, unbeknown to her hacker, showed her every keystroke the girl was making.

"Okay, I'm in. Now I have to trace and link back to his control program, and take control of it. Once I have that, I can send this thing anywhere you want."

"Fine, just do it in the next four minutes."

Kate watched the seconds tick away, knowing that the

rocket with its deadly cargo was racing closer and closer to her home, and that of about twenty million other people, with each passing moment. She pushed away the imagined carnage and destruction that something like this would spread in its wake. *Not on my watch,* she told herself. But at the moment, she was stuck in an all-too-familiar position—watching as one of her people tried to stave off disaster. Come on, girl, you can do it! Her screen flashed.

"All right, I'm in! I've got telemetry control of the rocket. Where do you want it?"

"Where is it right now?" Kate asked.

"At its current rate of speed, it's crossing out of Missouri and into southern Illinois. How about putting it down in a large body of water?"

With the tap of a finger, Kate brought up a map of the southern half of Illinois and highlighted every body of water. "The only problem is finding one that isn't right next to a populated area."

"You better find something fast, 'cause this sucker'll be hitting Indiana in about ninety seconds. Why not Lake Michigan? It's close enough by now."

Kate increased her scrolling, searching for any lake large enough to serve her purpose. "Now's who's putting the pressure on? Besides, I want that warhead, assuming it survives impact, and I'd rather have it not irradiating a Great Lake for about fifty thousand years." Kate scanned through huge swathes of land with finger flicks, trying to find the right combination of depth and remoteness. "Jesus, why couldn't they have flown over Minnesota? Wait a minute—I might have something. It's not perfect, but it'll have to do. Can you put it down in the westernmost fork of this lake?" She transmitted coordinates to B2S.

"I can try—you realize there's a good chance the whole

thing might burst apart on impact and scatter plutonium all over the place?"

"Better than plunging several million people into chaos. I'll fix it with the DNR later. Just do it now."

The hacker switched to a phone line so she could talk to Kate as she worked. "Okay, here goes…coming up on the coordinates…sending the new change of course. Guidance system has accepted it. According to my calcs, it should be hitting the lake right about…now. Hope we didn't scare the crap out of some early-morning fishermen."

As Kate watched, the red line abruptly terminated in the southeast quadrant of Illinois. She sighed with relief. "Congratulations, B2S, you probably saved about a million people's lives."

"I'll be sure to remind you of that at my next evaluation. You need me for anything else?"

"Yeah, as long as you're inside the Spaceworks network, make sure they can't destroy any of their data. I have a feeling the FBI folks are going to find it very interesting. Let me know when you've got it locked down."

"I'm on it."

Kate was already switching to another channel to the Super Hercules. "MR-1, this is Primary. Repeat, this is Primary. I am altering your flight plan, priority one. Change course and proceed to the downloaded coordinates. And tell the team to break out their hazmat gear and their scuba tanks, because they're about to go swimming."

Next, she dialed Tracy's line, wanting to tell her the good news.

41

Tracy noticed a dull ringing in her ears, accompanied by a throbbing behind her temples that felt like a hundred tiny men were playing drums inside her skull. An acrid smell invaded her nostrils, and her eyes fluttered open to see a SWAT team member crouched over her, holding something under her nose.

"Hey, you are alive." He helped her sit up slowly. "Careful, you took a pretty nasty jolt." His voice sounded muffled, as if he was talking through thick cotton.

Tracy tried to speak, but her throat felt as dry as the desert. "Water," she whispered. The SWAT officer produced a canteen, which she grabbed and lifted to her lips.

"Slow down, too fast and—"

"I know, I know, I might get cramps." Tracy took one more big gulp of water, then looked around. "What happened? The last thing I remember was Nate going into a small room…."

"We heard an explosion. When we found you, Briggs was knocked out, lying on top of you—we think he tried to get

you out of harm's way—and there was what was left of a
person blown across the hallway. Uh, don't look over there."

"Nate…oh, my God…" Tracy's gaze involuntarily went
to the red spray against the far wall. She winced and looked
away and swallowed, trying to control the bile rising at the
back of her throat.

"Was that his name? He must have triggered some kind
of booby trap on the hatch in the floor. It collapsed the
entrance to the tunnel or whatever's down there. He took
the brunt of the blast, too, actually ended up protecting both
of you. I'm afraid that's what's left—it was pretty nasty,
sorry."

"What about the rocket?" Tracy asked.

"We couldn't stop it in time. It's already launched."

"Can't we stop it from here?"

"They've locked us out of the system. No one's willing
to give up the codes to gain access. They say they're all
willing to die for Allah."

"Shit." Tracy pulled out her cell phone, hoping it hadn't
been broken in the impact. It rang just as she flipped it
open. "Stephanie?"

"Tracy, we've stopped the rocket. It's splashed down in
Illinois, and we've got people heading over there right
now. Is the compound secure?"

Tracy asked the SWAT member who nodded. "Yeah, but
al-Kharzi got away. He took off in a bolt-hole that led to
an escape tunnel—Nate was killed going after him."

"How'd you like to catch up with him?" Kate asked.

"What do you mean?"

"Our plans show the main tunnel under the building. It
goes north, and comes out near a normally unused access
road. If you hurry, you might be able to intercept him. Take
him alive, if you can."

Tracy rose, fighting off a wave of dizziness. "I'm on it. Thanks, Stephanie, for everything."

The SWAT officer eyed her dubiously. "Where are you going? You need to lie down, and should really have someone look at your head. You've probably got a concussion—"

"I've got one more thing to take care of. You got keys to a vehicle?"

"Well, yeah."

Tracy scanned the corridor for her pistol, finding it a few yards away. "Hand them over."

"What?"

"Listen, Officer, the man behind this entire plan, who almost destroyed half of the United States, is about to get away if I don't stop him. I'd hate to have to tell my superiors—and yours—that he got away because I couldn't get a vehicle. Now hand over those keys, dammit!"

Stunned by her commanding tone, the officer produced the keys. "The truck is out by the back entrance to the compound. Two doors down, turn right, go past the huge room and out the back—you can't miss it."

"All right. If your superiors ask, Agent Tracy Wentworth commandeered your vehicle. If they want to make an issue of it, have them contact the FBI. Who's your commanding officer, so I can let them know who to expect to hear from?"

"Lieutenant Marcus. Uh, ma'am, shouldn't I accompany you, for reinforcement?"

Tracy was already trotting down the hallway. "Thanks, Officer, but you'll probably be in enough trouble as it is." *Besides, I'm not planning on capturing him alive,* she thought.

Following the officer's directions, Tracy quickly made

her way out of the main building, flashing her badge at any SWAT or Border Patrol agent who even looked at her. Another minute brought her to the armored vehicle, which was being guarded by another officer.

"You Collins?" she asked, reading his name tag on his shirt pocket.

"Yes, ma'am."

Tracy showed her DHS badge again. "Your commanding officer, Lieutenant Marcus, is here. He wants to see you inside. I'll keep a watch out here."

"Thanks." He jogged inside, and as soon as he was out of sight, Tracy got into the truck, turned the key, strapped herself in, flicked on the headlights and gunned it into the desert.

The trip through the barren land was much like the first one she had taken only a few hours earlier, but now Tracy drove without hesitation, without any fear at all. The events of the past twelve hours had changed her in some fundamental way—shattered her preconceived notions of how things operated in the field. What she had seen had reshaped them profoundly. Everything she had seen and done, from the illegals to the break-and-enter to the assault on the compound, had altered her view on a lot of things, and it was all about to culminate in the next few minutes.

The truck dipped and bounced as it bulled its way across a rutted desert plain, carved out by a flash flood thousands of years ago.

Her phone rang, and Tracy risked taking one hand off the bucking wheel to flip it open, leaving it on the seat beside her. "Yeah?"

The cell automatically went to speaker. "Tracy, it's Stephanie. He's almost at the end of the tunnel, and will be reaching his truck soon. We're sending a helicopter to back you up."

"They already shot one down, but I'm almost there—just give me another minute. He's not getting away this time."

"Remember, take him alive if you can—he'll be a wealth of information if we can interrogate him," Kate said.

"That bastard just killed a Border Patrol agent, almost killed me and came within a hairbreadth of wiping out much of the East Coast, and you want me to go easy on him?"

Stephanie's calm voice almost soothed Tracy out of her plan. "I understand you're upset, but you have to look at the bigger picture. Al-Kharzi is a link in a bigger chain, connected all around the world. The people who took that bomb and sent it to his people in Texas, and the people all across the world who funnel them money, those are the people that we're trying to stop. The ones behind all of this. But we need the people who know them, who can tell us who they are, to get to them."

"Well, I'll see what I can do. I just found him." Tracy pressed the accelerator to the floor, and the truck leaped forward, its headlights illuminating an unarmored pickup truck. A startled face looked at her from the driver's-side window. "Yeah, you better look surprised, you prick."

"What was that?" The phone bounced on the seat, and Tracy thought Stephanie's voice might have taken on a concerned tone. She smiled grimly. "Have sighted suspect and am in pursuit. Will call after apprehension is made." Tracy flipped the phone closed and tossed it on the floor, removing the last distraction from the chase.

There was a small ditch separating the road from the desert, and she didn't hesitate, pushing the truck as fast as it would go to clear the obstacle. The plain she was on was higher and she cleared the trench and landed on the road with a bone-jarring crash, feeling the stiff suspension bottom out for a moment. Tapping the brakes just enough, she forced the truck into a bootlegger's turn, slewing it around ninety degrees and ending up facing the direction al-Kharzi had gone. The steering felt looser, and she thought she'd totally fucked up the alignment, but the truck was still moving forward, and that was all she cared about.

Stomping the pedal to the floor, Tracy shifted into two-wheel drive and raced after the fleeing terrorist. No doubt he was heading for the border, but if he thought he'd be safe there, she had a big surprise for him. Tracy had already made up her mind; she'd chase him all the way to Mexico City if she had to.

The modified Ford F550's powerful V-10 engine roared as it ate up the miles between Tracy and her target. Although the road was narrow and winding, her driving skills made all the difference as she navigated the dirt lane, gaining on the truck ahead of her with every passing minute. It helped that the terrorist was having a hard time controlling his vehicle, having to sacrifice speed for safety. Tracy powered around a final turn and her headlights lit up the back of the fleeing truck just as it sailed down a small hill. She followed, gaining enough speed to draw to within inches of his rear bumper.

Okay, now what? Tracy frowned as she realized she had been concentrating so hard on catching him that she hadn't thought out much of a plan beyond that. The road was too narrow to pull alongside and force him off the road. Shooting at him was also out of the question; not only would it be a wasted attempt here, but she needed both hands to control the steering wheel. That left only one thing to do.

Flooring the accelerator again, Tracy crept up to within

a yard of the other truck's bumper, then surged ahead, tapping the lighter truck with her much heavier vehicle. The pickup slewed from side to side as the terrorist fought to regain control.

One more oughta do it… Tracy pulled up and rammed the rear bumper just as they were about to head into a turn. The additional force kept the first truck going in a straight line. It crashed into the desert scrub, destroying trees and brush as it plowed across the land.

While Tracy had hoped to overturn it, she wasn't about to miss her advantage. Dropping the SWAT truck back into four-wheel drive, she followed the trail of destruction into the plain, scanning the hardpan for any sign of him.

About twenty yards ahead was the pickup truck, its driver's side facing the front of her truck. Al-Kharzi was trying to get back to the road. Every detail was highlighted as if the truck were parked in daylight, from its dust-caked fenders and windows to the face looking through the window at her.

Tracy grinned and crushed the accelerator to the floor. She surged ahead, aiming squarely at the midsection of the truck. Frozen between driving away and running, Sepehr made a halfhearted attempt to move the truck out of her path, then ducked out of sight a second before impact.

The big truck slammed into the pickup's side with a tremendous screech of crumpling metal and broken glass. It sent the smaller vehicle skidding across the ground with enough force to flip it over, crushing the roof of the cab as the truck completed its roll and landed on its side, the undercarriage facing her.

Thrown into the seat restraints by the impact, Tracy gasped in a breath before extricating herself from the straps and getting out. Her ribs ached each time she inhaled.

Drawing her pistol again, she approached the wreck, every sense alert, waiting for him to pop out and try something. A part of her hoped he would.

Leading with her weapon, Tracy came around the twisted and dented hood, covering the passenger compartment first. Sepehr was lying there, half in and half out of the truck. He had smashed out the shattered safety windshield, which lay in one huge, fragmented piece on the ground in front of him, but he hadn't gone any farther. His face was a mask of blood, and one leg was twisted under him.

Tracy aimed her pistol at him as he stared back at her. For a moment, the agent and the terrorist looked into each other's eyes.

Then Tracy lowered her pistol slightly. "Sepehr al-Kharzi, you are under arrest on the charges of intent to commit a terrorist act against the United States, conspiracy to commit a terrorist act against the United States and illegal possession of nuclear materials and a weapon of mass destruction. And by the time we're done, I'm sure the U.S. government will have come up with plenty more charges to pile on you."

Through the blood and broken teeth, Sepehr began to chuckle, then laugh. Tracy let him, figuring he'd let her in on the joke soon enough.

"Stupid American cow. There is no more American government. It has been destroyed. Washington, D.C.... New York...all burning now..."

Tracy shook her head. "I thought you might say something like that. But you're wrong. We stopped your rocket, brought it down in a lake in Illinois. That bomb never got the chance to take out those cities or anywhere else. In fact, we're recovering the warhead right now. It's over."

The terrorist pushed himself up on one arm. "You... lie...you're lying..."

"I don't have any reason to lie. You'll see that your mission has failed soon enough." Tracy produced a pair of handcuffs. "There are some people back in D.C. who can't wait to talk to you."

"No American woman is going to arrest me!" The wounded man grabbed the window frame of the truck, seemingly oblivious to the pieces of broken glass that sliced into his hand. He hauled himself to his feet.

"Stand right there and raise your hands over your head." Tracy adjusted her stance and aimed at his chest.

"No American whore is going to arrest Sepehr al-Kharzi!" Biting his lip, he took a step toward her.

"Stop right where you are!" Tracy ordered, lining her pistol sights on him. "Stop or I will shoot!"

Sepehr took another step, and as he did so, he brought his left hand out from behind his back, bringing up a small black pistol. Tracy squeezed the trigger of her SIG Sauer twice, the bullets entering the terrorist's chest and making him collapse against the hood of the truck. He tried to raise the pistol, and Tracy fired once more, this one carving into his neck. Sepehr al-Kharzi slid to the ground.

Tracy holstered her pistol. "No, but an American woman killed you, you psychotic fuck." She took a deep breath and walked back to the truck, spotting lights from the rest of the Border Patrol in the distance. Opening the passenger's door, she picked up the phone and flipped it over.

"Stephanie? It's Tracy. I'm afraid you're not gonna like this."

42

Tracy sat on a park bench, watching Jennifer play on the wooden equipment. Paul played with her for several minutes, until she joined a larger group of children on a merry-go-round. Then he let her run off, and walked back to Tracy. But every few seconds, Jennifer looked over, making sure she was still there.

Her return flight had touched back down in D.C. two days earlier, but Tracy still wasn't used to being back. The humid dampness seemed oppressive after the dry, hot desert, and the buildings and corridors of power no longer held the same interest for her. Even as she watched Jennifer laugh and run and play in the summer sunshine, even as she smiled and waved back at her near stepchild, her mind was more than a thousand miles away, at an abandoned barn in the middle of the Texas plains.

"Tracy?"

With a start, she realized that Paul stood next to her and had said something. "I'm sorry, Paul, I was—distracted."

"Yeah, much like you've been ever since you returned.

Look, I know you asked me not to pry but…is there any-thing you wanted to talk about? Anything at all?"

Tracy looked at Paul, secure and comfortable in his short-sleeved shirt and L.L. Bean chinos, with leather deck shoes on his feet. *Oh, Paul, there's so much I want to tell you—and so much you're not going to understand,* she thought. She shifted her position on the bench, wincing a bit as her sore shoulder twinged.

"Are you all right?"

"I'm fine, Paul." Tracy stared at Jennifer, her blond hair flashing in the sun, and tried to imprint the image in her mind, to take with her when she began her journey. "I resigned from DHS today."

Paul's eyebrows flew up in surprise. "What? When did you decide this? Why didn't you talk to me about it?"

She turned to him, about to retort, but simply smiled sadly. "Because it wasn't your decision to make—it was mine." She left out the part about Gilliam blocking her re-quested transfer to the Border Patrol, telling her she was far more valuable back in D.C. He had made vague noises about the transfer to Virginia, but she saw, with startling clarity, that he was never going to let her go. She had pulled out the second piece of paper from a folder and placed it on his desk and walked out.

"This is great! Let me make some calls, and I'll see about getting you an interview. I'm sure my company will snap you right up—what?"

Tracy had laid her hand on his arm, halting his plans for their future in midsentence. "Thanks, Paul, I appreciate your offer, but I'm not interested in pursuing a career with Globeview. In fact, I'm not interested in pursuing a career in Washington at all."

His brows dipped into a frown. "Not in Washington?

What do you mean? Are you thinking of heading to Langley, joining the Agency?"

"No, Paul. I want to go back down to Texas, to the border. I want to work there and try to help find a solution to what's happening there."

Paul stared at her, his mouth slightly ajar as he tried to fathom what she had just said. *Well, I guess I finally stumped you,* Tracy thought as she waited for him to reply.

"Okay, let's talk about this. You mean temporarily, right?"

"I'm afraid not, Paul. I'm thinking about staying there for several years. The situation there isn't going to change overnight. It's going to take committed people who are willing to stick around and get the job done."

"Jesus, you're really serious about this. So, where does that leave us?"

"I…don't know. This is my choice, and I can't ask you both to pick up everything and move there with me. That's not fair to you. But this is something I feel that I have to do. I've enjoyed my time with Homeland Security, but I always felt like I was sort of spinning my wheels and not getting anywhere, bogged down in the bureaucracy. Those people on the border are trying to accomplish something, and I want to be a part of it."

"Tracy, excuse me for being blunt, but you actually want to patrol the wasteland of the border and get shot at and save people who just want to sponge off our nation? I've been to those border towns—it's like stepping back in time. If you want to accomplish something, at least take a look at Globeview. They can station you around the world if you want to travel, and place you just about anywhere—even Mexico, if that's what you really want. But you'd have more flexibility in your schedule, be making a hell of a lot more money and, most importantly, we'd still be able to be together, as well."

"That's sweet, Paul, but you were already worried enough about me when I was in Texas. How would you feel if I took a two-year assignment in Mexico City, or the Philippines or in Colombia where women get kidnapped all the time?"

"GSS provides the best protection money can buy— you'd be safe at all times. They take care of their people really well."

"And also insulate them from the men and women that need help the most. That's not how things get done."

"What are you talking about? That's the only way things get done, by going to the top, by talking to the people who make the decisions in government, in politics. That's the only way to change anything down there or anywhere else."

Tracy smiled again, unsurprised by her fiancé's naiveté. "The only problem with that is those people tend to let the power they wield go to their heads, and spend too much time trying to extend or protect it, all at the expense of the people they're supposed to be serving. No, Paul, my mind is made up. You and I have different ideas of how to get things done. I'm tired of sitting on the sidelines and watching other people take the risks. I want to get in the game."

Paul ran a hand through his hair. "And there's no reason you can't do that at Globeview."

Tracy slipped her hand into her purse and brought out the engagement ring Paul had given to her eighteen months ago, and which she'd taken off on the flight down to El Paso and hadn't put back on since. She held it out to him. "I'm sorry."

Paul stared at it, seeing all of their shared plans and dreams disappear through the circle of gold. "There's nothing I can say or do to change your mind?"

"Only if you wanted to chuck it all and come with me." Her bright smile was forced, but she pasted it on nonetheless.

Paul met her gaze for several seconds, truly thinking it over, and Tracy found that she loved him even more for that. But then he dropped his head and looked back out over the playground. "I can't. I can't uproot Jennifer from school, her friends, to haul her halfway across the country. The divorce was hard enough on her, I couldn't subject her to that, not now."

Tracy placed the ring in his hand and folded his fingers over it. "Your daughter is strong, Paul, just like you raised her to be. I love you, and I love her, as well, but this just isn't the place for me right now."

"I can't believe this is happening. You go away on one field assignment, and you come back and want to go traipsing around down there like you've found your life's calling."

"Who knows, Paul? Maybe I have." Tracy stood. "I'm going to say goodbye to Jennifer."

"Maybe that's not the best idea—"

"No, Paul, it is. For her, and for me." She bent down and kissed him on the cheek, then lightly on the lips. His face had grown paler in the past few minutes, as if he had been drained of all his emotions. He sat on the bench, a shell of a man. "I'm sorry, I truly am."

"Not half as sorry as I am." He looked up at her with a rueful grin.

Tracy turned and walked across the park, stepping carefully on the layer of tree bark that covered the playing area. She knew this goodbye would be extremely painful but it had to be done.

THAT NIGHT, TRACY WAS trying to pack her things and not break down, but when she realized she had folded and repacked the contents of one suitcase three times, she took a break and sat at her kitchen table, resting her head in her arms. She had unplugged the phone, not wanting to have Paul try to contact her. She knew that for the rest of her life, a part of her would always wonder what might have been if she had stayed and made a family with Paul and Jennifer. Even though she knew she was making the right decision, her heart was going to take a while to come around to that fact.

An electronic chirping roused her from her fugue. Wiping her eyes, Tracy fumbled through her purse until she found the cell phone from the FBI. She flipped it open. "H-hello?"

"Tracy? This is Stephanie Cassell. Have I caught you at a bad time?"

"No, this is fine." Tracy took a deep, shuddering breath and leaned back in her seat. "I was just wrapping up some things here in town."

"Yes, I'd heard about your resignation."

Tracy frowned. "I didn't know word traveled that fast."

"Like I said before, there are some things that our government can do pretty well—like get information about certain people to those who need it the most. If you don't mind my asking, what are your plans?"

"I was going to head back down to the border to try to get a post there helping out."

"That's very commendable of you. Will you be joining the Customs and Border Protection?"

"To be honest, I hadn't thought that far ahead yet—I'm kind of burning my bridges here first."

"I understand." And the strange thing was, Tracy was absolutely certain that Stephanie did understand exactly what she meant. "I don't suppose we could meet—after all, I have to get that phone back. And I have an opportunity I'd like to present to you."

"Thanks anyway, but I'm not interested in another government job."

"Good, I was hoping you'd say that."

The words in Tracy's ear made her frown even more. "I'm afraid I don't understand."

"You are a very brave person. It takes tremendous courage to walk away from everything you know and face an unknown future like that. And that's why I want to talk to you face-to-face one last time. I want to offer you a very special opportunity to help people, many, many people."

"How?" Tracy asked.

"I'd rather not go into that right now. Tell you what, why don't we get together for dinner tonight, and I can explain in more detail?"

"I don't know—this isn't an offer from the government? I thought you were with the FBI?"

"No, it is not an offer from the government, and I might have misled you slightly about that. But I'd appreciate the chance to explain my actions, and also tell you more about what I can offer you."

"One more question before I answer you—could I be stationed on the U.S.-Mexico border?"

There was a chuckle from the other end. "We have three full-time operatives down there, and I'm sure they would welcome the help."

"All right, let's get together, and you can tell me how you're going to give me a chance to save the world," Tracy said.

Don Pendleton's Mack Bolan.

Havana Five

EXTREME MEASURES

Cuba remains volatile, and has the full
attention of the White House. Mack Bolan's
soft probe into a missing Pentagon official
inside Cuba goes hard when his cover is
blown. The connection between a notorious
Cuban underworld cartel, Havana Five, and
a growing army of leftist insurgents puts
Stony Man and Washington on high alert.
With U.S. and global interests in jeopardy
and a bloodbath just a hair trigger away, the
situation is critical. Bolan, flanked by two
of Stony Man's crack operatives, turns up
the heat with a battle plan that hasn't failed
yet—infiltrate, identify and destroy.

Available July 2008
wherever you buy books.

Don Pendleton
DARK STAR

Advanced rocket technology wreaks global hellfire...

A machine that defies logistics has become a grim reality.
A working X-ship can launch and land anywhere, is virtually
unseen and unstoppable due to stealth technology and sheer
velocity. Now a faceless enemy with a hidden agenda is
using X-ships to spread global fire and death like a tidal wave
from hell. Facing a crisis of unimagined proportions, Stony
Man is once again tasked with the impossible: unmask the
masterminds behind the attacks and take them out—fast.

STONY®
MAN

Available August
wherever you buy books.

JAMES AXLER

DEATH LANDS

Thunder Road

Fight or die in the raw and deadly frontier of tomorrow...

Thunder Rider is a self-styled superhero, prowling the Deathlands and serving up mass murder in a haze of napalm and nerve gas. Ryan Cawdor accepts a bounty from a ravaged ville to eliminate this crazed vigilante. But this twisted coldheart has designs on a new sidekick, Krysty Wroth, and her abduction harnesses the unforgiving fury of Ryan and his warrior companions. At his secret fortress, Thunder Rider waits—armed with enough ordnance to give his madness free rein....

In the Deathlands, justice is in the eyes of those who seek it...

Available September wherever you buy books.